DOUBLE TAKE

DOUBLE TAKE

JUDGE LAWRENCE WADDINGTON

Rev. date: 08/17/2016

To order additional copies of this book, contact:
Xlibris
1-888-795-4274
www.Xlibris.com
Orders@Xlibris.com
737804

To my wife, Jane, the love of my life

Chapter 1

Standing in his judicial robes and staring intently through rain-streaked windows of his third-floor chambers in the Los Angeles courthouse, Judge Roy Carleton surveyed a crowd swirling in the streets and sidewalks in front of an abortion clinic located down the street. Numerous young men and women among the throng slowly circled and proudly bore preprinted signs variously labeled Baby Killer, Women for Life, and Stop the Madness. Small children clung anxiously to the skirts of several women who gently nudged them along. Numerous elderly men flanked the pickets, forming a barrier between a separate line of women marching single file and parallel to the demonstrators. Displaying banners and signs identifying themselves as Americans for Choice, they jabbed their fists upward toward the sky and sang boisterously, "We shall overcome." Both groups sloshed through gutters bloated from water streaming down the side of buildings, drifting across sidewalks, and sprawling into the street.

1. Approximately fifty rain-coa]ted police officers were spaced intermittently along the curbs, another four mounted police sat on their horses at the intersection,

and numerous plainclothes officers wearing badges over their raincoats stood at the margin of the crowd. A man in police uniform wearing a hooded raincoat lettered SWAT knelt under an umbrella on the roof of an adjacent building, a rifle at his side, screening the crowd below with binoculars. A slate grey *sky* cast a pall over angry merchants scowling through shop windows while customers huddled in doorways, waiting helplessly for taxis unable to arrive through the congestion. But the sodden pickets, undeterred by a steady drizzle, continued shouting and singing. A flash of lightning scattered across the sky, and thunder rolled overhead. Resigned to this daily ritual near the courthouse, Carleton watched the rival groups occasionally shout slogans at one another, but neither had engaged in violence. Americans for Choice had sought a court order from Carleton prohibiting any interference with women seeking abortions at the clinic. During the court hearing, their witnesses had testified to observing pro-life picketers blocking entrances to the clinic, shouting pleas at pregnant women arriving in the company of "counselors," and vocally attempting to convince the arrivals not to abort. In defense of those who picketed, several police officers testified unanimously that pro-life demonstrators blocked clinic doors only briefly, cars entered the parking lot without interference, individual demonstrators never touched any of the pregnant women, and those identified as Americans for Choice shouted as loudly as anyone. At the hearing in the courtroom, Carleton had considered entering an order limiting the number of demonstrators and the specific hours they could picket, but as he frequently reminded the lawyers, his sensitivity to the role of free speech stayed his hand.

In the isolation of his chambers during a court recess, waiting for the court hearing to resume and shaking his head at the passion of the abortion debate, Carlton looked at the newspaper on his desk, reading, "President says Carleton 'strongest candidate' for vacancy on Supreme Court, but he did not want to compromise any judicial appointment pending the abortion ruling." A knock on the door to his chambers interrupted, and he responded, "Come in."

Art Matthews, a savvy political junkie, walked in.

"Did you read the paper, Roy?"

"Don't believe everything you read in the newspaper, Art. You know the president is pro-choice, and several other of my so-called friends are positioning themselves for the vacancy, waiting for my decision on issuing an order. A vindictive US

Senate would never confirm me if I issued an injunction prohibiting pro-life demonstrators from picketing."

Matthews replied, "I know, I know. And if you don't issue an injunction, the district attorney said he would file criminal charges against Women for Life. But hey, I just stopped by to say hello. I know you're busy. Call if you need me. I'll send you my bill as soon as you get appointed."

Matthews and Carleton both laughed. Mathews, waving good-bye, left the room.

The intercom buzzer on the desk sounded, signaling the return of the lawyers to the courtroom and a resumption of the hearing. On turning away from the window, Carleton noticed a local television news crew arriving in a truck, carrying cameras, cables, and floodlights. The crew immediately jumped out and set up their equipment, and a camera operator began taping the crowd. Channel 5 TV reporter Carmen Susa stood in front of a waiting camera crew while she angrily nudged a wisp of unruly, damp hair falling across her face. When the red signal light above the camera blinked, Susa changed expression instantly, looked assuredly into the camera, and assumed a grave and concerned manner. The two groups of demonstrators pushed closer in the background, each side shouting and defiantly waving their signs.

While Susa spoke, a car arrived, flanked by women bearing their Americans for Choice signs, the driver slowly parting the crowd and stopping in front of the clinic. A roar emerged from pro-choice partisans when a plainly dressed woman exited the car carefully, opened her umbrella, and cautiously stepped onto the drenched pavement. Both groups hurried toward the woman, while Susa trailed behind with microphone in hand, ignoring several women frantically waving their signs. A woman wearing a banner across her chest proclaiming Choice, Not Chance rushed to the new arrival's side, grasped her by the elbow, and led her through the crowd toward the clinic.

Carleton picked up his glasses and glanced toward the camera crew pushing through the crowd toward Susa and the woman. One of the crew, visibly limping and carrying television cables on his shoulder, walked next to the cameraman. His features were hidden by a hat and upturned raincoat collar. The logo on the back of his raincoat identified him as an employee of television station Channel 5.

The man turned quickly toward the arriving woman. Shifting the cables to his left hand, he held them over his shoulder, concealing the side of his face. While adjusting the cables, a heavyset woman in the crowd bumped against him, causing his hat to slip to the side, revealing a partially bald head and a short ponytail. Quickly replacing the rain hat, he eased back a few steps out of camera range, shielding himself from view to anyone on the other side of the camera. The crowd surged past him, while he continued to hold the cables over his left shoulder. Reaching inside the raincoat with his right hand, he removed an object. He shifted the string of cables on his shoulder and moved next to the unoccupied Channel 5 van. In the reflected backlight of the camera, the glint of a gun barrel in his hand equipped with a silencer eased into view.

Carleton watched the young woman now standing alone in the doorway to the clinic and surrounded by the crowd. The pro-choice crowd screamed, waved their signs, and cheered their motto. Pro-life members yelled back, "Save your baby! Save your baby!" Thunder rolled in the sky, followed by heavy rain. Umbrellas went up and out, hoods were pulled out, the crowd huddled in their raincoats, and women nurtured their children. The gun in the man's hand jerked upward, once, then twice. The pregnant woman crumpled onto the street and fell lifelessly into the gutter.

For a moment, the crowd continued to surge forward then halted. A wave of panic emerged, scattering everyone indiscriminately. Police attempted to control the fleeing bodies but were swept up in the maelstrom. Children screamed and cried, several falling onto the street. The crowd stumbled against the TV cameraman, who attempted to film the pandemonium. Merchants and customers scurried inside the stores. Susa, frantically attempting to maintain her balance, screamed into the microphone to describe the hysteria. She and the cameraman, unable to stem the tide of humanity flowing against them, surrendered to the hysteria and headed for the TV van. Bodies crushed against the cameraman, ripping the camera from his hands. The equipment dropped onto the street, careening wildly, the cables snapping and whipping aimlessly.

The chaos mounting as he stared, Carleton hurried across the room to the telephone, dialed the security office, ordered the courthouse closed, and instructed all court staff dispersed into courtrooms. Dialing 911, he heard the scream of sirens approaching. Replacing the phone without waiting for an answer, he returned to the window. The street, empty of people except for a few stragglers, was littered with signs, banners, and posters. Terrified merchants and customers peered nervously through windows. A handful of police officers surrounded a lifeless body sprawled in the street, lying in a pool of her blood trickling into the gutter choked with water. The assassin had disappeared.

Chapter 2

Judge Carleton closed the door to his apartment, sighed audibly, and walked wearily into his bedroom. Disrobing slowly, he hung his suit neatly in the closet, placed shoe trees into his shoes, removed his shirt and tie, and donned his sweat suit. Slowly arranging the loose-fitting garment, he slumped onto the sofa in front of the television. The telephone rang as he searched for the remote.

"Hello."

"Roy, this is Jean."

"Oh, hello, Jean."

"I just watched the news, and they reported a shooting outside the courthouse. Did you see what happened?"

Carleton hesitated. "Some of it. I was in my chambers but just saw the crowd running away."

"I see. I suppose you're not coming home tonight."

"No, I'm staying here."

"Roy, I don't see any reason for us to stay married. We've been separated for six months now."

"I'm still trying to sort things out."

"Like whether a divorce will interfere with your career? Or whether you can afford the spousal support I want?"

"Jean, please."

"Don't 'Jean, please' me. Look, either you file by the end of the month, or I do. We have only one child, and she's going to need money from you."

"Janice is going to college. She knows I'll support her."

"Really? When did you see her last?"

"I talk to her on the phone."

"Oh, wonderful."

"Jean, I'm very tired. Unless you have something constructive to say, I'm hanging up, as they used to say."

"I do. Good-bye."

The line went dead. Shrugging, Carleton replaced the phone and clicked the remote to activate Channel 5. The screen brightened, and the familiar voice of Carmen Susa reported the afternoon events, while the tape of the crowd ran in the background. In her voice-over, Susa described the chaos as the camera swung wildly, tape rolling, the cameraman trying to capture the action. The sound of screams, crying children, and shouting police officers matched the visuals. The camera jolted from side to side, crashing dizzily onto the street. The unmanned tape, through its rain-spattered lens, captured fleeing legs, flooded pavement, and abandoned picket signs. Susa briefly summed up, informing viewers she had not been injured but that the cameraman had been hospitalized. She added a sober footnote, deplored the death of the young woman, and urged anyone who had information about the assassin to call police. To emphasize this point, the tape rolled again in slow motion.

Carleton switched channels. Channel 8 always opened with local crime, and tonight was no exception. The anchor, explaining that their reporter was on the scene of the shooting, turned in his chair and shifted to watch the monitor behind him. The tape rolled, shot from a different angle showing the Channel 5 cameraman inching his way through the crowd, accompanied by a man carrying television cables. Although the camera shielded his face, the man appeared to limp markedly. The Channel 8 camera scanned the crowd, quickly focusing on the woman arriving in a car. Moments later, pandemonium broke out. The camera swept the scene but no longer taped the Channel 5 cameraman or his assistant. Carleton reached for the phone on the desk and called the police.

A voice answered, "Police department. Sergeant Higgins."

Carleton agonized.

The voice repeated, "Hello. Hello. Do you need help?"

Carleton hung up. He paused before he dialed another number.

"Yeah" came the weary voice of Art Matthews.

"Art, this Roy."

"Royal. I suppose you heard the news about the shooting at the abortion clinic?"

"Of course."

"But you really called to say the president just appointed you to the Supreme Court and you wanted to thank your old friend for helping you get there."

"No, not really. I think I might have a problem."

"You? Hey, it's in the bag as soon as the abortion case is over. I talked to the president's secretary yesterday. The president is out of town but should be back next week."

"Look, Art, having the abortion hearing at this time is not exactly convenient. No matter what I decide, there's going to be plenty of opposition."

"The president isn't worried about that. He knows you'll decide the right way."

"That's only part of the problem. I was watching the demonstration from my chambers today, Art. I saw the guy who killed that woman."

The phone was silent.

"Art, Art, are you there?"

"Yeah, yeah, I'm here. You're right. You do have a problem. That woman was three months pregnant. You're a witness to the murder of a woman about to have an abortion, and you're judging an abortion case."

"And that means I might have to disqualify myself. No one will believe I can be impartial with my appointment on the line."

"Which means the president will hold off your appointment until they arrest someone and prosecute the killer—that is, if they ever find him."

"Exactly. And if they do and then prosecute, the defense will scream bloody murder if the chief prosecution witness is a Supreme Court justice hearing an abortion case and testified just to make the DA's case look good."

"And nothing personal, Royal, but if the guy is found not guilty after you testify . . ."

"Then I'm not credible. If that's not bad enough, the president wants to make this appointment before his term ends next year. So he'll appoint Eddy Hiler, the original fruitcake."

"Which tips the balance on the court. Maybe we should change your registration."

"Art, this is not funny."

"Sorry, Roy. You're right. What are you going to do?"

"Why do you think I'm calling you?"

"Have you called the police?"

"Not yet."

"Look, can you really ID this guy?"

"Not positively. I couldn't see his face. But I saw a white guy, about forty-five and walking with a limp."

"That's it? That's your ID?"

"I told you I couldn't see his face."

"With all your years as a prosecutor, and you think you're a witness? You're not a witness. You saw a guy you can't identify."

"But the police might need this lead, particularly since this guy walks with a limp. You know how it works. Every detail helps."

"Look, Roy, let some time pass. See whether the cops come up with something. There might be another witness, an anonymous call, whatever."

"But I could be an important witness. The description is important even without an identification."

"I say again, wait. Sleep on it. I'll call you in the morning. Tell the cops the phones were jammed and you couldn't get through."

"Which also makes me a liar."

"Trust me. Sleep on it. I'll talk to you tomorrow. Gotta go. Bye."

Chapter 3

Judge Carleton had presided in the same courtroom for the last ten years. Although the courthouse itself reflected fading elegance, Carleton maintained his courtroom in its original condition. The ancient gas lamps on the wall bespoke antiquity and solemnity as all stood resembling sentinels above their burnished brass bases: maroon drapes, the folds encircled by gold sashes, flanked mahogany walls. An oak beam ceiling hovered solemnly over two massive counsel tables, spectator seats, and the elevated bench of the judge. For himself, Carleton had installed a high-backed swivel chair, its azure fabric edged in gold-plated buttons, the seat elevated to increase the perception of height and control. A colonial-era inkwell, unfilled but proudly mounting a feathered quill pen, rested silently on the right side of the bench. A walnut gavel lay on the left. The court clerk, Shelley Fields, worked quietly and efficiently behind a rolltop desk stuffed with files and legal papers.

Spectators, the press, witnesses, and police officers sat in original wooden courtroom benches shaped only for those with Spartan backs. Overhead lights flooded the worn and scarred but highly polished floors and aisles. A hard-backed wooden chair for witnesses sat next to the judge's bench but was positioned several feet lower, enabling Carleton to peer down over his half-glasses. The judge had acknowledged minimum needs for juror comfort by ordering installation of cushions for similarly uncomfortable chairs. An American flag and a Californian flag, carefully draped, hung from gold-plated poles standing on gold-plated bases at either side of the courtroom. The atmosphere exuded dignity and reason despite trials often tawdry, brutal, and senseless.

Frank Richardson, the lawyer representing Americans for Choice, had requested a court order prohibiting picketing or parading around the medical clinic and sought an additional order that none of the pickets approach women entering the premises unless invited. Richardson, having recently received substantial financial support from pro-choice groups, had seized the opportunity to file and argue the case himself despite his staff of experienced lawyers. He held daily press conferences and hired a press agent to regularly brief reporters on the substance of courtroom arguments.

Not a polished courtroom lawyer, Richardson was assisted by several aides who constantly advised him on strategy and points of law. Frequently uncertain of himself, Richardson would ask Carleton for a few moments to confer with one or more members of his staff, yet he had not entirely forgotten his trial skills and presented legal arguments in a professional manner. Contending that appellate courts had already authorized a trial judge to exercise judicial control over participants engaging in "freedom of speech" issues in similar cases, Richardson argued that Carleton should do the same.

Percy Amstead, who defended the pro-life defendants without fee, resembled film legend Cary Grant. Amstead presented a studious manner and formal bearing and spoke in a rich baritone voice radiating sincerity. His demeanor matched the ambiance of the courtroom, quietly responding to Richardson's frequent misunderstanding of the law. Amstead, arguing persuasively that his clients differed little from union pickets, contended the judge should not judicially shackle his clients any more than those on strike for higher wages or better working conditions. He had respectfully reminded Carleton that the community in general was sympathetic to strong unions who identified with the right of those on strike to yell, picket, and hurl insults at anyone who crossed the picket line.

"Even a little violence," argued Amstead, "regrettably caused by emotions, was familiar to battle-scarred union members, but demonstrators in our case had not engaged in any violence."

With a touch of dramatic silence, he paused.

"And police have arrested no one in this case."

Amstead had conceded that not everyone in the community agreed with the demonstrators but nevertheless understood their right to chant, issue warnings, parade with signs, and generally mimic union activity. Amstead had frequently and passionately played this chord to Carleton. Pausing again, as if merely collecting his thoughts, he looked around squarely at reporters from the sympathetic local *Times-Register* newspaper and resumed his argument, comparing parallels between his clients and unions. Unsurprisingly, editorial support for his case occurred frequently throughout the several days of the hearing. After both sides had completed their arguments, Richardson asked, "Judge, there is one additional matter that I need to bring to your attention."

Carleton stiffened slightly. "Yes."

"The murder of the young woman that occurred. Based on that incident, I intend to request a more stringent order than I previously requested."

"Mr. Amstead, any objection?"

"Yes. Your Honor, this is most inappropriate. Counsel has already prepared an order for your signature. I have opposed it. He must either withdraw his request and submit a new order or seek permission to amend his original proposed order so I can respond."

Carleton looked at Richardson. "Mr. Amstead is correct, Mr. Richardson. What do you want to do?"

Richardson looked helplessly at his aides. One signaled to withdraw the pending request.

Richardson nodded. "We will withdraw the request, Your Honor, and submit a new order for your signature today."

Amstead jumped to his feet. "Your Honor, then I insist that Mr. Richardson serve the proposed order on me and allow us time to respond in the statutory time, ten days."

Dismayed, Richardson replied, "Ten days? We have a murdered woman, and you want ten days to think it over, Mr. Amstead?"

"It's called the law, Mr. Richardson. I only want the statute to apply."

"Your Honor—"

Carleton interrupted, "Counsel is correct, Mr. Richardson. Serve your papers on Mr. Amstead and set the hearing ten days from that date. Court is adjourned."

Carleton glanced at the clock, its antique roman numerals barely visible, and noted the late hour. Swinging his chair around slowly, he nodded briefly to Shelley, handed her the file, and returned to chambers.

Chapter 4

Judge Carleton stood facing the elevator located down the hall from his courtroom, staring idly at the panel light displaying descent. Lost in thought, unaware of the staccato approach of high-heeled shoes striding down the hall, he vaguely noted an approaching woman who interrupted him from his musing. He looked up toward the court administrator.

"Oh, Kelly. I'm sorry. I didn't realize it was you."

Kelly Francis smiled, tilting her lightly tanned face in recognition. Administrative assistant to the chief judge, her managerial skills were as renowned as her taste in fashion. Her shoulder-length auburn hair, highlighted by streaks of blond, flowed over her shoulders. The tailored tan suit caressed her hips and clung effortlessly as she moved. A soft orange scarf curled around her neck, securely fastened by an emerald pin. Over her shoulder, she carried a sleek black leather purse stitched thinly with gold threads. Despite a ten-hour working day, Kelly Francis never displayed fatigue. Pushing the already illuminated elevator button with a manicured fingernail, she sighed.

"I always give the elevator a second chance, Judge. Just in case."

"In case the elevator didn't hear me order it down?"

"Exactly. Judge, are you all right? You look like you're a thousand miles away."

"Oh, no, I'm fine. Just concentrating on that case I'm involved in."

"The abortion case? That is a tough one. Is it almost over?"

"It was, until the shooting occurred."

"Of course. Terrible. Just terrible. Will that affect the hearing?"

Carleton paused for a moment, lips tightening slightly. "Folks on both sides argue about it and stoke up their emotions. Pro-choicers will point to the murder, demand more protection, and Richardson will probably seek an order from me prohibiting pro-lifers from even coming near the clinic. Pro-lifers will argue abortion is murder, and that's what happens when you legislate morality. Plus, they will contend they have a right to picket and no one has been injured by their picketing."

"But you've been there before. This is not your first high-profile case. In fact, you've tried more controversial cases than any other judge."

"I know. But somehow, I'm a little more involved here."

"What do you mean?"

"It was raining. I was watching the demonstration from the window during recess. The police were doing a pretty good job of control. They had a special-weapons officer on the roof next door, when I saw a man . . ."

He backtracked. "I mean, I saw lots of people running and screaming. Shouting. Bedlam. Sort of makes me a witness in a general sense."

"Yes, but no different from hundreds of other people on the street. The only difference is, you were on a higher level."

"Of course. That's how I see it too, just that it's a little unnerving that this happened during our hearing."

The elevator light flashed, and the doors opened slowly.

"Kelly, you go ahead. I just remembered, I left my briefcase in chambers."

"OK. See you tomorrow."

Kelly Francis stepped into the elevator, turned, and smiled at Carleton, who managed a weak return nod. The doors shut, and Carleton stood alone, watching the panel light go dark. He waited a moment, reached forward, and pushed the button again.

Chapter 5

By the time of the next hearing date in court two weeks later, the police had made no arrests. The FBI entered the case under authority of a new federal statute, to the disgust of local police who inferred that the Feds thought them incompetent. Relations between police and the FBI had degenerated, strained by prior federal investigations of alleged civil rights violations, as their respective investigations crisscrossed each other. Outwardly cordial, the FBI agent in charge and Police Chief Willard Riley held joint press conferences without criticizing each other or displaying hostility. When the press and TV had gone, the tension continued between the two men.

In the resumed hearing in court, both sides concluded presenting their evidence, and Judge Carleton had taken the case under submission. Based on recent court decisions, Carleton had told both lawyers he had legal authority to issue an injunction against the demonstrators, but the order must be narrowly tailored to avoid suppressing freedom of speech. He planned to walk a middle course, allowing limited picketing to continue, but under tight restrictions on the time, place, and manner of the demonstration.

Sitting in his chambers that evening, staring occasionally into the night at city lights, Carleton drafted and redrafted the order, struggling to find the right balance. He glanced at the clock: seven forty-five. A gentle knock on the door startled him.

"Come in."

Kelly Francis poked her head around the door.

"Sorry to bother you, Judge. I thought I might get some food for you from the deli across the street if you were hungry. I'm going anyway, working late, so it's no problem."

"Oh, thanks, Kelly. No, I'm almost finished. Thanks anyway for asking."

"OK. By the way, a couple of police officers came by today. They wanted to know if I'd seen anything on the day that woman was shot at the medical clinic. My window faces the street just like yours. It seems the police had identified everyone who worked in an office that had a window facing the street. Naturally, they picked the chief judge and me first since we both have the same views. I told them I was in the ladies' room at the time and didn't see anything. Did they talk to you?"

"No. Not yet, anyway. But I can't be of any help either since I was in trial."

"I thought you said you were at the window at the time of the shooting."

"Um, I did. I did. I meant we had just taken a recess, and when I came back here in chambers, waiting to resume, I just saw a lot of people running and screaming. Too late to see anything except the police and the poor woman who was lying in the street."

"I see. You actually don't know any more than I do. Sure you won't change your mind about the food?"

"No. I'm almost done here. I'll get a bite later."

"OK. Good night."

"Good night, Kelly."

Carleton finished the draft of the court order and read it one more time. Sitting back for several minutes, he reached for the phone and punched in numbers.

"Hello," came the perennially tired voice of Art Matthews.

"Art, it's Roy."

"Oh, hi, Judge. On a Friday night, you're calling me? You should be at home."

"Not tonight. I just got word the police are interviewing everyone who had window views of the street in their offices to find out if they saw anything during the demonstration. I can't decide whether to tell them I saw the shooter."

"Tell you what, maybe you should file your order and take a three-week vacation. The police can at least look at your chambers while you're gone. Tell your clerk you're on vacation and 'not available.' By the time you get back, they'll have somebody in custody, or at least this thing will have cooled down."

"I'm not sure about that. But the vacation part sounds good. The chief judge told me to take some time off after I finish this case."

"There you go. Perfect."

"OK. I'll sign the order and leave in a few days."

"Sounds good. You going to your favorite hotel in Mexico?"

"Yeah. Villa Annunciator. Very quiet. Isolated."

"Good. Call me if you need to. Bye."

Hanging up the phone, Carleton thought he heard a slight click on the line. He picked up the phone. Nothing.

In another hour, Carleton had signed the order and deposited it in his secretary's box to format in final form. Glancing out the window, he could see rain slowly falling in the starless night, glistening under streetlights. Putting on his coat, he pulled gloves out of the pockets, shoved his fingers deeply into the woolen lining, buttoned his coat, and walked out the door down the empty hall toward the elevator.

On a Friday night, the elevator arrived almost immediately. He strode into the empty car, the elevator descending to the parking garage without interruption. Only a few vehicles remained, mostly owned by custodial personnel who parked after-hours. Government auditors had adopted a policy to save electricity by illuminating every other overhead light inside the bare cement parking structure. Dimly lit exits and entrances open to the street offered targets for wind howling through the garage, dropping rainwater on the floors. Two security guards at each end of the garage huddled in their booths, portable heaters plugged on High.

Carleton walked to his car under the scattered lights, his footsteps echoing throughout the empty, cavernous cement walls, the sound amplified by the screaming wind. Searching for his keys, he heard a sharp, metallic sound behind him. Instantly, he turned and stared into the gloom. From the corner of his eye, he glimpsed the shaft of an overhead light reflecting on a sedan parked against the wall. Instinctively, he ducked behind his car but heard nothing. In a moment, a car motor roared to life. The driver reversed, and the car careened out toward the street. Screeching tires pierced the air as the car raced out of the garage, never slowing nor turning on its lights. In a moment, the night swallowed it up.

Chapter 6

Entering the courtroom together on Monday, lawyers Richardson and Amstead asked Shelley Fields to schedule an emergency hearing that afternoon. At one thirty, Carleton took the bench. The press and spectators occupied every seat. Shelly handed Carleton the file. He glanced at his notes and looked up.

"Counsel, I understand you have asked for a hearing on an expedited basis. Is there a problem with the order I drafted, Mr. Amstead? I'm leaving on vacation shortly."

"Your Honor, Mr. Richardson and I have discussed the order, and we have reached an agreement that we would like to recommend."

"What is it?"

"We both request a brief continuance to suspend enforcement of your order. My clients realize that the murder of an innocent woman has severely affected our position in this case, and they have voluntarily agreed to discontinue picketing for three weeks. They deny any knowledge or complicity in that heinous act that killed an innocent woman and deplore the violence at the clinic but are willing to cancel any further demonstrations.

At the end of three weeks, both sides would return to court for further argument."

"Mr. Richardson, is that your understanding?"

"Yes, Your Honor. But we reserve the right in the interim to reinstate issuance of the order you have signed if there is any violation."

"We agree with that, Your Honor," replied Amstead.

Carleton studied the amended order submitted by both lawyers. "All right. This sounds like a good temporary measure. I will suspend the original order for three weeks and schedule another hearing on that date. If there is any violation of this agreement, my order will go into effect, Mr. Amstead."

"We understand, Your Honor."

"Do both sides agree that the chief judge can substitute if necessary during my absence?"

"Yes, Your Honor," both lawyers replied simultaneously.

"Court is in recess."

Courtroom security guards, allowing only enough spectators to fill all the seats in the courtroom, stood prominently in the aisles to assure no disturbance. A few reporters jumped up to file their reports after Carleton granted the request to delay implementing his order, but a polite and firm, uniformed hand reminded them they had agreed to remain seated until the parties and their lawyers had left the courtroom.

Stepping down from the bench, Carleton glanced toward the departing crowd. Out of the corner of his eye, he saw a man shuffling eagerly toward the door, pushing aside others in his haste. Blocked briefly by the crowded aisle, the man looked in the direction of the judge. Their eyes met. Instantly, the man turned his slightly balding head and ponytail, but not before he saw a startled look in Carleton's face. Carleton stopped to get a better view, but the crowd parted, and the man limped out of the courtroom hurriedly. Carleton quickly returned to his chambers, gulped down a glass of water, and sat down heavily in his chair. A gentle knock on the door interrupted him. Kelly Francis opened the door slightly and peered in.

"Judge, excuse me. Can I come in?"

"Kelly, hi. I was just considering that agreement to continue the case. Come on in."

"Of course, I'm sorry. Shall I come back later?"

"No, no. Come in."

"Well, Judge, have you decided where to go?"

"What do you mean?"

"On your vacation. I just submitted your request to the chief judge."

"Oh, yes, of course. Mexico. A place on the beach to sit and watch the waves."

Kelly laughed. "While you read decisions of the Supreme Court."

"You know me too well, Kelly."

"Just teasing. This is a good time to get away. When do you leave?"

"Tomorrow. It's about a three-hour flight."

"I envy you. Do you need an administrative assistant?"

"Oh, yes. But I'm not sure the people would understand why I need an administrative assistant on my vacation."

"Particularly for the next Supreme Court justice."

"Now, now. Nothing is definite yet."

"Oh, sure. Judge, would it be an imposition to ask if you could bring back a few pictures?"

"Sure, no problem."

"Good. Have a nice trip. See you when you get back."

"Thanks, Kelly."

"I know you're on vacation, but do you want to leave a phone number in case of an emergency?"

"If there's an emergency, the chief can handle it. You don't know where I am."

"Somehow I knew you'd say that. Bye."

Kelly closed the door quietly. Carleton picked up the phone and dialed. The voice mail activated. Carleton waited through the recorded answer then spoke.

"Art, it's Roy. I'm going to the Annunciator, my usual villa in Mexico. You have my number and can reach me there. Otherwise, I'll call you when I get back."

Staying on the line, he listened carefully. Another click.

Chapter 7

Sergeant Basil Slonsky, affectionately known as BS to his colleagues in the police department, slumped in the officer's lounge chair, watching a tape of the demonstration at the clinic. Formerly a competitive weight lifting champion, Slonsky had tired of the unending grind of training for contests that award the winner only one thousand dollars and lead to a nowhere career. When his personal trainer was shot and killed in a robbery, Slonsky abandoned the gym world and joined the Los Angeles Police Department. Easily passing the rugged physical exam, he toiled in the mean streets of South Los Angeles, gaining a reputation as a tough enforcer. Several months of sustained judo training enabled him to disarm drunks, drug addicts, and muggers without inflicting bruises, abrasions, or injury to their skin. The department quickly recognized his skills and assigned him to Homicide, where he experienced the daily world of passion, intrigue, and hate.

Personally opposed to abortion, he nevertheless accepted assignment to investigate the medical-clinic murder, another of his never-ending high-profile cases. From experience in the department, he learned the value of never talking to the media on or off the record. The media had the advantage of the so-called shield law preventing courts or the public from compelling them to disclose their sources of information, but reporters never hesitated to reveal news to the public when it suited their self-interest. Slonsky dismissed most media types as unabashed liberals intent on embarrassing the police, and he ignored them when they shoved microphones in his face and asked questions. But in this case, someone had killed a pregnant woman seeking an abortion, and the universally pro-choice media immediately offered the department full cooperation. One of their own—so to speak—had been killed. When Slonsky asked for the tape of the shooting, Channel 5 television messengered it over immediately. Usually, the television station needed a subpoena.

Slonsky studied the tape intently, scrutinizing each frame in slow motion. Most of the scenes depicted men and women shouting or arguing with one another. When the camera focused on the two women walking toward the clinic, Slonsky sensed the timing of muffled gunshots and saw one of the women jolt backward and collapse. Seconds later, screams split the air. The cameraman, jostled by the frenzied retreating crowd surging around him, let the tape run as he struggled to remain upright with the camera on his shoulder. The camera swung wildly into a semivertical position, erratically sweeping across the people, buildings, and sky.

Weary of watching this dizzying scene, Slonsky reached for the remote to turn off the TV set when something caught his eye as the camera careened upward, taping the side of the courthouse. The cameraman had obviously lost control of the camera, and the tape haphazardly recorded a figure looking through a courthouse window on one of the upper floors. Although the features were blurred by the rain-streaked glass, the observer clearly was watching the scene below. Slonsky stopped the tape and rewound. A second look confirmed the scene, and he reached for the phone and buzzed the lab. When a voice answered, Slonsky shouted, "Get the tech guys ready! I'm coming down with a tape."

Slonsky stood up, walked over to the VCR, checked the tape number, and pushed the Eject button. Grabbing the tape, he hurried down the hall to the lab. The forensics expert, Billy Forsyth, was ready.

Slonsky handed him the tape.

"Put this in."

Forsyth inserted the tape, and the scene came to life on his computer.

Slonsky interrupted, "Freeze the frame."

The tape stopped, and Slonsky leaned forward. "Zoom in."

The camera had fallen onto the street, continuing to run, and it depicted a figure standing behind a courthouse window. But without enough light and rain streaming down the glass, Slonsky could only see a blurred and indistinct face.

"Sharpen it."

The scene sharpened. Slonsky could see empty bookshelves in the background behind the figure in the window. He squinted at the screen.

"Can you get it any sharper, Bill?"

"Hey, BS, we can only do so much. This ain't gonna get any sharper."

"Can you brighten it at all?"

The picture brightened but washed out the face.

"Best I can do, BS."

"Print it for me."

The laser printer spit out a hard copy. Slonsky grabbed it. Ejecting the tape, he slipped it into his coat pocket. Forsyth looked surprised.

"Where you going in such a rush? You couldn't see anything."

"To do a room check in the courthouse."

"Sure, but what for?"

"So I can see who doesn't have books on their bookshelf."

"You know, BS, you can never tell what turns cops on."

Chapter 8

"I'm sorry, Detective Slonsky," said Kelly Francis, "but the judges have all gone home, and the chambers are locked. I know they don't want anyone in there while they're gone, and I just don't have the authority to let you in. The police have already been here, but is there anything else I could do to help?"

Francis smiled sweetly.

Slonsky's face tightened around the mouth. "No, not at this time. Tell you what, suppose I just stand in the doorway with you and look inside the room. No entry. We're trying to determine whether anyone might have fired a shot from this building. We still don't know if there might have been another person involved."

"Surely you don't think any of the judges are suspects, do you?"

"Oh, no. We're just trying to cover all the bases. The courthouse is the only one of the few buildings tall enough in the area for anyone to see clearly what's going on in the street below. Just routine."

"Well, maybe if I was with you and you just stood in the doorways, that would be all right."

"Good. That's fine."

"Mr. Slonsky, there are ten judge's chambers on this floor. Pretty much all alike. Please follow me."

Kelly ushered Slonsky toward the door, reaching inside her jacket pocket for the keys. They walked silently together down the long hall, stopping first at the chambers of the chief judge. Kelly opened the door, and after Slonsky surveyed the room, she started down the hall, opening each door, while he stopped and peered inside. Although some chambers were more personalized than others, each was almost identical in size and furnishings. All had bookshelves on one side of the room or the other, every one stuffed with books—except one: the chambers labeled Honorable Royal Carleton. Slonsky removed a photograph from his coat pocket depicting the indistinct figure standing in the window, but the bookshelf in the background was clearly visible and displayed no books on the top two shelves. He glanced back and forth between the photo and the bookshelves.

"You found something," said Kelly.

"No. Just trying to keep the rooms straight. Say, is that a picture of the judge on the wall showing him holding a fish? Looks like he's pretty tall."

"About six foot two. Played tight end in college."

"Hmm. Anyway, that's the last one. I took some mental notes on the angles from each room, but it looks like they all have about the same vantage point. Sorry for the inconvenience."

Kelly closed the door.

"No problem. I'll just lock up all the doors. Would you mind seeing yourself out?"

"Not at all. Thanks again."

Slonsky handed Kelly his card and started down the hallway, the sound of his retreating footsteps clicking on the floor. Kelly opened the door to Carleton's chambers, walked over to the telephone on Carleton's desk, and called on the phone.

A voice answered, "Yes."

"We've got a problem. I think this cop I told you about is on to something, but I'm not sure."

"Meet me tonight. Same place."

Chapter 9

The sullen foreman of the janitorial service in the courthouse scowled at Slonsky. He waved his dirt-stained hands wildly when he talked.

"Why do you want to see the building plans at this hour? The courthouse is closed, and we have strict orders not to allow anyone inside the building without the consent of the judge."

"Mr. Butler, I just want the blueprints to the building. You know, the ones you are required to keep for inspection."

"Inspection, yes, during business hours. Why can't you come back when the courthouse is open tomorrow?"

"Look, I don't want to be difficult. Should I get a subpoena to order you to court or not?"

The hands came down in disgust over the blue overalls. The weathered face creased with exasperation. "All right. I'll get 'em. You stay here."

The foreman turned on his heel and headed toward the clerk's office at the end of the hall. Slonsky watched him unlock the door, turn, scowl, enter the room, and slam the door behind himself. The lights flickered on, and through the glazed window in the door, the shadow of the foreman opened a file drawer, reached in, and removed papers. Slamming the drawer shut, he stalked back through the door and thrust the blueprints into Slonsky's outstretched hand.

"Here you are. How long you gonna be looking at 'em?"

"Not long."

"Terrific. I gotta stay here while you look through all the blueprints. 'Not long,'" he mimicked.

Slonsky smiled. "Just about ten minutes."

"Ten minutes. OK. I'll just sit here and watch. Real exciting." Slonsky laughed briefly. Quickly thumbing through the blueprints, he pulled out the design for the third floor judges' chambers. Tracing the line from each window toward the general location down the street where the woman was shot, he marked at least three courtrooms as possible vantage points. He rolled up the plans and handed them to the impatient foreman. He reached in his pocket.

"By the way, my friend, here's something for your trouble." Slonsky handed two twenty-dollar bills to the foreman, who stuffed the money in his overalls.

He looked at Slonsky. "Oh, you don't have to do that," he replied incredulously.

"I know. But you've been a big help. And I know how hard your work is. Moving furniture, books, chairs, and all that stuff."

"Well, I got lots of help."

"How do you move so many lawbooks? The chambers are filled with them."

"Some judges keep everything. We like those guys. Others throw a lot of stuff out. About two weeks ago, we carried out whole shelves full of books from one judge's chambers. Not only that. We took some he had stacked on the top shelf."

"Whoa. Is that part of the job?"

"No. But Judge Carleton is a generous guy. Always gives us a big tip at Christmas."

"The judge that's hearing the abortion case?"

"That's him. You know him?"

"No. Sounds like a straight shooter though."

The foreman looked around slowly and spoke in mock confidentiality.

"Yep. He might even be on the Supreme Court someday. That's probably where the books are going."

"Really? Well, thanks again. Here's my card if I can ever help you out."

Slonsky smiled at the speechless janitor, who accepted the business card. Slonsky turned and walked away, smiling as he spoke, "Don't bother, my good man. I'll see myself out."

Chapter 10

Standing on the sidewalk near gutters trickling with rainwater, Slonsky waited for several cars to pass then walked out to the yellow dividing line painted on the street. Scanning the courthouse, he counted windows until he came to three that had a line of sight to the street, overlooking the location where the woman was shot. A leafy oak tree on the parkway obstructed his view of two windows. Only one window enabled a viewer to clearly see the shooting—if the viewer was looking. Scanning the photographs taken from the tape, someone was indeed looking from the only window facing the street with a clear view: the chambers of Judge Royal Carleton, room 13.

Walking toward the sidewalk to avoid approaching cars, Slonsky studied other photographs of the scene. Despite the rain, the faded chalk lines drawn by police marked the outline of a dead body. Hurrying to his car, he punched the computer, searching for the home phone of Judge Carleton. The monitor blinked: unlisted and classified. He punched another key enabling him to avoid the regular listing. Up came the number. Slonsky reached for his cell phone and punched in the number.

"Hello," answered Helen Morris, housekeeper to Judge Carleton.

"This is Detective Slonsky, LAPD. I'm conducting an investigation of a recent killing outside the courthouse. Is the judge at home?"

"No. He's on vacation. Won't be back for a week."

"Do you know where he went?"

"No, I'm the housekeeper. Somewhere in Mexico. He didn't tell me."

"What time did he leave?"

"Sometime after six o'clock last night."

"OK, I'll call him when he gets back."

Slonsky tapped on the phone in silence. Running down his list of numbers, he stopped at Tammy Moreno. He punched in her number.

A voice answered, "World Travel. This is Tammy."

"Tammy, hi. This is Basil Slonsky from LAPD. Do you remember me?"

"Of course. I'm happy to hear your voice. You helped me escape from my abusive husband and got me into a woman's shelter. No news about my husband, I hope?"

"No, he's long gone."

"Good. And you're calling because I suppose you need a travel agent. I'm available."

"Actually, Tammy, I need a little expert information."

"Oh, and I thought it was something else you needed. Well, I'm available."

"I need some airline schedules for last night's flights out of the city going to Mexico."

"No problem, but my computer system here at the office is down. If it's important, we can run it on my computer at home. I was just leaving the office anyway."

"If you don't mind."

"Not at all. You have my home address. I'll meet you in an hour."

"I'm on my way."

* * *

Slonsky stood outside the gated and locked apartment building. He punched in Tammy's apartment number on the directory and announced himself. In response, a buzzer unlocked the door, and he entered the ornate lobby, looked around approvingly, squinted at the chandelier, and admired the leather couches and exotic plants. He entered the elevator, exited on the eighth floor, and walked down the corridor, to be greeted by a smiling Tammy Moreno standing in front of her apartment. Dressed in black pants and a white blouse, her blond hair cascading over bare shoulders, she ushered Slonsky inside.

"Come in. Come in. What a pleasant surprise. I thought maybe you had forgotten about me."

"Not a chance."

"Why haven't you called?"

"I just did."

"That was a business call."

"You're right. But there's lots of folks out there shooting each other. Too much work."

"You can't work all the time. Here, come in and sit down. Loosen that power tie and take your coat off so I can admire those biceps."

Tammy walked over and helped Slonsky off with his jacket. He could feel her hands slide gently down his arms. Her perfume drifted across his face. She brushed her breasts across his back.

"Sergeant, I see you still buy your suits off the rack. You need a woman's help. But enough of that. What can I get you to drink?"

"I'm on duty. How about a soft drink?"

"Coming right up. With plenty of ice, as I recall."

Slonsky nodded. He watched the slender figure, her waist cinched by a silver belt, her high heels clicking on the tile, hips swaying slightly, disappear into the kitchen. He looked around to study a comfortable and tastefully decorated room dimly lit. Soft carpets. Overstuffed furniture. He sank into a sofa. In minutes, she returned with a glass of ice and a can. She poured the liquid slowly over the ice, leaned over, and handed him the glass and the can. She wore no bra.

"Here you are. The good stuff," she smirked, "if you know what I mean."

"Right. Here I am, alone with a gorgeous woman, and I order a nonalcoholic drink. Not too romantic."

"And you're not here for romance."

"Unfortunately, no."

"Yes, unfortunately."

Tammy grinned and sat down next to him. Her perfume wafted across his face again. Slonsky sipped his drink slowly, feeling her arm against his shoulder.

"Tammy, I need help from a good travel agent."

"And I need help from a good man, someone who works out at a gym, say, like you."

She ran her hand across his arm, pressing ever so slightly. Slonsky tensed. "I'll keep my eyes open for one."

Tammy sat back and pouted. "OK. I can see we're not getting anywhere tonight. What do you need, and why do you need it?"

"I really can't tell you the details because I may be off the track."

"I'll accept that. It's a little sensitive?"

"A little. I need to know whether a certain person left the city last night."

"What's her name?"

"Not *her. His.*"

"Good," she beamed.

"Judge Royal Carleton."

Tammy sat up. "A judge? The one on the abortion case?"

"I said it might be a little sensitive."

Tammy blinked, rolled her eyes, and grimaced. Standing up, she walked over to a mahogany secretary, lifted up the desktop, and pulled out her computer. Activating it in a moment, she spoke over her shoulder, "What airline?"

"At that time of night, probably Mexicana."

"Spell his name."

"C-a-r-l-e-t-o-n, R-o-y-a-l. Or it could just be Roy Carleton.'"

Clicking, scrolling, Tammy waited for the computer to catch up.

"Here he is. Mexicana. Flight 709 to Acapulco."

"Can you find out where he's staying?"

Clicking some more, she said, "Villa Annunciator. About five miles from Acapulco in a village called San Tomas."

"Tammy, I could kiss you."

"Why don't you?"

Slonsky just smiled and gulped down his drink.

Chapter 11

Chief Willard Riley leaned forward in his chair, his florid face deepening around unamused eyes.

"So, Slonsky, you want to go to Acapulco to investigate the abortion case and talk to a witness. And I want to take a cruise to the Bahamas to see who shot John Kennedy. Look, Slonsky, for twenty years, I worked detectives, solved more crimes than any other dick. But never, never did I feel the need to investigate by going to Mexico, swim in the ocean, and sleep all day. That's what the Feds do, waste taxpayer money."

"Chief, this is really sensitive. I wouldn't ask if it weren't important."

"Oh, how considerate. Am I allowed to know whom you're investigating?"

"Judge Roy Carleton."

Riley, seldom at a loss for words, could only stutter.

"A judge? You think a judge is responsible for a murder? Slonsky, now I know why they call you BS for short. Have you thought about retirement? I can get you a disability for mental strain."

"No, Chief, not as a suspect. As a witness."

"A witness to what?"

"The abortion murder."

"How the hell would he know anything about it?"

Slonsky stood up and laid out his report on the desk, including the photos of the figure in the window and the empty bookshelves. He explained his investigation. Riley was not impressed.

"And you think that's enough? You tell me somebody standing in a room whom you can't identify, don't know whether he, or she, saw something and didn't tell anyone about it, and you think it's Carleton? If it was him and he saw something, why didn't he report it? Or if it wasn't him, why wouldn't some other person in the room report what they saw?"

"That's just it. Why didn't they?"

"Why don't you just call him on the phone?"

"Chief, you know face-to-face is better."

"This makes a wild goose chase look like shooting fish in a barrel. OK. You got two days. Understand? Two days. Read my lips. By yourself. Clear?"

"Thanks, Chief. You're a prince."

"I'm an idiot."

Chapter 12

Accustomed to gritty urban streets and unending traffic, Slonsky surveyed the broad, uncluttered, quiet village of San Tomas. An uneventful afternoon flight landed him at a pristine airport in Acapulco obviously designed for American tourists. All signs in Spanish were also written in English. An impeccably dressed taxi driver delivered him to the Villa Annunciator, where an obsequious clerk checked him in efficiently. Without request, a bellman appeared, carefully placed Slonsky's luggage on a cart, and beckoned the detective to follow him outside.

Sitting in the cart while passing several villas, Slonsky marveled at the clipped shrubbery, the verdant grass, and the trimmed trees. The bellman smiled broadly, stopped the cart, removed the luggage, and signaled Slonsky to follow him into a bleached white villa facing a swimming pool. Softly lapping water caressed the side of the pool, glistening under stately lit lights. Mesmerized by the scene, Slonsky dimly heard the voice of the bellman in the background.

"Over here, Senor. Welcome to the Villa Annunciator."

Slonsky turned to see the smiling bellman standing in the doorway of the villa, nodding for him to come inside. Trailing the bellman, who had opened the door more widely with a flourish, Slonsky stepped into a spacious living room professionally decorated in Mexican motif. An immense window on the far wall overlooked the Pacific Ocean, its shore slightly graded into a private beach, deserted except for a handful of beach chairs shaded by umbrellas and a cabana set for two. On the walls, Mexican art, subdued and tasteful, adorned the polished plaster. The tile floor, beamed ceilings, and casual furniture clearly invited the occupant to relax. Slonsky handed a few coins to the perpetually smiling bellman, who busily fussed with the luggage. Bowing his head deferentially toward Slonsky, he accepted the money, walked to the door, and quietly closed it behind him.

Slonsky stood in front of the window, his eyes sweeping the grandeur of the ocean. Removing his jacket, he slumped onto the sofa, loosened his tie, and stared out into the endless space. Interrupting his own reverie, he picked up the phone and called the front desk.

"Front desk," answered the desk clerk.

"I don't think I gave the bellman a big-enough tip. Hard to figure out the exchange rate."

"That's perfectly all right, sir. No need to bother."

"No, no, I insist. Besides, I might need some other service."

"Of course, sir. I understand. Ramon will be right over."

Within minutes, a knock on the door announced the quickly responding bellman.

Slonsky motioned him inside, reached into his pocket, and pulled out several American dollars. Handing the money to the obviously delighted bellman, he said, "Ramon, I need some information."

"I understand, sir. I know several women—"

"Not that kind of information."

"No?"

"I need to know if someone else is staying here."

"I am sorry, sir, I cannot give out that kind of information to—"

Slonsky waved his hand casually in the air and pulled out a few more dollars from his pocket.

The bellman smiled. "Of course. Perhaps in this case, we could make an exception."

A few more bills changed hands. The bellman folded the currency carefully.

"Now I am sure we can make an exception. Let me see what we have."

Removing a guest list from his vest pocket, the bellman ran his finger down the lines.

"How do you spell the name?"

"C-a-r-l-e-t-o-n."

"Sir, there is no one here registered under that name."

"Let me see that."

The bellman handed Slonsky the list, modest in length, but Carleton's name did not appear. He looked again. Under the letter *R* was listed "Royal, Carl, villa 22." Slonsky feigned surprise.

"I guess he's not here."

"Sorry, Senor. Maybe he will arrive later."

"That's probably it. Thanks a lot."

Slonsky handed the list back to the perpetually smiling bellman, who quietly closed the door behind himself and retreated down the pathway. Only twenty-five villas comprised the Villa Annunciator, and Slonsky easily found number 22. He surveyed the surroundings and waited a few minutes, studying Carleton's villa as well as those on either side. Nothing of significance occurred while Slonsky strolled around the grounds for half an hour, but dusk began to shroud the sun, and lights from inside the villa blinked on. Moments later, ground lights illuminated the paths.

Slonsky, moving casually behind a tree, attempted to look inside the villa. A figure walked across the room in front of the window, but the evening sky too dark to identify. Moving toward the partially shaded window, he peered inside. Judge Carleton was engaged in animated conversation with another man. The exchange stopped; the man shook hands with Carleton reassuringly and grasped his shoulder warmly. He briefly said something and strode toward the door. After a few more words, he walked outside, stopped briefly on the steps, and set down his luggage. He turned toward the door and spoke, "Judge, don't worry. Hey, maybe I should call you Justice Carleton. No one knows you're here except me. Get some sleep."

"Thanks, Art. I really appreciate your advice. And thanks for coming down here at the last minute."

"You're welcome. Art Mathews, political hack, at your service." Judge Carleton closed the door, and Mathews stood silently outside the villa. The sound of tires running over stones signaled an approaching hotel cart. A different bellman arrived, parked the cart, and walked toward the door. Picking up the stacked luggage and placing it on the cart, he waited briefly until his passenger climbed in. The cart drove off, its electric motor humming, and only the tires crunching on the path broke the stillness of the approaching night.

Slonsky walked slowly toward the villa under a canopy of enormous oak trees. While placing his badge conspicuously on his suit, he heard the sound of another cart approaching from a different direction. In the glare of the headlights, his bellman drove up toward villa 22. A single passenger in the cart sat silently, apparently waiting to get off. The cart stopped short of villa 22, and a man wearing a long-sleeved dark shirt eased himself out. Carrying no luggage, he handed something to the bellman, turned, and stared intently at the villa. When the cart drove away, Slonsky retreated behind the trees. The stranger moved slowly, limping toward the doorway to the villa. He slipped one hand under his shirt. The porch light shed enough illumination to disclose the unmistakable glint of a revolver. The man reached into his pocket, removed another object, and attached it to the end of the weapon. For a moment, the rising moon slipped out from behind the clouds to reveal the man held a revolver equipped with a silencer. The moon vanished, and under darkening skies, the figure walked toward the door, looking around and slowly reaching for the door handle.

Slonsky reached for his holstered weapon, stepped out from behind the trees into the open, and shouted, "Drop it, or I'll shoot!"

Stunned, the man stood up and turned toward the sound of Slonsky's voice.

Slonsky shouted again, "I said drop it. Police."

In response, the man raised his weapon and fired two shots, muffled by the silencer, in the direction of Slonsky. One bullet tore into a tree and shredded the bark. Slonsky jumped back then fired twice at the now-moving figure, the sound of gunshots ripping through the stillness of the night. Slonsky crouched, struggling to see his target and simultaneously concealing himself. The sound of running feet retreated into the darkness. Slonsky wavered, trying to decide whether to follow and risk ambush. He heard the door to the villa open, and carefully stepping out from the safety of the trees, a man rushed out.

"Get back inside!" shouted Slonsky.

The man froze.

"Get back inside, or you'll get shot."

The man turned on his heels, rushed inside the villa, and slammed the door shut. Slonsky stood erect warily. Other villa doors opened, and guests looked around anxiously. Slonsky replaced his weapon in its holster, walked toward the door to villa 22, knocked, and waited. He shouted, "Judge, you're safe now! It's Detective Basil Slonsky, LAPD. Open the door."

Slonsky held his badge up high in the air.

The door stayed closed. Slonsky walked to one of the overhead lights by the pool in front of the villa and stood underneath it.

"Judge, I'm Detective Slonsky, LAPD. Everything is OK. Please open the door."

The door opened slowly. An anxious Judge Carleton squinted in the darkness, looked out warily, and beckoned Slonsky to come in.

Chapter 13

Bewildered and frightened guests who had poured out of their villas upon hearing the sound of gunfire stood around uncertainly. Slonsky lifted both hands toward the crowd and signaled for quiet.

"It's OK, folks. I'm a police officer. I fired my gun in the air because I saw a coyote apparently wandering down from the hills."

Those guests who had brought their dogs and cats thanked him profusely. One of the guests, an ecologist, mumbled about nature and the wilderness but was universally ignored. After calming everyone's nerves, Slonsky reassuringly told them to return to their villas.

Now he sat in an overstuffed chair facing a distraught Judge Carleton, both sipping iced tea and sandwiches prepared by the hotel. Having introduced himself and explained his presence, he asked, "Judge, do you have any idea who might try to kill you?"

"Lord, no. But I suppose it's someone who feels strongly about abortion—one side or the other."

"But you haven't made your final decision yet. Why would anyone want to kill you before then?"

"Sergeant, you don't know the people on both sides of this issue. Some think the murder of that young woman should result in me throwing the book at the pro-lifers. Others would say that's exactly the reason the pro-choice crowd set it up."

"Or it could be some nut."

"Or someone I sentenced in another case."

"Maybe we should assign some men to you for protection."

"No, that's not necessary. Whoever tried to kill me tonight got thoroughly scared and assumes I have protection. Unlikely he'll try again."

"But, Judge—"

"Sergeant, in order for you to assign protection for me, you need my consent. Correct?"

"Yes. All right, but consider it an open offer."

"Fair enough."

"One more thing. The Feds are involved in this abortion case. Since you're the judge, they'll probably contact you. I'd appreciate it if you kept me informed."

"No problem."

Slonsky paused.

"Judge, you probably don't know it, but I went to the courthouse a couple of days ago and looked at all the judges' chambers."

"You what?"

"Don't worry, I just stood in the doorway and looked. We wanted to make sure no one in the courthouse or any other building had a vantage point in a room acting as a lookout, even in the courthouse. Then I watched a tape that the TV cameraman took during the shooting. In the tape, you can see a figure standing in the window of your chambers. Any idea who that might be?"

"It could have been me. I did come to the window after all the screaming started. But people were just running away."

"How could you have heard screaming through the window? It's double-pane glass, according to the blueprints."

"Sergeant, you can hear demonstrators chanting and shouting even through the window. I know the difference between shouting and screaming."

"So you only saw people running? Nobody with a gun?"

"Correct. I had no idea what had happened."

"But the tape shows the figure in the window watching the picketing, then the shooting occurred, and people running away."

"Maybe my law clerk was at the window. Did you interview him?"

"No. I didn't know you had one."

"I can't explain it. Sergeant, I've told you what I know."

Slonsky stood up, moved his plate aside, and extended his hand.

"Good enough. Thanks, Judge. Pleasure meeting you. Here's my card. Call me if you think of anything else. I'll see myself out."

"Thank you, Sergeant. I am most grateful to you."

Slonsky waved his hand casually, shook hands with Carleton, and walked toward the door and out into the night.

Chapter 14

Jean Carleton stood impatiently in front of the elevator doors, staring at the blinking light signaling the approaching elevator. The doors opened to disclose several men exiting, who eyed her approvingly. Age had damaged her face, but plastic surgery had restored it. And faithful to her diet and personal trainer, she maintained a figure that continued to attract the male glance. Outwardly indifferent, she stepped demurely into the elevator and pressed the button for the eighth floor. At 6:00 p.m., everyone crowded the down elevator, and Jean rode up alone. The door opened to a corridor with a list of room numbers fastened to the wall. She searched the names and found "Paul McClosky, private investigator: room 808." Walking down the hall, she opened the door to room 808 slowly and entered. The receptionist, Janice Weston, was putting on her coat, about to leave. She looked up.

"Mrs. Carleton?"

"Yes."

"I'll tell Mr. McClosky you're here. I'm just leaving, so please sit down."

"Thank you."

Janice pressed the intercom. "Mrs. Carleton is here."

"I'll be there in just a minute," replied a voice.

Janice smiled and picked up her purse.

"He'll be right out. Please excuse me. My husband is waiting."

Jean Carleton nodded indifferently.

Janice, picking up her umbrella, walked out the door, while Mrs. Carleton surveyed the office. Plaques and awards, carefully arranged, hung on the wall. The police department had awarded him numerous honors, the city had commended him, and the district attorney presented him with the prestigious Outstanding Investigator Award. Several newspaper articles, laminated and framed, were interspersed among the photographs. A photograph of the chief of police shaking hands with a man hung over the transom to the office next to a pair of .45s, crossed with loaded clips. The office door opened, framing the six foot lean and elegantly tailored McClosky. Physically impressive and possessed of a disarming smile, he held out his hand. "Mrs. Carleton?"

"Yes."

"I'm Paul McClosky. Please come in."

Standing aside to let her pass, McClosky closed the door, eyeing her languorous gait approvingly.

"Sit down, please. Can I offer you something to drink? Coffee? Tea?"

"No, thank you. I'm fine."

As she started to sit down, McClosky grasped the chair and slid it gently underneath her. He walked around behind his desk and sat down.

"I got your message, Mrs. Carleton. I understand you are Judge Carleton's wife."

"Legally, yes. But we are living apart."

"I see. How can I help you?"

"I need someone who is not intimidated by power and who knows the inside workings of the courthouse. I was told that you were formerly a high-ranking police officer, had investigated major cases with the district attorney's office, and testified frequently in court."

"If I may say so, in all modesty, the above is true."

"My husband is a very influential man. The president has his name on the short list for a vacancy on the United States Supreme Court."

"So I understand."

"I don't think he is an appropriate candidate."

McClosky folded his hands in reply.

"He has an excellent reputation among lawyers, Mrs. Carleton. Why do you say that?"

"Because he is having an affair."

"Why do you think so? Are you sure?"

"Not entirely, which is why I want you to check it out."

"Without seeming rude, Mrs. Carleton, if you are separated and, I presume, contemplating divorce, why does this concern you?"

"Mr. McClosky, don't you think that a prospective justice of the United States Supreme Court should be faithful, at least until there is a divorce?"

"Yes, but if he is having an affair, the information would sink his appointment."

"That's a risk he has to take."

"I suppose so. Still, how does this affect you?"

"If there is a divorce and I can prove infidelity, the court will certainly consider the division of property differently for me and my daughter."

"That's so. How old is your daughter?"

"Eighteen. She lives with me."

"I see. What do you want me to do?"

"Find out if I'm right."

McClosky frowned, pursed his lips, and leaned forward slightly in his chair.

"I'll be frank with you, Mrs. Carleton. I like Judge Carleton. I testified in his court many times, and they don't come any better. And he sentences big-time. Most of all, he's fair. If I took your case, it's on the basis of his possible infidelity as it relates to his profession—not to satisfy any vindictive personal reasons."

Placing her hands on the arms of the chair, signaling her departure, she started to stand. But she wavered for a moment before sitting down.

"Understood. Here's a file for you to read."

She pulled out a large manila envelope from her purse and handed it to McClosky.

"Mr. McClosky, read this over. Then call me."

She stood up, without offering him her hand.

"My telephone number is in the file."

"Don't you want to know my fee and how I'll proceed?"

"Just send me your bill. I don't care what you do or how you do it. In fact, I don't even want to know."

She turned sharply and let herself out.

Chapter 15

Slonsky sat down heavily in Chief Riley's office, twisting his burly hands and looking absently out the window while waiting for the chief to finish a phone call that had interrupted him. Riley slammed down the phone.

"Those damn reporters think we have nothing to do except work on this case. It's not the only homicide in town."

He paused.

"All right, Basil, tell me how well we're doing."

"Going nowhere. No leads. No witnesses. The usual informants in homicide cases came up dry. Nothing on the Channel 5 tape showed who fired the shots that killed the woman. The camera was focused on the pregnant woman when someone shot her."

"Anyone with cell phones taking pictures?"

"Rain was too heavy, and people, including the photographers, were rushing toward the victim. The crowd pictures from the TV camera show no one taking pictures."

"Anything else?"

It's my opinion that Judge Carleton stood at the window and witnessed the shooting but inexplicably refused to cooperate.

The video shows him standing by the window before the shooting started."

"OK. OK. You told me about your talk with the judge, but he told you nothing. If the judge saw someone, even if he couldn't identify the shooter, why not say so?"

"Good question. His law clerk was on vacation at the time of the shooting, and the registration desk at the courthouse showed no visitors to him."

"That doesn't mean he saw the shooting."

"No, but why didn't he at least what he did see prior to the shooting?"

"In a crowd during rain, he's supposed to see someone with a gun?"

The sound of the intercom interrupted them. Riley pushed the button to the intercom. His secretary spoke on the line, "A Mr. McClosky would like to speak to Mr. Slonsky whenever it's convenient."

Slonsky shrugged his shoulders at Riley.

"Go ahead, Basil. Basically we've made no progress."

"That's about it, Chief. I'll call you tomorrow."

Slonsky opened the door and walked out of the room to see Paul McClosky sitting quietly in a chair. Slonsky stopped.

"McClosky. What the hell are you doing here?"

"I just came up to visit a former colleague."

"Oh, sure. You came here without calling me because you knew I'd say no to whatever you wanted."

"Hey, BS, I used to work in the same department with you, remember?"

"All too well. The glory hound."

"Look, I didn't come here to open old wounds. In fact, we might have a joint investigation going. Can we talk?"

Slonsky only grimaced and pointed to a nearby room. McClosky entered and looked around briefly.

"I'm not interrupting anything, am I?"

"Do you care?"

McClosky smiled.

Slonsky closed the door behind him, and both sat down. Slonsky waited, while McClosky opened his briefcase and removed a file. Spreading it out on the table, he pointed to a sheaf of papers.

"I read your so-called supplemental homicide report. You interviewed Judge Carleton."

"How did you get a hold of that? Those reports are confidential."

"Basil, please. Instead of questioning me, maybe I can give you some answers."

"Same smart-ass as always."

McClosky waved off the insult.

"Based on your notes—which you did not include in your original report—and the photos, you speculate that Carleton saw the shooting. So why didn't he volunteer the information?"

"You tell me."

"Basil, I have a client. You need a suspect."

Slonsky sniffed. "OK, McClosky. What's your offer?"

"I don't know exactly what Carleton is doing. He's up for the Supreme Court. And he's probably going through a divorce."

"So?"

"Maybe Carleton is involved in the shooting."

"Are you nuts? Why?"

"Look, BS, someone shoots a pregnant woman during an abortion protest. Who gets the blame?"

"Theoretically, the protestors."

"Right. The pro-life crowd. Now Carleton can decide the protest is getting out of line and shut it down. He does the politically correct thing and orders the demonstrators limited so severely they are ineffective. Who can complain? Pro-lifers are way off-balance. They can't defend the shooting, and Carleton gets his job on the Supreme Court."

"I don't think Carleton is the type. Somebody from the pro-choice crowd could have set this up."

71

"I thought of that. But either way, Carleton wins. Look, you have no persons of interest for the media. By the time you guys find the shooter, if ever, Carleton has gone to Washington. Even if you find the shooter, the case will be continued in court for years before the trial even starts. You're appointed already. Case closed."

"I just don't think a guy like Carleton would do something like that."

"Maybe not. But I have a client who thinks Carleton is involved in something else."

"Naturally, I can't know who your client is or what the information is either."

"Naturally. But I can share some of what I come up with. If so, I satisfy my client, maybe you get the shooter."

"Maybe."

"Yes, maybe. But you don't have any better ideas, or you wouldn't be here loafing."

"OK. Deal."

"Give me some time to check some stuff out. I'll see you at the funeral for that woman who was killed."

Chapter 16

The congregation sat silently inside St. Catherine Church, awaiting the start of the memorial service for homicide victim Maureen McCullough. The memorial had been delayed while police searched unsuccessfully the area for family or relatives. The pastor had banned press, radio, and television coverage inside the church, but on the crowded front steps, a gaggle of reporters and photographers hovered, while men and women entered the venerable St. Catherine. The media, consigned to wait until the service ended, milled around aimlessly, constantly inspecting their watches and talking on cell phones. Staff writers wrote editorials railing against this wanton act of murder committed by a crazed lunatic undoubtedly associated with the antiabortion crowd. Front pages announced the hunt for the suspect had focused on the most vocal pro-lifers, but police had made no arrests.

Slonsky stood in the back of the church, while the priest recited prayers and the choir intoned hymns. No member or relative of the McCullough family attended, the homily mercifully short, and no one delivered a eulogy. Slonsky moved forward down the side aisle and stood near a pillar adjacent to the altar.

Father Dan Braun smiled slightly at him in a sign of recognition as the choir concluded the service.

Slonsky returned to the rear of the church and waited, while the choir began the recessional hymn, joined by the congregation in singing "Holy God, We Praise Thy Name." The congregation filed out, struggling through the media who were attending a memorial of a woman virtually unknown in life who had become an overnight celebrity in death. Photographers pushed people aside and repeatedly flashed pictures of various city officials. Slonsky inched his way through the crowd out of the church and walked to his car. Unlocking the door, he entered, sat down, and reached for a large brown envelope. Opening its contents, he removed a photograph and a report received from an FBI agent he had met in New York. He read the report again.

> BS, good to hear from you. In reply to your fax: Read your report on a Maureen McCullough. Enclosed is her photo from high school. Born in upstate New York, not far from the Canadian border. Graduated from high school and went to Canada. No work record there, and she lived in an apartment under an assumed name. Both parents are dead. No relatives or siblings as far as I know. How she got to California is a good question. Lived in Vegas for a short time.

Cops think she got married by some drunk who has
no records, and the city has no proof. Nothing in the
DNA base. One set of prints. No New York driver's
license. No job. Dead end.

Not much here in the Big Apple. Good luck.

Agent Frank Abrams

Slonsky stuffed the photograph and report back into the
envelope.

Chapter 17

The court bailiff opened the morning session to a packed courtroom after quieting the spectators. Slonsky and McClosky sat in the last row on different sides of the aisle as Judge Carleton stepped up to his chair and sat down. He nodded to lawyers Amstead and Richardson.

"Good morning, counsel."

"Good morning, Your Honor," replied both lawyers.

Carleton folded his hands and leaned forward. "Mr. Amstead, I know your clients have agreed to withdraw from the clinic area for a short period of time. Thankfully, no further violence has occurred. I am confident, however, that they will want to resume demonstrations at the expiration of the time period you both agreed upon. But I cannot make my ultimate decision necessarily influenced by their cooperation. In this matter, I have given careful consideration of the request to issue a court order banning demonstrations outside the medical clinic. I need not remind you that the United States Supreme Court has repeatedly guaranteed the right of the people to assemble and demonstrate their political convictions. This country has always afforded dissenters the right to disagree with the majority, no matter how odious their views, even to the point of protecting them from violent suppression. Civil rights demonstrations and union picket lines were protected against violence even when causing widespread opposition to their cause. The court has been a bastion against governmental suppression of speech.

"But free speech is not a license to violate the law. And in this case, the evidence clearly establishes that pickets marched peacefully, blocked no entrances, and only attempted to persuade people to agree, or at least understand their point of view, by singing and chanting. The volume of their voices was matched by those who opposed them. In a word, prior to the shooting of an unfortunate woman, the police had not made a single arrest. No injuries. No violence. This demonstration was conducted respectfully and responsibly."

Carleton paused briefly and pushed his chair forward.

"But I cannot ignore the premeditated and unjustified act of violence that caused the death of an innocent person. And it is obvious that this court cannot overlook the increased tension among the public subsequent to that homicide. Although no violence has occurred as of yet, the public needs assurance that the demonstrators will not resume picketing in the absence of a court order. I am not implying any bad faith on the part of the demonstrators who now have voluntarily discontinued their picketing. But I think all parties will be better served if there is an order submitted by Mr. Richardson. Without a court order, the temptation to resume may be too great. Accordingly, I will issue a temporary order effective for fifteen days banning any demonstration on the premises of the clinic. At the end of that time, I will reconsider my order. This order should not be interpreted as an indication of my final decision, and I will also entertain additional argument and rule at that time.

"I appreciate the efforts of both counsels to agree on a voluntary withdrawal of all demonstrators for both sides. Perhaps the lull in demonstrations alone will be helpful. Issuance of the order applies to all sides, and there have been no arrests for evidence of unlawful activity. Since both counsels have voluntarily agreed to do what the order says, I think we might come to some agreement. See the clerk for the terms of the order. Court is in recess."

A shifting of seats and a low hum of voices swept through the courtroom. Carleton stood and exited, while the court bailiffs restrained the media briefly, but upon their release, reporters raced out, pushing and shoving while calling on their cell phones. In the hallway outside the courtroom, Paul McClosky smiled smugly and waved to a departing Slonsky.

Chapter 18

Underneath the old Criminal Courts Building, the Los Angeles County Morgue hid resolutely from public scrutiny. Originally built in 1925 to house cadavers in a sleepy town struggling to exist in a desert, the explosive growth of Los Angeles after World War II strained the facilities of the coroner beyond its capacity to conduct autopsies. Friends and relatives of a deceased often retched when entering the building to identify a body riddled with bullet holes or slashed by a knife. The overwhelming stench of death, coupled with the odor of sterile chemicals, had sickened numerous inexperienced young police officers and attorneys. County officials ignored the necessary evil of a besieged coroner's office, but the population explosion forced the board of supervisors to reallocate its resources.

The coroner's office received an influx of young men killed during gang wars or in the newly invented art of drive-by shootings frequently destroying the lives of innocent people. Sullen gang members who came to identify one of their own at the morgue, if they came at all, departed with threats of retribution and a constant stream of loud profanity. Coroner staff members demanded—and received—police protection whenever a gang member was killed. Detectives observing autopsies always carried weapons despite a county ordinance prohibiting firearms in the morgue.

Although the media had generally ignored the routine daily work of pathologists, for obvious reasons of taste, coupled with public indifference to gang killings, a few dedicated reporters attended autopsies often enough to learn the routine of this morbid work. These media men and women, having earned the trust of doctors and detectives, could jump-start stories with their advance knowledge of the facts. In particular, violent deaths of prominent entertainment figures gave reporters a head start despite hazy or incomplete details. A tiny circle of reporters had developed relationships with watch commanders at police stations and hospital staff who alerted them to shootings or deaths. The former police-blotter press corps of another time no longer bore the stigma of the stodgy, jaundiced old reporter. In a television and Internet age and through careful nurturing of relationships, the new reporters became personalities themselves.

Carmen Susa belonged to that select circle. On a Friday afternoon several weeks later, she stood behind Slonsky at the morgue, silently observing Dr. Fred Southers, the leading pathologist in the county, conducting an autopsy. She looked at her notes. A late-morning telephone call from a coroner insider alerted her to a subsequent file review requested by Detective Slonsky. A displeased Slonsky glowered when she arrived.

Southers was reading the autopsy file on a woman "tentatively identified as Maureen McCullough." Southers, a consummate professional, tersely read his findings as he simultaneously identified photographs and named various parts of the body: "White female, approximately thirty. Two gunshot wounds entered the abdomen, lodged in uterus. Weapon unknown, although likely a handgun; slugs visible but without x-rays and removable. Woman pregnant with male child. Fetus not examined. No other wounds on body or extremities except around both eyes and a contusion on the right wrist. None of the extremities distended. Internal organs intact."

Southers droned on, pausing for a moment, when Slonsky interrupted, "Fred, how do you think she got those black and blues around the eyes?"

"I noticed that. Maybe she fell against something when she was shot."

"She was shot on a parking lot. Just fell down on the street. Are those marks from hitting the cement?"

"Not a chance. The marks would be entirely different."

Both men looked at each other.

Slonsky cocked his head. "Somebody hit her?"

"Yes. Or she ran into something."

"When?"

"I can't tell. It's hard to say."

"Have the photographer take some close-up shots of her face."

"Sure. Pick 'em up tomorrow."

Susa signaled she had to go the restroom and hurried out. Southers put away his tape recorder and turned toward Slonsky. "All done, BS. Nothing new. This was a little unusual. How come you asked for another review?"

"I needed to consider the angle of the entrance wounds on her body again, Fred. We can't tell whether she was shot from the ground or from a building. We have no witnesses. I was hoping the media types wouldn't show up."

"Pretty hard to tell, BS. I'll have to do some more homework if you think it's important."

"Would you, please? I don't know, but right now, we're stumped."

"Give me a week or so."

"Good enough. By the way, the cops found her ID card in her purse. Do you still have the purse?"

"Sure. In the locker. Why?"

"Can I see it?"

"Of course."

Southers walked over to a bank of lockers, checked the number of one of them, twirled the combination, and removed the purse. Handing it to Slonsky, he asked, "Strange request, BS, but here it is. Just put it back and twirl the lock when you're done. I gotta start another job."

"Thanks, Fred. I appreciate it."

Slonsky rummaged through a sparse number of items: comb, brushes, lipstick, and empty wallet revealing an ID card. Inside the purse, he felt a separate lining. Reaching in, he felt a piece of paper and removed a marriage certificate signed by a justice of the peace in Las Vegas. The license confirmed a marriage between Eddie Mathes and Jeri Mathes, a.k.a. Maureen McCullough, and included two sets of fingerprints. He folded the document carefully and placed it and the prints inside his jacket pocket. Replacing the purse and closing the locker, he sauntered back to Souther's office upon hearing the sound of shoe heels clicking on the floor.

Carmen Susa frowned as she approached.

"What are you doing, BS?"

"Just thinking. Just thinking."

Wearing a skeptical face, Susa walked outside the morgue with Slonsky.

"BS, what do you make of those bruises around her eyes you asked Southers about?"

"You heard Southers. He doesn't know."

"Well, I do. I've seen hundreds of women who look like that. She's been abused."

"Which means?"

"A husband or a boyfriend."

"That's always a possibility."

Susa touched Slonsky's arm, and both stopped walking.

"BS, you're hiding something."

"Is this a test?"

"Not funny. I have connections. I can help."

"We can always use help. Call me anytime."

"I will. But you need to work on your candor. By the way, did you know we had a mugging a little while ago at the Channel 5 studio?"

"No."

"Not a big deal, but on the day of the murder outside the medical clinic, our cameraman's assistant was found unconscious in the men's room. The staff thought he had a heart attack and took him to the hospital. When he awoke, he told us someone in the men's room hit him from behind and knocked him out. Whoever it was stole his raincoat and hat. Is that strange?"

Slonsky nodded thoughtfully.

"Yes, very strange. Did he report it?"

"No. He wasn't hurt badly. He couldn't identify anyone, so we just dropped it."

"I'd like to talk to him."

"Sure. Anytime."

Susa walked away. Slonsky waited until she disappeared into the crowd. He removed his phone from his pocket and called Channel 5.

Chapter 19

The death of the murdered young woman continued to stir the pro-choice group into a frenzy despite lack of evidence the homicide had been committed by any of those picketing the clinic. Hastily calling press conferences and shrilly denouncing another "senseless act of violence against women," they pulled out all the stops. Every politician in sight jumped on the bandwagon, and the president issued another call for more federal legislation. The media talking heads screamed that Judge Carleton should issue a permanent injunction against any picketing within one hundred yards of the clinic "to stop the violence." The temporary order issued by Carleton would expire shortly, and Richardson had filed a motion seeking a permanent injunction. Amstead, in his courtroom argument objecting to the injunction, again reminded Carleton that similar injunctions against unions limiting their picketing had been stricken by the Supreme Court in the past despite violations directly committed by union members. Judge Carleton listened politely then issued the injunction.

Sitting in the back of the courtroom, Slonsky listened carefully to the arguments of the lawyers. When the spectators in the courtroom had cleared, he approached a glum Amstead, who was busily collecting his papers and stuffing them into his briefcase.

"Nice argument, Percy."

"Hi, BS. Thanks, but this case was lost before I even opened my mouth."

"I sensed that. Say, have you got a minute? I might have something useful."

Amstead shut his briefcase and locked it.

"Sure. Shoot. Pardon the expression."

Slonsky laughed as both sat down at the counsel table. Slonsky removed several photographs.

"Percy, these are autopsy photos, and a little gruesome, but you prosecuted homicides when you were a prosecutor in the DA's office."

Amstead nodded. Slonsky laid out several photographs on the table, studied each one carefully, looked up at Amstead, and pointed to the faces of the same woman photographed from different angles.

"Percy, this is the woman who was shot at the clinic. Look at her face and right wrist."

"Black and blue. So?"

"Southers told me he couldn't tell when those marks had been made, but they had nothing to do with her fall in the street when she was shot."

"Those marks could have come from anywhere or anything."

"Or anyone."

"What do you mean?"

"Domestic violence. Some guy holds the woman with one hand and smacks her with the other."

"So you think there's a connection with the murder?"

"Look at this file."

Slonsky handed Amstead the autopsy file containing several documents. He pointed to the name Maureen McCullough on the file.

"Her married name is Jeri Mathes. She had an ID in her purse identifying herself as Maureen McCullough. The ambulance driver brought in her purse, and the coroner listed the contents, but I found a marriage certificate with her fingerprints on it concealed in the lining. I went to the abortion clinic outside of where she was shot. Two days before her appointment for an abortion at the clinic, the staff had taken her fingerprints. They gave them to me after a little persuasion."

"Like issuing a subpoena if she refused and a report to the judge that they were concealing evidence?"

"In a word, yes. I also added that a lawyer might be interested too."

"BS. Now I know how you got your nickname."

Slonsky laughed and continued, "It'll be easy for forensics to match the medical-clinic prints with the prints on her marriage certificate. Nobody knows this, Percy, so it's confidential. I haven't even filed a report because the Feds get to look at all our records under that stupid court decree."

Amstead scratched his head. "So her married name is Jeri Mathes. Where does that lead? Did you follow up?"

"I did. The press and the media don't know this, but the police reports bear a certain file number when no arrest ensues after a crime has been committed. We call it an incident report. It means nothing to the average person or the media or the Feds. But I found it. Under her former name of McCullough, she reported two domestic violence cases within the last year. She told the police she would refuse to prosecute either case, so the cops only took an incident report. I temporarily removed the report from the file and deleted it from the computer. I can recover it if necessary."

"BS, is that protocol?"

"I said *temporarily.*"

Amstead laughed. "You are a piece of work, even if it's illegal. So there is no public file on her reports?"

"Correct. But look at this one police report she filed two months before she was killed. Not only did she agree to prosecute. The case is set for trial next week. It's on the court calendar."

"And the connection? She's dead. The judge will dismiss the case."

Slonsky pulled a copy of a court file out of his vest pocket and handed it to Amstead. The lawyer scanned it and looked up. "*People v. Mathes.* So?"

"Look who the defendant is."

"Eddie Jefferson Mathes. Wait a minute. The victim's name is really Jeri Mathes? Maureen McCullough is really Jeri Mathes? Is the defendant her husband?"

"Strike one. I found her marriage certificate in her purse."

"Pitch me another fastball."

"Eddie Jefferson Mathes is a police officer."

"Oh, oh. Strike two. How do you know that?"

"The victim talked to Father Braun at St. Catherine's Church several months ago. He called me on this case and said he couldn't tell me what she told him at that time, but now that she is deceased, he was sure the seal of the confessional did not prevent him from identifying her husband as a police officer. Braun didn't want to go to public. I confirmed Mathes's name in our department records."

"And for strike three?"

"Southers reported the presence of the fetus during the autopsy. He did not remove it, although he could identify its race. The fetus and the mother are both white. Mathes is black. I told Southers to hold off on filing his final report."

"Somebody else fathered the child."

"Home run, Counselor. I think we better look for the pitcher. Percy, this is not public knowledge. But it may affect your case. I'll call you."

"BS, if you can prove someone had a motive to kill her, the demonstration in front of the clinic was a perfect time and place for cover. But why tell me?"

"Because I trust you after working with you all those years when you were in the DA's office. And you may know something I might need to know."

"Which might help your case."

"And yours too."

Slonsky smiled, shook hands, and walked away to a grinning and knowledgeable Amstead.

Chapter 20

Walking into the reception area of the Los Angeles County District Attorney's Office, Slonsky smiled broadly at receptionist Cindy Border, who sat behind a desk, filing her nails. He leaned over the counter, surveying her with playful lust. "How soon you gonna divorce that husband of yours?"

"When I see you get a decent job." She laughed.

"Well, keep me in mind if you leave him."

"I'll put you on the list. You want to see Mr. Marcum?"

"Yes. Is your chief executioner in?"

"Probably not for you. Just kidding. Go on in. I'll buzz him and tell him you're on your way."

Slonsky, winking wickedly at the twenty-one-year-old receptionist as she buzzed him in, walked down the hallway to the last door. With a brief courtesy knock, he entered the office of John Marcum, chief deputy district attorney and currently a candidate for the office of district attorney to replace the retiring incumbent. Photographs lined the walls, laminated newspaper articles lay underneath glass tabletops, and various trophies and awards sat on bookshelves lined with lawbooks and statutes. Marcum, his tie loosened over his shirt, walked around the desk and shook hands with Slonsky.

"BS, good to see you, old friend. I figured you'd be around to chat. Anything yet that I can use in my campaign? I need all the help I can get."

"OK. I'll kick in five bucks, John. Actually, as you might expect, that's not why I came to see you. I think we may have a problem."

Marcum waved Slonsky to a sofa, and the two men sat facing each other.

"John, I know you've made a lot of statements about how you're going to start a new section in the office to prosecute assaults on women. And this abortion business is like throwing meat to you."

"In a word, yes."

"You know we don't have a suspect in the abortion case yet?"

"Are you here to tell me we do?"

"Not yet. We have identified the victim. Her true name, or at least her married name, is Jeri Mathes, not Maureen McCullough. This is not for publication."

Slonsky paused for effect. Marcum sat back.

"We got the wrong person?"

"No. Just a different name. She was married to a police officer. Eddie Mathes."

"A police officer? My deputies didn't tell me this."

"They wouldn't know. They don't have the information. We'll talk about that later."

Slonsky handed Marcum a file highlighted for quick reading. After a quick review, Marcum blanched.

"Two withdrawn domestic violence reports by her against Mathes and another one set for trial?"

"Next week. But the file name is under McCullough."

"Which court?"

"Judge Carleton."

"The judge who is hearing the abortion case and just issued an injunction?"

"Yes. And who is also in the running for the Supreme Court. But that's not all. The bottom line is, I think he might have been a witness to the murder."

"A witness? How?"

"TV tapes. They show someone in his chambers watching the demonstration at the time of the murder. I talked to him, but he says it must have been someone else. I'm not so sure."

"Why would he deny it?"

"Good question. Unless he's involved."

"Whoa, BS. This is getting to be heavy-duty."

"Look at it this way. He needs to justify issuing an injunction for political reasons. Up to the time of the murder, the pro-life folks were just a nuisance. If he had issued an injunction when the cops say there had been no arrests and no violence, the court of appeals would have reversed him in a heartbeat. He looks ridiculous, the president is embarrassed, and the Senate jumps all over him for punishing free speech. But with the murder, the injunction can be easily justified."

Marcum shook his head slowly.

"An interesting theory, BS. Where's the evidence?"

"You're right. Just a theory. But believe it or not, I got some help. Paul McClosky is working this case from a different side of the street."

"McClosky? He's a private detective now. What's he got to do with it?"

"Divorce time. He gives me the usual 'confidentiality' bullshit, but I can guess."

"Carleton's wife?"

"Bingo."

"What's the connection between Judge Carleton and the guy who pulled the trigger?"

"Another good question. But here's another one. Jeri Mathes was pregnant with somebody else's child."

"You think Mathes knew about it?"

"I don't know. But we can't rule him out either."

"Have you talked to him?"

"Not yet. I need to do some more work and need more time. That's why I'm here. I don't think Mathes pulled the trigger. He's black, but the tapes that I have don't show a black guy anywhere near the murdered woman. Anyway, take a look at the police file on the day of the shooting."

Marcum looked at the file and read, "Officer Mathes off duty, on leave." Marcum looked up at Slonsky, who took back the file and pointed to the report.

"Look, I think Carleton was in his chambers looking out the window, watching the demonstration. He's in the clear himself. Mathes is not working that day, maybe angry about his unfaithful wife, but somebody else in the crowd kills her."

"Are you saying either Carleton or Mathes hired some hit man? I don't think Carleton is the type."

"I'll admit it's a little thin. I just don't think it was some crazy pro-lifer type."

"Thin? Thin? B.S, to be honest, it's translucent."

"Just one more thing. Someone tried to kill Carleton."

"Kill the judge?"

"Yes."

Marcum waited.

"I can't tell you about it just yet, John. No press releases. No contact with your prosecutors about this. Tell them not to dismiss the Mathes case. I need time. But you'll be the first to know. Who's the prosecutor?"

"I am."

"Big surprise, but I gotta have some time."

"You got it, BS."

Chapter 21

The following day, Slonsky told Lieutenant Sam Tolley, department records supervisor, that a case he had was set for trial and that he needed to look at personnel records because the public defender had a court order to inspect them. Tolley waved him over to the computer, and Slonsky clicked open the Mathes file. Scrolling down to the day of the abortion shooting, the screen read "Injured on duty. On leave of absence. Department doctor to examine."

Slonsky printed out the text from the screen, folded it carefully, and inserted it in his file. He walked over to a phone and called Marcum's private line.

"This is Marcum."

"John? BS here."

"BS. Anything new?"

"The case on your domestic violence calendar we talked about is next week."

"Right."

"John, do me a favor. Get a continuance on the Mathes case."

"A continuance? Do you have something new?"

"I can't answer that right now. But it just might help me out in the abortion-homicide case."

"How can I get a continuance if the victim is dead? We have no witnesses. What will I tell the judge?"

"Judge Murphy is in the calendar court with a heavy caseload, but the case is tentatively assigned to Carleton for trial. Tell Murphy you have a golf date."

"Come on."

"OK. Tell him we're trying to sort out some record problems and we just need a little more time."

"Is that the truth?"

"Close enough."

"Done."

"And, John, one more thing. Can I see your file on this case?"

"No problem. Anytime."

"I'll see you at the courthouse in a little while."

"You got it, BS."

Marcum picked up the file from Records and walked across the street to the Criminal Courts Building.

* * *

The burgeoning crime rate in Los Angeles had forced the board of supervisors to also budget a new Criminal Courts Building, but they had not appropriated the funds to replace the ancient Hall of Records, an indestructible gray edifice resembling a prison. Into its dispiriting ground floor walked the detritus of Los Angeles, gang members, petty thieves, prostitutes, and their friends and relatives. Police officers often rode up in elevators with men they had arrested; prosecutors stood shoulder to shoulder with battered women and children, all enduring the stench of liquor and cigarettes. The master calendar court was jammed, and the jury box was stuffed with men in orange jumpsuits stamped LA Co. on the back. Shackles wove them all together in a train of steel links that jangled every time someone moved. Criminal-defense lawyers hovered over their clients, if they could find them, prosecutors thumbed through a stack of files, and detectives checked in with the court liaison officer. Clerks, buried under mounds of papers, were unapproachable, and no one dared ask them questions. The court reporter sat in front of the bench, sullenly surveying the barely restrained chaos.

Ultimately, the board appropriated the necessary money, and the county built a new Criminal Courts Building. The chaos remained substantially the same, but safety had improved, more courtrooms had been built, smoking was disallowed anywhere, elevators operated more smoothly, and a modern atmosphere appeared. All trials were assigned to a calendar court where the judge distributed the cases to trial courts.

The current calendar court judge was Brian Mulcahy, one of the last liberals appointed by a governor who had filled the courts with civil rights activists, feminists, gays, and minorities. Except for Carleton, none of these judges had any trial experience or significant professional records, and prosecutors had achieved little success in trial for the last four years.

Mulcahy, the consummate liberal, refused to believe no such thing as a "bad boy" existed—until his daughter was assaulted. A trial judge had excluded the confession of the defendant on grounds the arresting officer had failed to tell him he had a right to a lawyer before he answered questions. When the defendant walked out of the courtroom a free man, bailiffs had been forced to restrain the jurist. After that, he was more understanding.

The court bailiff bellowed to the people in the crowded courtroom, "This court is now in session! The Honorable Judge Brian Mulcahy presiding."

The din eroded, lawyers took their seats, and the jangling of chains on prisoners subsided. Mulcahy strode into the courtroom from his chambers, sat down, adjusted his half-glasses, and scanned the crowd.

The bailiff resumed, "All please remain seated and come to order."

Years of hard drinking had colored the jowls on the face of an old liberal given to activist causes. In his early years on the bench, he had sentenced leniently, often imposing terms of probation on defendants and subsequently monitoring their progress—or lack thereof. Within a few years, he abandoned his rehabilitation programs, all having universally ended in failure, and began giving straight sentences to jail or prison. He scoffed at so-called domestic violence cases that never went to trial because women always withdrew their complaints or failed to appear. Politically minded prosecutors railed at this policy, but he reminded them that if they weren't ready to prosecute a defendant in the absence of a witness, he would send the case out for trial and call the press to complain about wasting taxpayer money while more serious offenders were ready for trial. No one took him up on his threat, and publicity died down. Easing his two-hundred-pound frame into an antique chair he had refused to replace, arguing to court personnel that he had worked for years to shape it according to his size, Mulcahy fingered his half-glasses on the end of his nose and picked up the daily calendar. He started to call the cases when he noticed John Marcum and Slonsky standing by the side of counsel table.

"Well, Mr. Marcum, we are not executing anyone today. What are you doing in this courtroom?"

"Your Honor, I wonder if we might approach the bench."

"We?"

"Detective Slonsky and myself."

"Your sidekick there, old BS?"

"Yes, Your Honor."

"All right, come on up."

Marcum and Slonsky walked toward the side of the bench, and Judge Mulcahy swung around to meet them.

"BS, you son of a bitch, what are you doing here? Get out in the street and arrest someone."

"I tried that, Your Honor, but got sued for using excessive force."

"Some black guy you harassed, I suppose."

"I don't remember. The paramedics took him away in an ambulance."

"So now Internal Affairs is on your ass."

"What else is new?"

"I love you Fascists. Anyway, BS, thanks again for working up that case on my daughter. Not your fault that some rookie cop screwed up."

"Thanks, Judge."

"OK, Marcum, what's the problem?"

"Judge, we have a sensitive case on your calendar next week, and we need a short continuance."

"Sensitive case? Where are all those jackals from the media?"

"That's why we wanted to talk to you about it in private. The name of the case is *People v. Mathes.*"

Mulcahy leafed through the docket sheets and folded them back.

"*People v. Eddie Mathes.* One count of assault. One count of battery. One witness. Looks like a domestic violence case. What's the problem?"

"The witness is the victim in the abortion killing."

Mulcahy leaned back and removed his glasses.

"OK, but why do you need a continuance? If she's dead, there's no trial. Why not just move to dismiss the case?"

"Judge, this is highly confidential. We think there may be a connection between the homicide at the clinic, the domestic violence case on your calendar, and the defendant Eddie Mathes."

"It might be the same guy?"

"Maybe. That's why BS needs a little more time."

"What good does a continuance do?"

"BS can explain."

Mulcahy turned toward Slonsky.

"Judge, the defendant Mathes is a suspect. We need to keep him on a string for just a little while."

"The public defender will raise hell."

"Judge, the public defender doesn't know why the victim won't be here. She and her staff got so many cases they won't recognize any connection, and she hasn't even assigned a lawyer to defend Mathes yet. The police department redacted the victim's name on the police report at my request. The file shows her name now as Mathes—not McCullough. As far as anyone knows, it's just another case. So far, the media doesn't know Mathes or the victim except as Maureen McCullough. And, Judge, one more thing."

Slonsky leaned forward.

"Mathes is a cop. We need a little time to see if there is a connection."

Mulcahy leaned forward.

"Mathes is a cop? OK, I owe you one, BS."

"Thanks, Judge. We never had this conversation."

Judge Mulcahy swung around in his chair and faced Public Defender Eleanor Dean, the leading feminist in the city.

"Ms. Dean, number 33 on your calendar for next Tuesday will have to be continued for two weeks. The district attorney indicates he needs a short time for additional investigation. Is your client in custody?"

Dean opened her calendar and read the routine entry to herself, "Defendant not interviewed. Released on bail, available by telephone."

"He is available, Your Honor. On call."

"All right, two weeks continuance. Get a date from the DA, and I'll sign the order."

"On what grounds, Your Honor? If the district attorney can't proceed, let's dismiss this case."

"Ms. Dean, this is a domestic violence case. If I dismiss the case, the DA will just refile it, and your client will be rearrested, and he can put up bail again."

"Oh. In that case, I have no objection."

"Thank you, Ms. Dean. Very considerate of you. Please notify your client. Just confirm with me that you have notified him."

Marcum nodded slightly to the judge, Slonsky smiled, and the clerk summoned Public Defender Dean and Marcum to his desk for both to agree on a new date.

Chapter 22

Some cops you can trust; some you can really trust when it comes to keeping things confidential. Slonsky knew retired Sergeant Barney Hoffman from the old days when they were partners, long before affirmative action and minority preference. Whenever Barney drank a little too much, he would give his speech to anyone who would listen.

Raising his glass, he shouted, "Partners together! From the old days when the courts would let you convict guilty defendants, before the judges invented all the rules on search-and-seizure bullshit and Miranda crap, and without every arrest leading to some civil rights demonstration or a lawsuit!"

But Barney had always been there for Slonsky, never lied under oath, lost cases he could have won because he told the truth, and never circumvented the new rules. His reward? Assignment to the Department of Internal Affairs investigating complaints against cops. Hoffman knew where all the skeletons in the police closet were buried, but no one could get a word out of him—except Slonsky, when he really needed to know something. And Slonsky needed to know about Mathes.

The two old friends sat in an obscure coffee shop several miles away from downtown and located where few other cops patronized. Hoffman, who needed to remain involved without being involved, had an encyclopedic memory and an army of contacts, informants, and friends. Only a few detectives knew where to find him, but Slonsky was one of them. Both men sat in a booth, clasping hands around steaming coffee cups, chatting about the old days, until Hoffman broke the stream of conversation.

"Now that we've reminisced, what do you want, BS?"

"Tactful as ever, old buddy."

"And none of that old-buddy stuff either."

Slonsky smiled, leaned forward, and stirred his coffee.

"Barney, do you know about that murder at the abortion medical clinic in LA?"

"Sure. You're on the case, which is why you're here."

Slonsky swirled the coffee around the cup and looked at Barney.

"The victim was married to a cop."

Hoffman paid attention and looked up.

"A cop? The papers didn't say anything about that."

"Because she didn't use her married name when she made an appointment with the clinic. And she carried misleading identification in her purse under the name of Maureen

McCullough. I found her marriage license in her purse dated in Vegas two days before the murder. We can't find anyone in California who knew her or met her."

"OK. I'm sorry she was killed, but what's the point?"

"The victim had filed a domestic violence case against the cop."

"She's dead. The DA will dismiss the case. What's that got to do with her murder?"

"Barney, if that's the case, why would I be here?"

"OK. I get it. What's the cop's name?"

"Mathes. Eddie Mathes. The victim's married name is Jeri Mathes. Prior to her death, she filed a criminal complaint against him. The case was set for trial, but it got continued."

Hoffman sat up, folded his arms, and looked out the window. Slonsky knew the signal, and he continued.

"I got the incident file from the Records Department. A Maureen McCullough called police two times for assault but refused to make a report when officers arrived, so they filed it as an incident report. But the third time, she filed a complaint against Mathes under her name as McCullough. The police report shows that the officers arrested Mathes a few days later, but it says nothing about him being a cop. This department is so big you can't know everybody. They booked him at the station, but he posted bail and was released. The public defender appeared for him in court, pled not guilty, and got him a trial date. Nobody knows he's a cop."

"How come no preliminary hearing?"

"The DA filed it as a misdemeanor. The prosecutor said not enough injury to make it a felony. So just a misdemeanor trial."

"What do you need me for?"

"Some information on Mathes before I talk to him. We all know that 99 percent of the time, the victims in these domestic violence cases have no witnesses, except maybe the cops that responded. Maybe a neighbor. But usually the cops."

"Talk to the officers who responded to the complaints."

"I tried. The same two officers responded in all three cases. One has since died in a traffic accident. The other one retired and went to Europe. No phone, no PO box for mail. Checks deposited directly in his Swiss bank account."

Barney took a note on a paper napkin.

"How about personnel files, BS? Under that stupid federal court decree, the arresting officers are supposed to file a report domestic violence stuff in their personnel files."

"I looked. Nothing there about that. Even if they did know, Mathes was hired under a special-recruitment program. Lieutenant Tolley told me they treat those guys with kid gloves because they don't want to get sued. Solution? Unless someone submits a complaint directly against an officer, or the cops make an arrest, delete any reference to a police officer in the file. Just note the incident was resolved. In the one case the victim did report, there is still no reference to Mathes being a cop. Either the officers didn't know who he was, and you can't know everyone in as big a department as ours, or they just omitted it on purpose to avoid filing a report."

"Does Mathes live in an apartment?'

"Yes."

"I presume you didn't talk to the landlord, who would have told Mathes you asked about him."

"Just so. One more thing. When I looked in Mathes's personnel file, I saw 'Marital Status: Unmarried.'"

Slonsky waited. Hoffman twisted his cup around in his hands.

"There might be another way. You have the dates of all the assaults and the time reported on the two incidents and then the arrest. You can look up payroll records and find out who were the watch commanders on duty on the dates for all the incidents. Those guys review the incident reports and arrests for everyone. The watch commander would know Mathes even if the arresting officers didn't. If he's the right kind of guy, he'll tell you what happened."

Slonsky reached for his file, opened it, and thumbed through the reports. He pulled out a report, read it, and looked up at his old friend.

"It says 'Watch Commander: Sergeant Bill Asquith.' On duty all three dates of the contacts. Where does that get us? I don't even know him."

"Basil, when I worked Internal Affairs, we were death on cops who beat their wives. If they had any kind of prior record, that would have been enough to terminate them. If the files in your case are incomplete or not filed or whatever, something is wrong. And the watch commander, if anyone, would know. Maybe you'll get a lead."

"Maybe."

"Lots of cases are solved on maybes. I know Mathes. He got in a little drug trouble, and the brass swept it under the rug. If he were to be convicted in the domestic violence case, the department would terminate him."

"So he has a motive."

"Maybe. There's just one problem. Mathes is black."

"So?"

"Sergeant Asquith is president of the Black Officers Union."

Chapter 23

LAPD Wilshire Division was not located on Wilshire Boulevard, and the decision to name the building was clouded in history. Originally designed to serve the mid city and its affluent population, the changing residential patterns had placed the station in a war zone of black gangs. Most detectives, like the city of Los Angeles generally, took scarce interest in gang killings, concluding it was one less gang member on the streets. The constant stream of petty thieves, prostitutes, and drunks mingled inside the station along with gang members arrested for a variety of crimes. The building had steadily deteriorated under the mass of the shiftless and the criminal, but the city council remained indifferent to this temporary warehouse for human refuse. Officers assigned to that division considered it the "dark hole" and schemed for a transfer to anywhere else. Slonsky had been previously assigned to Wilshire Division and knew the territory. He parked his car in the fenced and guarded lot, carefully switched on the alarm system, and walked up the stained, decrepit steps to the station. Inside, the entry hall swarmed with sweaty black and brown bodies, the stench reeked throughout the room, the noise level laced with profanity, threats and incoherence among the swirling surge of bodies. Several burly officers armed with billy clubs stood guard and repeatedly intervened to separate macho types among different gangs.

Slonsky, not dressed in uniform, moved cautiously around the edges of the room, ignoring sneering black faces and leers from prostitutes. Several surly black teenagers stepped in front of him, blocking his way. When one of them approached, Slonsky opened his hand in greeting, but quickly his outstretched fingers darted straight to the Adam's apple under the scowling face, and simultaneously, he kicked the groin of the startled teenager. The young body shuddered and crumpled to the floor in pain. The others quickly retreated, and Slonsky walked uninterrupted to the desk occupied by a sergeant arguing with a young man tattooed with gang symbols. Slonsky walked unseen to the side of the desk and touched the officer in uniform on the shoulder. Sergeant Joe Rutledge, annoyed and only slightly turning aside his head, noticed the intruder was wearing a suit. The sergeant snarled over his shoulder without looking at Slonsky.

"You must be the mouthpiece."

Slonsky laughed, pushed back his hair, puffed up, and replied, "Yes, sir, brother. And I hopes you done read this poor boy his rights."

Sergeant Rutledge wheeled, stared, then roared. "BS, you old bastard! What are you doing here at the animal farm?"

"Training for a job in Internal Affairs."

"And you'd flunk out in one week."

"But if you were my only case, you'd be gone."

Rutledge howled, released his hold on the adolescent, threw out his arms around his old friend, pulled him closer, and hugged him. Backing away, he held Slonsky by the arms.

"It's good to see you, Basil. I read about your investigation of that snuff of the pregnant babe. But why come here? I know it's not just to see your old friend."

"To be honest, you're right. Can we talk?"

"Sure. Come on to the lunchroom. I'll get Chuck to take my place talking to this dipshit."

Rutledge signaled his exit to one of the other officers, turned, and faced the gangbanger.

"Put your ass in one of those chairs. When your mouthpiece gets here, you can talk to him."

Turning toward Slonsky, Rutledge grabbed him by the arm, and the two men chatted while walking toward the lunchroom. When they entered, a handful of motor officers sitting in the back of the room were drinking coffee and talking. The voices stopped, each man studying the new arrival in the suit closely, looking for signs of an investigator, civilian inspector, or civil rights lawyer. Rutledge, sensing their apprehension and accustomed to constant surveillance by politically correct types from the mayor's office, waved to the group reassuringly and shouted, "Just a detective from homicide! Not to worry."

The faces relaxed, visibly relieved, and conversation resumed. Slonsky smiled. "Talk about paranoia."

"Unfortunately, it's rational. We're under constant surveillance, and don't think it doesn't take its toll. Cops look the other way on patrol down here and only get involved in major crimes. As a result, the idiots get away with the small stuff, which leads to the big stuff. And the real victims are the folks that want us to crack down. The innocent people have to put up with all this crap."

"What does the chief say?"

"Nothing he can say. They got him on a string. Some pantywaist lawyer watches everything, sticks his nose in all over the place. Typical liberal-guilt type."

"Not like the old days."

"Amen. We used to protect other people. Now we got to protect ourselves. Hey, you need something, right?"

Slonsky nodded. Rutledge pointed to a table in the back of the room, and both men walked over and sat down. Slonsky pulled his chair closer to the table.

"Joe, I've got a sensitive matter. I really can't give you all the details, but you'll be the first to know if anything pans out."

"Shoot."

"I want to check up on the watch commanders for certain shifts."

"Gee, BS, I'm not sure we keep those records here. They all go downtown. You know, payrolls, overtime, reprimands, all that stuff. The guys want it private."

"I know. But I don't want to get it from downtown. Someone will ask questions. Don't you keep local records?"

"Hold on. I'm not good on this stuff. Let me call somebody."

Rutledge went over to a battle-scarred, worn, rotary phone and dialed. Seconds later, he spoke into the phone.

"Jugs, it's Rutledge. Could you come down here for a minute?"

Rutledge paused, listening. Grinning at Slonsky, he laughed into the phone.

"I love it when you talk dirty. Thanks, babe."

Rutledge walked back to an amused Slonsky, who asked, "Was that a woman? They're gonna get you on a sexual harassment beef."

"Are you kidding? I haven't had sex for a week. In fact, I only wish someone really would harass me, especially Jugs. Trust me, BS, this woman is good."

Moments later, the door swung open, and Honey Wissman walked in. All the motor officers, Rutledge, and Slonsky stared at a six-foot blond woman with breasts under her blouse struggling for freedom, hair sprawling around her face, and wearing a skirt that ended at the knees. She walked over to Rutledge and stood directly in front of him, hands on her hips, the outline of her breasts pointed at his face.

"You called? You want something? What can I do to you, big boy?"

Rutledge struggled to control himself, speechless but loving it. The motor officers howled when she leered at them, shifted her hips, and purred.

"Hi, boys. You want to ride my bike? Or we could take yours, and I'll shift your gears."

Everyone broke up, including Honey. She pulled up a chair and sat down. Rutledge, clearly amused, looked at Slonsky.

"BS, we want Honey assigned to our own 'Internal Affairs.'"

Rutledge nodded toward Honey.

"Honey, this is Detective Basil Slonsky, also known to his friends as BS. He's in Homicide. BS, meet Honey Wissman. She's the best vice officer in the department."

Honey nodded to Slonsky and shook hands. "BS? Interesting name."

"Stands for Basil Slonsky."

"Basil? They named you Basil?"

"My folks liked Sherlock Holmes."

"So?"

"An actor, Basil Rathbone. He played Sherlock Holmes in the movies."

"Before my time. Anyway, pleased to meet you. Are you here to investigate someone?"

"No, no. Just visiting."

"You came to the right place. We have showtime every half hour down here."

"So I understand."

"Wait a minute. You look familiar. Aren't you the detective on the abortion case?"

"Hey, not bad. Looks like you keep up with the news."

"Try to."

She turned toward Rutledge. "Joe, why am I here? This guy doesn't look like a john."

"Honey, BS needs help on that abortion-murder case. He's the lead investigator and needs some very sensitive information. And it's gotta be confidential."

Rutledge leaned forward on the table and faced Slonsky.

"BS, Honey is one of the best computer nerds we have. She has saved our ass more times than I can tell you by retrieving records of some of these punks that claim police harassment."

"Good. But I don't want to get her in trouble."

"Honey can take care of herself. If she can't do it, believe me, she'll let you know."

Slonsky paused. "Ms. Wissman—"

"Call me Honey."

"OK. I need to find some internal records that Joe says aren't kept here. Everything is downtown."

"What records?"

"I need personnel records written by watch commanders who were here on duty on specific shifts."

"That's no problem."

"Well, this isn't just ordinary records. These are records of incident' reports in domestic violence cases."

"Still no problem."

"Of women who reported getting beaten up but refused to make a report."

"Give me something difficult."

"OK. Beaten up by a cop."

Honey said nothing for a moment.

"That is a problem. Those records are erased."

"So it is difficult?"

"In a word, yes. Blacks and browns get those records erased, which really pisses me off, by the way. Those guys get at least one free hit."

"Maybe there is some incentive for you here?"

"You bet your ass there is."

"Can we find out?"

"We could get in big trouble."

"I don't want that to happen to you."

"I said we *could*, not *would*. I've got two big computers that both work."

Rutledge and Slonsky howled.

"All we have to do is 'boot up' and 'click Enter.'"

The two veterans collapsed in laughter.

Rutledge pushed back his chair. "I told you, BS. This woman is dynamite. I'll leave you two alone. I gotta go back to the animal farm. Basil, just give Honey what kind of information you need. On the case, I mean."

Chapter 24

Slonsky watched Honey Wissman lead him through computer records, explaining briefly where she was headed. But each time she searched for records described by Slonsky, the computer screen displayed an error message that the program she sought was classified. She pulled up records of desk officer sergeants assigned to Wilshire for the last two years, but the list contained no dates of assignment. In searching for anything with the word *minorities* or comparable titles, she came up blank. Frustrated, she leaned back on her chair and stared at the screen.

Slonsky hesitated, then remarked, "You know, I don't know much about computers, but I do know cop lingo."

Honey ignored him.

Slonsky studied the screen and scrutinized the menu of word searches that Honey had entered.

"Why not try *duty roster*?"

"I tried that."

"How about *payroll*?"

Honey looked over her shoulder disdainfully.

"Oh, sure. Paychecks will identify watch commanders."

"Honey, there are only six sergeants here at Wilshire that rotate watch commander duty. We know what regular sergeant pay is, but watch commanders get a bonus. I used to pass out paychecks. I've seen the code for it."

Honey stopped typing. She looked at Slonsky.

"You know, BS, that's worth a BJ."

"Really?"

"Yep. And I know there'll be plenty of ladies to accommodate you. I even know the best ones."

"Just type."

Honey clicked, and the screen scrolled down to the day of the homicide.

The computer clicked to Wilshire Division, clicked to Watch Commanders, clicked to Graveyard Shift: Bill Asquith—with a code word for bonus on his paycheck.

"Bingo. Honey, I could kiss you."

"Please, not here. Besides, I have a date waiting upstairs."

Slonsky moved closer to the screen.

"Anything else on his paycheck or file that might be helpful?"

Honey clicked. Arrest Reports Filed on Shift. *Click.* Incident Reports Filed on Shift. *Click.* "Eighteen."

Slonsky counted the names on the list.

"Only seventeen."

Honey counted.

"You're right. One is missing."

"Can you retrieve it?"

"If it was entered in the system, it has to be somewhere. Let's see how they dump files."

Click. Deleted Files. *Click.* Type Name of File. *Click.* Erased. Honey turned to Slonsky.

"Double bingo, BS. Whoever entered this file typed in the word *erased.* You have to give the computer that order. That means it's somewhere, but I don't know if I can find it. Hey, you want to look now or buy dinner?"

"Let's eat. Business with pleasure."

Chapter 25

Most cops ate near the Wilshire station at a café owned by a retired police captain. Honey knew its rowdy and all-male clientele better than to suggest it for quiet conversation. They drove down Wilshire Boulevard to a small Mexican restaurant owned by her sister and her husband. A phone call in advance assured them discretion and avoided the constant scrutiny that everyone gave Honey. Parking in the back of the restaurant, they entered through the rear door to an awaiting Marilyn Hathaway. The women hugged each other affectionately, Honey introduced Slonsky, and they all walked through the kitchen. Marilyn led them to a quiet side table and waved to the waiter, who responded quickly.

"Jimmy, don't seat anyone around them."

The waiter nodded.

Marilyn spoke to her sister, "I know you two need to talk. I hope it's not business."

"I'm afraid so," replied Honey.

Marilyn frowned, blew a kiss to Honey, and moved away.

"My little sister. Married to a great guy who owns this place."

"Nice lady. Runs in the family."

"Why, Detective Slonsky, I thought this was business."

"It is. But she's still a nice lady."

"Thank you."

The waiter appeared with two cups of coffee and placed them on the table.

Slonsky looked up. Honey chuckled.

"Every cop drinks coffee. Marilyn ordered for us. We can order dinner later."

"OK. Thank you."

Slonsky sipped his coffee; Honey stirred a little cream in her coffee and cradled the cup in both hands. She looked up.

"BS, can you tell me what this case is all about? It might help me."

Slonsky put his cup down and leaned forward.

"Yes, you probably should know, but it's strictly confidential. I can tell you this much. I think the abortion killing is a cover for something else. And it may involve a cop."

"Whoa. What do I need to know?"

"I did some checking, and the woman's husband is a wife beater."

"You think the cop killed his wife?"

"I don't think he was the shooter, but I gotta start somewhere. He might have hired a shooter. He's not the only suspect."

"BS, I've seen these guys and what they can do. I'll try to find the guy for you."

"You know, Honey, I don't doubt it for a minute. Incidentally, where did you learn to use the computer?"

"My little brother is a techie. The little snot uses the computer as a toy. Naturally, he wasn't too keen on teaching his older sister. But I fixed him up with a few of my friends, who gave him a real good time. After that, no problem."

"But with your computer skills, you could make big money. Why a cop?"

Honey put down her cup.

"I thought this was a business meeting."

"I lied. You're an interesting lady."

"Lady? Are you kidding? I'm working as a whore."

"OK. An interesting whore."

"All right. You told me something in confidence. I'll tell you something personal. When I was eighteen, some punk killed my father in a bank robbery. Dad was president of the bank, talking to a customer, when three guys came in, and one of them shot him. At his funeral, I vowed I'd find those guys if it took forever. Of course, I couldn't do much at the time. When I was twenty-one, I applied to the department. That was a couple of years ago. One of those guys is dead, but the other two are around somewhere, and I'm still looking for them."

Slonsky said nothing when he saw tears forming in her eyes.

Honey reached for her napkin and dabbed her face.

"Sorry, I just haven't talked about it for a while."

"No reason to apologize."

Neither spoke for several minutes while Honey regained her composure.

Slonsky ventured, "Maybe I can help."

"How?"

"I do robbery and homicide in this department, you know."

Honey leaned forward.

"Looks like nice guys run in your family too."

Chapter 26

At 3:15 a.m., the phone rang in Slonsky's bedroom. Struggling to awaken, he picked up the phone and grumbled, "Don't tell me somebody just killed somebody."

"BS, hi. It's me, Honey. What are you talking about?"

"Oh, Honey. Sorry, I thought it was the detective squad calling for one of the usual late-night homicides."

"No. But maybe I'm close to the one you're investigating."

Slonsky sat up.

"Go."

"I remembered that the captain at Wilshire has a password for security clearance. The brass knows nothing about computers. They just stick the password in their drawer. Anyone can find it easily."

"Of course. Why didn't I think of that?"

"Spoken just like a man."

"Do I detect a sexist remark?"

"You do. Would you like some harassment too?"

"Harass me."

"When the cleaning lady went to the office at midnight, I followed her in. I said I left my keys in the captain's office and just needed to look around. Sure enough, the card with the password was in the first drawer I opened."

"You actually went into the captain's desk?"

"Of course."

"Why didn't I think of that too?"

"Of course. Why not? So I memorized the password, went home to my computer, and the rest is history."

"You have access to all department files in your computer?"

"Yes. The captain had so many problems with his computer he gave me access. But the department changes the password every month, and he's on vacation, so I didn't have the new one. That's why I had to go into his office."

"Of course. Rutledge was right about you. Amazing."

"Anyway, the responding cops in the domestic violence case had filled out two incident reports and one arrest report on the woman who was killed at the clinic. The victim said her name was Maureen McCullough. The lady was hurting on the first two cases but wouldn't authorize an arrest. The beater just stood around and said nothing, but the woman wouldn't let anyone in. Both cops wrote out an incident report and submitted it to Bill Asquith, the sergeant on duty that night as watch commander. Asquith filed the report under a separate code name: AA. The letters stand for affirmative action. He did the same with the arrest report."

"So we can talk to him."

"Not so fast. The AA file shows Asquith filed the incident reports in file 13."

"The wastebasket."

"Exactly. But Asquith is no dummy. He wants coverage, so he duplicates the files and puts them under his own name."

"And . . ."

"I opened his files but came up empty."

"How do we get them?"

"With great difficulty. I didn't know his password. But on the back of the captain's card with his own password are the passwords for all the watch commanders. When I punched in Asquith's password, the files came up, but his computer flashed to show an unauthorized user logged on. I couldn't find his files because he probably added a firewall or something. If he's good enough, he can find the computer the department assigned to me here at home."

"Oh, jeez."

"Oh, jeez is right."

"Do you know Asquith?"

"Yes. He's not a bad cop actually. But there's just one problem, Basil. This is serious. If Asquith can trace this back to my computer, he will certainly tell the captain. And that will lead to an investigation. They'll find me, and there goes my job. I will never be able to find those men that killed my father. I need this job."

"Honey, I understand. Let me work on it. I have an idea. After all, I got you into this."

"Thank you, Basil Slonsky. Thank you."

Chapter 27

Sally Thompson had worked in the Procurement Department of the city for thirty years and was scheduled to retire in one month. A stickler for rules, she watched the budget like a hawk and nursed every penny in her department. The death of her husband last year convinced her it was time to spend time with grandchildren. She wanted no retirement dinner, no lunch, just say good-bye. A skinflint with taxpayer's money but possessed with a heart of gold, she devoted her weekends to St. Anne's Home for Women.

Slonsky quietly opened her office door and peeked around inside to see a woman reading reports.

"Ms. Thompson, it's your boyfriend. I need a new undercover car with mag wheels, air-conditioning, loaded with extras and plenty of horsepower."

Sally Thompson looked up, laughed, and shook her head. "I'm sorry, Sergeant, you can have a Yugo."

Slonsky walked in and embraced his old friend, who immediately started sniffling. Slonsky held her by the shoulders.

"Oh, now come on, I'm not that bad looking."

Smiling through the tears, she hugged him warmly.

"I promise not to talk about Harry."

And she broke down and cried. Slonsky held her, not saying a word. She stepped back and looked up at him, smiling through the tears. She dabbed her eyes with a small handkerchief.

"Whenever I see you, I think of my husband. Both of you half potted at his birthday party. And then you invited him to sit down so you could talk . . . where you had placed a whoopee cushion. He was so embarrassed I thought he would die. And then he did."

Her body shook as she sobbed. Slonsky held both her hands.

"Sally, you two had thirty-five good years together and a passel of kids that all love you."

"I know. I know. I'm sorry to be like this. God, I miss him."

Slonsky just held her, waiting. She stepped back and wiped her eyes again.

"I know you didn't come here to see an old lady cry. You want something."

"I plead guilty. Sally, I need some help on a case I'm working. Domestic violence."

"Oh, dear. Was she hurt bad?"

"Killed."

"Oh, lord. But why do you want to see me?"

"I need a favor, a money favor."

"What is it?"

"Do you have any money to buy six new computers?"

"Six computers? Are you serious?"

"Yes, I am. A female police officer is helping me investigate a case, and she's in jeopardy. I can't explain. I just need to replace old computers issued by the department and change the passwords. I need to hide her computer."

"Is it obsolete?"

"Of course."

"Let me look in my obsolete file."

Sally walked over to the window, looked out for a moment, and laughed.

"I just remembered. I do have new computers to replace obsolete models. Who is requisitioning them?"

"Wilshire Division."

"Is tomorrow too soon?"

"I knew you could do it. Will there be any trouble?"

"Of course. But I retire next month."

Slonsky kissed her on her cheek. She giggled.

"If you're in the market for a hot widow, give me a call."

"Sorry, I don't date young women."

Sally Thompson beamed.

Chapter 28

Sergeant Bill Asquith called roll of the officers on the graveyard shift, identified numerous suspects active in the area, and listed several recent crimes. The 1:00 a.m. shift allowed him several hours of quiet time with nothing but reports to fill out. He wrote an article for the Black Officers newsletter, read the paper, and started on the comics when he remembered he hadn't paid his bills this month. Turning to his department computer, he opened the program and called up his files. The screen came on but displayed no text. Instead, a flashing red light identified a hacker signaling that someone had entered his files. He immediately began a security search. The screen displayed a computer model number issued to Wilshire Division but on loan outside the department. Asquith reached for the phone and called. A voice, obviously awakened and displeased, answered. Asquith whispered into the phone, "Somebody got a hit on my computer. No, I can't track it down until later. I don't want to hang around too long and be obvious. I'll call you tomorrow." Asquith sat down in front of his computer, entered the captain's password, and logged in. The hacker's computer was checked out to Sally Thompson in the Supplies Department.

Slonsky arrived at Wilshire Division shortly after 7:00 a.m. to see a large delivery truck unloading supplies. The open trailer held several large boxes identified as computers on the side of the containers. Smiling approvingly, he walked inside the building while the graveyard shift was checking out, and day-watch personnel entered for roll call. Walking over to the lobby pay phone, he pretended to make a call, keeping his eye on the truck. City personnel, not noted for their accelerated work habits, slowly unloaded the computers and hauled them into the captain's office. Slonsky decided to approach one of the workers.

"New computers, eh?"

The deliveryman just shrugged.

Slonsky tried again, "Who puts these complicated things together?"

"Downtown programmed everything. Here, give this envelope to the captain, would you, please? Passwords for the new computers."

"No problem."

With that, the deliveryman walked away.

Slonsky took the envelope, walked into the captain's office, and tossed the envelope on the desk. No need to talk to Captain Martin, an old-school type who still used pen and paper and probably would not even notice the change in computers or the new passwords. Slonsky reached for his cell phone and called. "Can you come down here for a minute? I've got something for you."

One hour later, Honey Wissman possessed a new computer and a new password.

Chapter 29

At 2:00 a.m. the following night at Wilshire Division, a black Porsche eased into a parking space at the far end of the lot and away from streetlights. Officer Eddie Mathes turned off the engine and sat in the darkness, scrutinizing the parking lot. Satisfied, he slumped down in his seat and waited. Footsteps approached, and moments later, Bill Asquith tapped on the window. Mathes unlocked the doors, and the sergeant slipped into the passenger seat.

"I've only got a few minutes. We had a robbery last night at a convenience store."

"You called me for that?"

"Just shut up for a minute. I ran my computer tonight and found out who hacked me. Somebody named Sally Thompson. She works at Supplies and Procurement downtown. It could be a mistake because we got new computers today with new passwords, but I don't think so."

"Who the hell is Sally Thompson?"

"I checked her out. Her husband was killed during an ambush of motor officers by a black gang last year."

"What's that got to do with me?"

"I don't know, but for some reason, she wanted to read my files about the fights you had with your wife and your arrest. The file shows the dates and times. You told me that."

"She's working for someone else."

"Maybe the DA is checking you out."

"On the wife beating? They don't even know who I am. You fixed that when you erased the reports. What else?"

"I don't know. Who had access to your password?"

"No one except the captain, and he doesn't even know how to type."

"Where did you say this woman worked?"

"Downtown. Supplies and Procurement."

"Thanks, man. I appreciate it."

"What are you gonna do?"

"Dunno. Probably nothing. See what you can find out about her."

"OK. But I gotta be careful. I'm going back to work."

Asquith opened the door and slid out. Mathes started the engine and slowly drove around the margin of the lot and out into the starless night. He parked his car several blocks away, turned on the dome light, reached into the console, removed a laptop computer, and punched in his password. In minutes, the entire roster of civilian personnel in the department appeared on the screen. Mathes scrolled down: "Thompson, Sally; chief clerk, Supplies and Procurement, third floor, police building. Home address, 8400 Kingston Avenue, Los Angeles."

Mathes picked up the car phone and punched in a number.

A voice answered, "Yeah."

"I'm calling in my chit. Meet me at noon. Same old place."

Mathes hung up the phone.

* * *

With the advent of strip malls, discount stores, and catalogs, the neighborhood Mom-and-Pop stores had slowly disappeared on Kingston Avenue. Unable to maintain competitive prices against cost cutters and with the emergence of discount sales and shopping centers, the worn old stores were only patronized by elderly men and women with time on their hands and the need for recognition by the owners. Sally Thompson had shopped at Max's Grocery and Deli for twenty years. Every Wednesday, Max would shop for her, pack the groceries in a bag, and ceremoniously hand her a bill.

Few other patrons shopped regularly, and she would routinely enter an empty store. Max, on the brink of selling the market, had listened sadly as Sally told him she would retire soon and move away. She promised to write, but they both knew the reality of modern life. Her memories of Max weeping while serving as a pallbearer at her husband's funeral still resonated. Working late again as usual on Wednesdays, Sally exited the police building in the evening at six thirty, reading her TV guide in search of an old movie on television. She stopped at Max's for her supplies and a corn beef on rye for dinner. Max stood alone behind the counter, smiling as usual, the groceries neatly stacked.

"Good evening, Mrs. Thompson. Looks like you're going to party tonight with the corn beef sandwich. I made it extra special good."

"Oh, Max, I hope you didn't pour too much mustard on it."

"Mrs. Thompson, would I put mustard on your corned beef and spoil the rich taste of prime meat?"

"Max, you're teasing me."

"I am, Mrs. Thompson, I certainly am. But I gotta charge you. Here's your bill."

"Thank you, Max."

Sally reached into her purse and withdrew her wallet. While removing the cash, the main door opened, and she glanced at a man wearing a coat partially covering a ponytail enter and limped toward the counter. He disappeared inside the store briefly but returned carrying a bag of potato chips. Setting the bag down on the counter while the two old friends talked, he slowly stepped beside her. Without a word, he removed a gun from under his coat and fired twice, the silencer muffling the sound. Sally Thompson slumped against the counter and collapsed on the floor. The gunman wheeled and fired at Max, who lurched backward against the shelves, spilling cans and bottles over his body as he fell. The shooter, concealing the gun in his coat, rifled through the cash drawer and stuffed bills in his pocket. Looking around again at an empty store, he limped toward the door, stopped at the security camera, and fired a shot into the lens. He reached up to the shattered camera with his gloved hand, pulled out the tape, and stuffed it in his coat. Limping badly, he walked out the door.

* * *

Driving home that night, Slonsky's radio crackled. "211 armed robbery. Shots fired. Location at Max's Delicatessen, 893 Kingston Avenue. Dead victims identified as the owner and one Sally Thompson, an employee of the police department. All units in the area report." Slonsky jammed his portable red light on the car roof, activated his siren, and drove rapidly to the location. His headlights shone on flashing blue lights and the familiar yellow tape that cordoned off the delicatessen. He skidded to a stop, waved his badge to the officer in charge, and hurried inside the market. Detective Frank Howard and Bobby Fairburn were taking notes. Howard looked up.

"BS. Hey, man, go home. We got this one covered."

"I knew the victim. Can I see her?"

"Oh, sure. Sorry, BS. Over here."

Howard removed a sheet, and the dead body of Sally Thompson stared vacantly into space. Slonsky turned away, wiped his eyes on his sleeve, and tried to speak. Howard put his hand on Slonsky's shoulder.

"Excuse me, BS, one of the cops wants to talk to me."

Slonsky nodded and looked at the tired face of his deceased old friend. He kneeled down beside the lifeless body and murmured, "Only a month before retirement. Don't worry, Sally. We'll find whoever did this."

Chapter 30

Honey Wissman stared out the window of her house during a Southern California drizzle.

"Sally Thompson was killed because of me. She used her password for my computer."

Slonsky stood next to her, a copy of the crime report in his hand.

"No, Honey. It's my fault. I was the one who told her to change computers because I thought someone could trace you."

"But she must have known someone would track my password to her."

"Yes, she probably did. And that someone works in the department. I had forensics check it out, and she had inputted all kinds of security protection. Not enough, but she wanted us to find the killer of the young woman, no matter what."

Honey wheeled around.

"Get me assigned to this case."

"What? You're working vice."

"Find a vice angle."

"Impossible."

"For someone who can get new computers, you don't sound very smart."

"Honey, I can't take you off vice. The captain will never go for it. He's not too pleased with me right now because I borrowed you for this case."

"Then how did you get authority to request new computers?"

"Well, Captain Martin had a little problem several years ago. I got him out of trouble. I fired my gold bullet, and he approved the order for the computers but used my name as the recipient for Homicide, but not any transfer of personnel."

Honey sat down. She looked up at Slonsky.

"You got profiles of homicide suspects, right? The department uses computers to find suspects, right? Do you know how to use computers? No. I do. That's your angle for the transfer."

"This is a robbery murder, not an abortion case."

"I don't care. Murder is murder. A woman is dead because she exposed herself to protect me. And an abused woman is dead. I want results."

"And I thought women needed affirmative action."

"Not in this case," she snapped.

"We can talk about that later. Look, Honey, help me out here. When you found Asquith's password, could anyone in the department have known you were searching files?"

"These days, anything's possible, but who would be interested in his files?"

"Someone in the department who has access."

"You mean a cop?"

"Exactly.

Honey handed Slonsky a printout. He stared at it.

"What's this?"

"It's called a printout. It shows whose computer in the department intruded on files."

"What does this say? It's just numbers."

"The numbers show the code for the department and the user station."

"So?"

"This computer was used at Wilshire Division. Assigned to the watch commander."

"What are you saying?"

"Asquith is a watch commander. He found out his computer was hacked and located the source. Easy to trace inside the department. The printout shows invoice number 1899 was approved by Sally Thompson for computer shipment to Wilshire Division. Order of Sergeant Slonsky. Six new computers and passwords. Sally Thompson was the director of supplies and inventory. She approved all orders. But the order was filled under your name. We both know that computer orders are issued by the division commander, in this case, Captain Martin. Now why would a Sergeant Slonsky, investigating a homicide and not assigned to Wilshire Division and who is computer illiterate, make this kind of request from Sally for new computers and new passwords? To cover tracks for someone."

"Yes. In this case, me. Sally bailed me out."

Slonsky looked at the printout again.

"My name is on the invoice for the computers. So Asquith knows I'm looking for a cop's records."

"But how would he trace his computer that you hacked?"

"Because he knows the ID number on the computer assigned to him as watch commander. When the city workers took away the old computers, including his, they stored them somewhere downtown. He probably knows people in that Supplies and Procurement Department who received the old computers. They dig it out. He goes downtown and plugs it in. There I am."

"Get your coat. You're transferred to homicide."

Slonsky grabbed his cell phone and called Chief Riley's office.

Chapter 31

"What? Transfer Honey to homicide? She's the best whore I've got, Slonsky."

"Chief, trust me. This woman is good. Off the record, I think I've got a lead on the medical clinic murder, thanks to her."

"What are you talking about?"

"Chief, I think it may be someone in the department."

Riley leaned across the desk.

"Slonsky, if it was anyone but you, I'd transfer him to pedestrian intersection control. The last I heard, you went flitting down to Mexico. You found nothing. Then you ordered new computers nobody needed. Then the woman who sent the computers got killed. What the hell is going on? No one has told me anything about this."

"Chief, look, I can't advertise. Honey did some digging and found some dirt. I can't explain. All I know is, it's a really solid lead."

"You getting any on the side, BS?"

"Chief, I'm serious. Help me out on this."

"One month. That's it. The vice commander will scream."

"Murder is more important, Chief. Look, I just got the ballistics report. The bullets that killed the pregnant woman at the medical clinic are both from the same gun that killed Sally Thompson. Whoever killed both women is the same guy."

Riley sat back.

"Don't blow this, BS. We don't need any killer cops."

"Trust me."

"The last time some guy said that, he went to jail."

* * *

Sergeant Asquith led roll call, excused the officers and went immediately to his computer, scrolled down department daily records, and scrutinized every item. Nothing unusual; only committee meetings, civil service hearings—routine stuff. Clicking on Personnel, he noticed a vice squad transfer to homicide—Wissman, Honey. Opening her personnel file, Asquith noted her original assignment to vice. The transfer order read "Excellent work ethic and trained in computer research. Transfer requested by Sergeant Slonsky."

Asquith deleted everything and walked casually out to the desk. Signaling the desk officer he was going to the men's room, he strolled toward the back of the building, removed a cell phone from his pocket, and punched in a number. The voice mail

150

activated. Asquith said, "I forgot to pick up milk at the market. I'll be home a little later."

Walking back to the station, Asquith waved again at the desk officer and knocked on Lieutenant Albright's open door. Albright looked up.

"Lieutenant, it's pretty quiet. I think I'll check and see if anybody's sleeping."

Albright smiled and nodded. In minutes, Asquith checked out a patrol car and drove to the All-Nite Market. Parking in the rear, he looked at his watch. Moments later, a beam of car lights swung across his windshield. Officer Eddie Mathes opened the door to his Porsche and hurried toward the patrol car. Asquith leaned across the seat and unlocked the door.

Mathes seated himself in the front seat.

"What's wrong?"

"Something's going on. I'm not sure. Your friend Honey Wissman got transferred to Homicide Division."

"From Vice to Homicide. That's highly unusual. But so what?"

"The request came from Sergeant Slonsky."

"The same guy who requested the new computers?"

"Just so. Wissman's personnel file shows her as computer literate. Now why would a vice cop with computer experience transfer to Homicide at the request of a homicide detective?"

"She found something."

"And that something may be somebody: you."

"This is getting serious."

"You bet your sweet bippy."

"So we don't use the computer anymore."

"You got that right."

"What do we do?"

"Not *we*, brother, *you*. It's time for you to go on sick leave. Maybe permanently."

"Quit the department? We'd lose our inside knowledge."

"Maybe. Or would you rather be with the brothers in prison."

"When do I leave?"

"Get your act together. Apply for sick leave. I'll approve it. I'll give you medical leave tomorrow. Then get out of town for a while until your trial date in the domestic violence case."

"What trial date? The DA's got no witnesses."

"The DA asked for a continuance. Why would they do that?"

"OK. I'll go feel sick."

"I gotta get back to work. Later, bro. And by the way, you better have a little talk with Honey."

Chapter 32

"Whoever it is, Basil, they've stopped using the computer." From her chair in front of the computer assigned to the absent captain, Honey Wissman turned her head around to talk to Slonsky. He looked at the monitor.

"How do you know?"

"Not one message, not an e-mail, nothing. So they probably meet and talk somewhere. Probably don't even use the phone."

"Why are you using the captain's computer? Won't Asquith find out?"

"I talked to the captain. I told him my computer was down and could I use his. He said 'Sure, I don't use it anyway.'"

"So if anyone wants to know who the hacker is, it's from the captain's computer."

"Good thinking."

Slonsky looked over Honey's shoulder.

"Maybe they're using a different password or changed their e-mail address."

Wissman turned around sharply.

"How would you know that?"

"Know what?"

"That they've changed passwords or e-mail addresses."

Slonsky laughed. "Just a hunch."

"Oh, no. You know more than you're telling me."

"Nope, just a guess."

Honey Wissman grimaced. Returning to the keyboard, she began manipulating passwords. Nothing. Slonsky walked over to the computer.

"We know it's coming out of Wilshire. Why not try several computers other than the one at the desk of the watch commander? Others have passwords."

"You knew how to use computers all the time."

Slonsky smiled. "Try it."

Honey reached in the desk drawer and removed the captain's list of passwords.

"Here we go," she said.

Honey began to run the computers one at a time and scrolled down all e-mails.

"Bingo."

She scrolled up on the screen to reveal a note on the computer clearly unrelated to department business. The e-mail address was listed as "Interdepartmental." No reply.

"Found address. 134 No. Belmont, Chatsworth."

Honey sat back in her chair.

"Son of a bitch. Someone used the captain's computer to find my home address. I forgot about that."

Slonsky read the message. "What time was the message sent?"

"Two a.m. Last night."

"Asquith."

"What?"

"Sergeant Asquith. I got a copy of the duty rosters. He's been watch commander every night this week. Watch commanders have access to the captain's computer if they need it."

"What's he got to do with all this?"

"I don't know. But we're gonna find out."

Honey stood and put her hand on Slonsky's arm. "BS, I need help on this."

"No problem. I already got a place for you to stay."

"What? How did you know?"

"Twenty-one years on the force, Honey. Sometimes you just work on intuition."

"Where is it?"

"On a lake. In the mountains. Way out of town. Oregon."

"I'll have to talk to the captain about taking time off."

"I already have. Get your coat, and we'll go see him together."

Honey logged out of the computer and stood up.

"You know, BS, you are some kind of cop and some kind of guy. When do I leave?'"

"Tomorrow on the train. I don't want you to fly. Too easy to track, and most stalkers wouldn't think of the train. Stay in your compartment, order meals from the steward, get off at the wrong stop, then jump back on the train as it starts to leave the station. I'll fly to Portland and drive to the cabin as soon as I can. Here are the directions.

Slonsky handed her a piece of paper and added, "Pool in the backyard. Tennis court down the street."

Honey Wissman took Slonsky's hands in her own.

"Thank you, Basil, thank you very much. I'll talk to you tomorrow."

Chapter 33

Honey Wissman knew how to pack in a hurry. Breakfast took fifteen minutes. Grabbing fruit from a bowl on the table and a bottle of water from the refrigerator, she locked the doors to her house and hurried to her car. In moments, she was on the freeway, driving toward the Amtrak station and the 10:00 a.m. train to Oregon.

She picked up her cell phone and called Slonsky.

"BS, I'm driving, so I only have a minute. I really would have preferred to fly rather than take the train."

"Honey, no one will think you're taking the train. It's much safer. Remember, stay in your compartment, order meals there, and check the aisles before you go out.

"I think you're paranoid."

"Probably. But you'll still be alive."

"See you there. Bye."

Replacing the phone, her mind wandered as she drove down the freeway. Changing lanes for the off-ramp to the Amtrak station, she saw a flashing police motorcycle light in her rearview mirror. She slowed down, but the light continued to flash directly behind her. Annoyed, she pulled over on the shoulder of the off-ramp. The motor officer stacked his bike, began pulling off his gloves, and walked toward her. She rolled down the window.

"Officer, was I speeding?"

"No, just a little tailgating. May I see your license and registration, please?"

Wissman fished around in her glove compartment and removed the registration. From her wallet, she removed the department badge. The officer smiled.

"Oh, police officer. I've been around so long I never expect to see a woman as a cop."

"Yes, times are a-changing. And I don't expect black police officers either."

"Indeed. Hey, no problem. But you know, I think your tires are low. Wanna take a look?"

"Sure."

Wissman exited her car and walked around inspecting the tires but saw nothing unusual. While she was bending over a front wheel, the officer quietly attached a small round object underneath the rear quarter panel of her car. She stood up.

"They look OK to me."

The officer looked surprised then studied the tires himself.

"Ah, radials. I wasn't sure. Those things always look flat to me. Sorry about that. Have a nice day."

Tipping his helmet, the motor officer walked back, mounted his bike, revved up the engine, and waited for her to leave. Wissman activated the turn signal, carefully looked in the rearview mirror, and pulled her car away from the edge of the off-ramp. The motor officer immediately reached for his cell phone. Watching the car merge onto the freeway, he spoke into the phone.

"She's alone. One suitcase. She took the off-ramp for Amtrak. I'll pick her up in a few minutes and confirm."

Honey mumbled to herself about the stop. She entered the Amtrak parking lot, parked her car, grabbed her suitcase, hurried into the station, and checked the departure gate number. Walking down the ramp to the train, she showed her ticket to the steward, boarded, and found her compartment. From behind the baggage carrier, a man walking with a limp and wearing a ponytail emerged and approached the steward. One hundred dollars changed hands.

* * *

Slonsky called Lieutenant Albright, the watch commander at Wilshire Division.

"Hi, Jimmy. Slonsky here."

"BS. Hey, man, how come you're hanging around here? No one else does."

"Nostalgia, Jim, nostalgia. Hey, listen, I need some information. Can you tell me the names of the officers on graveyard duty last night?"

"Sure. I got it right here. Anyone in particular?"

"Mathes. Eddie Mathes."

"Let me see. No. He's on sick leave authorized by Sergeant Asquith."

"Thanks, old buddy. That's all I need."

"Hey, call anytime for nostalgic purposes."

"You got it, man."

Slonsky ended the call, ran to his car, started the engine, accelerated, and burned rubber out of the lot as he headed toward the Amtrak station in Santa Barbara. He picked up his cell phone and punched in Honey's number but got no answer. He called the Amtrak station and got a recording. Slonsky knew the train stopped briefly in two cities before arriving at Santa Barbara at noon for a twenty-minute stop. His clock on the dashboard read eight thirty. He headed toward the freeway.

Chapter 34

Honey Wissman settled into her compartment, hung up clothes, stored her suitcase, changed into her sweat suit, and laced up her running shoes. Reaching into her purse, she removed a cordless phone, replaced the battery, and punched in a number. Allowing it to ring four times and after waiting for the voice mail message to conclude, she said, "Hi, Kelly. It's Honey. I'm on my way to Oregon. Tell the girls I said hello. Bye-bye."

The haunting sound of the diesel horn, followed by a slight surge forward, signaled departure. The train cautiously snaked its way out of the Los Angeles yard, wheels grinding on switches, swaying around curves, sliding past the graffiti, trash, and abandoned cars of East Los Angeles. The steel jungle of railroad tracks switched and crossed, the train wheels clacking on the rails as the diesel engine hauled the passenger train north to Oregon. Cement, dirt, steel, bridges, and towers clashed in the background while the train inched through the railroad yard toward its ultimate destination. A distinct odor of diesel smoke hung in the air, drifting over passenger cars, and the occasional mournful horn sounded at street crossings lined with their impatient motorists. Children stopped their play to wave innocently at the train whose comfortable passengers waved back.

Honey smiled at the incongruity of children playing among the grime and filth of their surroundings. She mused, "In a few years, they would start shooting each other."

Within forty-five minutes of departure, the intercom squawked to announce the train arriving at Glendale for a five-minute stop. Why anyone would take a train from downtown Los Angeles to Glendale was a mystery, but apparently, passengers boarded there. Honey watched several elderly couples waiting on the platform. With the help of obliging porters, the passengers struggled up the steps, lugging their suitcases and belongings. The train resumed a few minutes later, and Honey settled back to read her mail. Mailers, feminists to the core, sought her money, her membership, or her assistance. Tossing the financial appeals aside, she opened her policewoman newsletter and perused the latest litany of complaints about sexual harassment, glass ceilings, and other assorted gripes. Setting the papers aside, she lay back on the seat and closed her eyes. The soothing motion of the train after it left Los Angeles lulled her to sleep. She was awakened only by the sound of the conductor's voice announcing arrival in Santa

Barbara within thirty minutes. She stretched, yawned, and leaned back in her seat again.

Slonsky drove in excess of the speed limit and arrived at the Santa Barbara train station ten minutes before the train was due. Glancing at a copy of Honey's ticket, he paced restlessly on the platform until he heard the sound of the diesel horn. The train slowly curved around the tracks, wheels grinding, and pulled into the station. Scrutinizing the car numbers on the side of each car while the train ground to a stop, he found Honey's compartment. The porter opened the door to allow several passengers to exit but stepped aside as Slonsky flashed his badge and jumped aboard. Searching for compartment C, he looked inside to see Honey getting ready to step out. He knocked on the door. She looked up, surprised to see the rugged face peering in, and quickly opened the door.

"BS. What are you doing here? Why didn't you call me?"

"I tried but couldn't make a connection. I didn't want to call the police because they might make a big deal out of it."

"You are a little paranoid, but I appreciate it. What's the urgency?"

"I found out that Asquith authorized Mathes for sick leave. Did you tell Joe Rutledge or anyone else you were taking the train to Portland? Perfect time and place for someone to finish you off."

"Have you been smoking some of that stuff in the property room? And why would Rutledge tell anyone where I'm going? What reason would he have? And I didn't say when I was going."

"Just the same. Someone is out to get you. If not Mathes, someone else."

"I can take care of myself. I'm a big girl, Mr. Macho Man. No. Wait. I'm sorry. I'm flattered, but why the hurry? You could have called me in Oregon, unless someone is going to rob the train."

"Call me paranoid. I got your car license plate from the captain. He just kind of winked, but he gave it to me. I called security on the way up here and gave them your car license numbers. They found your car. I know the head guy there who used to be a cop. I asked him to check your car for bugs. He found one under your car."

Honey paused, concentrating, then looked at Slonsky.

"The traffic cop."

"What?"

"A cop stopped me on my way to the station. Said I was 'tailgating' and then asked me to check my tires. He probably stuffed the bug under the car while I was in looking at the tires."

"Honey, they know where you're going, and someone is going to follow you. Practice your evasive techniques on the train and in Oregon. When you get to the cabin, check in with the local cops. Close your doors to the cabin. I'll be up there as soon as I can."

Honey looked at BS, took him by the shoulders, and hugged him. "Hey, big guy, you better get off the train, or something might happen."

Slonsky beamed. Honey smirked.

"Otherwise, we'll both be going to Portland."

"Not a bad idea."

"Probably not. But we should be partners."

"You're right. Call me when you get there. I'm going back to LA now."

"OK. And, BS, we're partners now. It doesn't always have to be that way. Let's solve this case first."

A broad smile swept across the face of the veteran detective as the diesel horn sounded and the train lurched forward. Slonsky hurried down the aisle toward the vestibule. Flashing his badge again, the porter opened the door, and Slonsky jumped out onto the platform. He turned and waved at a smiling Honey Wissman. Pumping his fist in the air, he walked to his unmarked police vehicle and drove out of the parking lot. From inside the station, a taxi driver watched Slonsky enter his car. The driver picked up his cell phone.

"She's on the train. The cop just entered the freeway going south. Tan Chevy, license TTF 229. Unmarked police car. Probably down the 101 Freeway or Pacific Coast Highway."

He hung up.

Chapter 35

Slonsky lounged behind the steering wheel, driving down the Pacific Coast Highway toward Los Angeles. The afternoon sun reflected off the Pacific Ocean as the road paralleled the coastline and wound down along endless beaches. Big wheelers toiled in the slow lane as the drivers hauled local freight to small beach towns. Slonsky exited on an off-ramp to find a burger joint, where he wolfed down a cheap hamburger while sitting in the car, gulped a soft drink, then slumped behind the wheel, and fell asleep. After a short nap, he resumed the drive under a late-afternoon sun and darkening clouds. Approaching the city of Ventura, he checked his gas gauge. Close to empty and not enough to make it to LA. Sensing the need for a little exercise, he stopped at a dimly lit gas station and got out of the car. Another car pulled off the road behind him, but the driver went directly to the air pump, one of the last stations on the freeway offering that service. From inside the station, a young man walked out toward Slonsky, simultaneously wiping off the grease from his hands. His dirt-stained shirt identified him as Al. Slonsky rolled down the window when Al approached.

"Fill 'er up, sir?" he asked Slonsky.

"Yes, please. And check the oil and water. Where's your restroom?"

"In the back. The key's inside on the counter."

Slonsky nodded, opened the car door, handed Al his credit card, and headed toward the station. He grabbed the key, hurried around the back, unlocked the door, and entered the restroom.

At the gas pump, Al stuffed the hose into the gas tank. He set the handle lock, walked to the front of the car, and pulled open the hood. He checked the oil dipstick, opened the radiator cap, and checked the water level. The sound of another car pulling into the station briefly diverted his attention until he filled the radiator and started to replace the hood. The sound of footsteps interrupted him, and he looked up. In the fading light, he could not make out the features of a man approaching Slonsky's car, limping slightly while adjusting his baseball cap partially concealing a ponytail.

The stranger leaned on the front fender, but without looking at Al. He said, "Sorry to be so nosy. I used to be a mechanic. I still love to check out engines."

"Yeah. I love cars too. Drivin' 'em. Fixin' 'em. And out here, you can drive at a pretty good clip."

"I'll bet. I remember the old days when they used to have carburetors."

"That sure was the old days."

"Yeah. Say, as long as this other driver is inside, could I get some black coffee to go?"

"Oh, sure. You need any gas?"

"No, thanks. I just need to stay awake."

Al shrugged, shut the hood, and removed the line from the gas tank. He walked toward the office while the stranger returned to his car. Inside the office, Al turned his back to pour the coffee when he heard a motor start and the car drove out of the station. Surprised, he frowned and began pouring the coffee back into the pot when Slonsky emerged from the restroom.

"How much for the gas?"

"Fifty-nine dollars and ninety cents."

"Hmm. Gas cost is lower than I thought. Add a cup of coffee to that."

Al nodded, poured a cup of black coffee, and handed it to Slonsky, who surveyed its sloshing contents.

"Got a lid?"

"Let's see. They should be here somewhere."

Al fished around the coffeemaker, looking in drawers, and finally noticed the lids next to the artificial cream. He handed one to Slonsky.

"Thank you. Can I have a little cream, please?"

"Sorry. Most of us drink it black around here, and we—"

An explosion ripped through the air. Shards of glass tore through the station windows and rained on the building. A ball of fire mushroomed above Slonsky's car and expanded into the air. Suffocating heat and dust choked the lungs of both men as they jumped up and raced out the back door of the gas station to the sound of exploding rubber and fabric. Huddled behind the station until the noise subsided, they looked carefully around the side of the building. An incinerated police vehicle burned furiously.

Chapter 36

A team of paramedics transported a bleeding and protesting detective to a small country hospital staffed at night with only one doctor and two nurses. The doctor listened to Slonsky's heart, palpated his back, and examined his hands and feet. Slonsky muttered under his breath. The doctor removed his stethoscope and helped the detective to the floor.

"Mr. Slonsky, everything looks OK, but you have a lot of cuts from the exploding glass that came from the windows. We better keep you overnight. Just in case."

"Overnight? What for, if everything is OK?"

"Detective, sometimes your body holds off the shock for a while then relapses when the adrenaline stops pumping. We need to monitor you."

"Someone tried to kill me, and you want me to hang around to see if something might go wrong?"

"Mr. Slonsky, in your job, you learn from experience. So do we. Just one night."

"No."

"Well, are you going to leave dressed in a hospital gown?"

Slonsky looked down at the white gown hanging around his knees, tied in back tightly, but exposing his butt and legs.

"Shit."

"I'll have the nurse walk you to your room."

"Shit."

The doctor smiled and summoned a waiting nurse, who took Slonsky by the elbow and walked him toward a room. Moments later, he lay alone in a hospital bed, dressed in a flimsy white gown with air flowing up his ass. The unsmiling nurse placed his clothes in a closet. Slonsky struggled to sit up.

"Detective, in case you want to leave in the middle of the night, let us know, and we'll call one of the farmers to bring over a horse."

"Shit."

The nurse left the room. When the door closed, Slonsky slid painfully out of bed. Almost falling on shaky legs, he looked out the window from his room on the ground floor. Three cars were parked next to the hospital in a darkened lot. He saw no guards, no hospital personnel, and no fences. Through the window of the single-story hospital, he could see the doctor and two nurses attending to Al in another room. Walking unsteadily to the closet, he removed his clothes from the hangers. Untying the knot on his gown and shedding it on the floor, he dressed himself unsteadily. With shaking hands fumbling with his shoes, his fingers trembled while trying to tie the laces.

He pulled a wire coat hanger off the clothes rod in the closet, folded it, and stuffed it into his pants pocket. Opening the window in his ground floor room, he climbed out slowly, pain shooting through his legs, and dropped the three-foot distance to the ground. In an awkward landing and struggling to find his balance, Slonsky lurched toward a nearby low-level wall and clawed his way upright. Leaning on the side of the wall, he surveyed the darkened parking lot. Turning around, he could see the doctor examining Al in a different room and talking to the nurse.

Slonsky clambered clumsily over the wall, limping in pain, walking across the parking lot toward the three cars parked next to one another. Gambling on the heat of the countryside inducing drivers to leave a window partially open, he approached an older-looking car. An inch of open space at the top of the window was enough to insert a bent coat hanger. With decades of experience behind him, he removed the wire hanger from his pants pocket, folded it into a loop on the end, and inserted it inside the window around the door latch. A slight tug, a click, and the lock released.

Slonsky opened the door and climbed into the driver's seat, the pain searing through his body. Reaching under the dashboard for ignition wires, he could see their individual colors in the dim glow of the overhead parking lights in the lot. Bending the wires back and forth repeatedly in his shaky hands, the strands broke. Pausing to see if anyone was looking, he returned to the task. Touching the ignition wires together, the car started. Slonsky sat up, closed the car door, and activated the headlights. Sixty seconds later, Detective Basil Slonsky drove the stolen car out of the parking lot and back toward Los Angeles.

* * *

"You're damn right you'll pay the damages for this, Slonsky. All the press needs is for us to be stealing cars."

Chief Riley stared at his bandaged detective, who stood grimly before him. Slonsky mumbled.

"It was an emergency."

"Oh, right. How many times have you heard that in court from some dip?"

"I said I'd pay the damages."

"You bet your sweet ass you will. The only reason I don't suspend you is because you almost got yourself killed. By the way, how are you?"

"I thought you'd never ask."

"OK. OK. I'm sorry. Why don't you go home and get some rest? You look like you need it."

"I'll be fine. But I don't have a car."

Clark clenched his teeth then relaxed.

"Go downstairs. Check out another car. But go home."

"Right. Maybe I should take a few days off."

"Now that makes sense. Come back next Monday."

"Deal."

"Now get out before I change my mind."

Slonsky left.

Passing through the crowded lobby, Sergeant Rutledge yelled at him, "BS, you got a message!"

Slonsky walked over to the grinning sergeant, who feigned drawing a gun.

"Hands up. You're under arrest for car theft. You should call the ACLU to make sure we give you your rights."

"You cops are all alike, harassing us poor, underprivileged folks who just need wheels for a little while."

"Man, you are something else, stealing a car. But hey, how are you?"

"A little tired and shaky. The chief gave me a few days off."

"Great. Hey, you got a message from that TV broad, Carmen."

"Carmen Susa?"

"Yeah, that's her. She said she had a tape you might want to see."

Slonsky grabbed his phone.

"Give me her number."

"310-221-7776."

Writing down the telephone number on his business card, Slonsky went over to an unoccupied desk and called on the phone.

"Carmen, it's BS. What's up?"

"Normally, someone asks me how I am first."

"Sorry. I'm just a little tired."

"I'll bet. You almost got killed. How are you?"

"OK. But I think I need a few days off."

"Good idea. Here's why I called. When I was at that abortion protest, we taped the shooting, but the place was chaos, so the stuff didn't come out too well. You saw it. Seems like Channel 6 also got some pictures, but they were cut and never shown. Just a bunch of people protesting while the cameraman panned the scene before the shooting started. Frank Milke, the Channel 6 guy, was filling time, talking about the abortion hearing that was going on. The cameraman pointed the camera at the courthouse and zoomed in for background. Guess who was standing at the courthouse window, loud and clear."

"In the courthouse? Probably a judge."

"Lucky guess. Judge Carleton, big as life. The Channel 6 camera guy probably didn't know someone was shooting a gun equipped with a silencer, so he just kept taping background while Milke was talking. All of a sudden, he switches the camera to the crowd running and screaming. The judge must have seen the whole thing."

Slonsky feigned surprise.

"Interesting. Interesting. For once, you helped us, even if you don't like us."

"Well, I don't dislike all of you."

"Thanks, babe. I owe you one."

"I'd like that. Call me anytime."

"You're beautiful. When can I see the tape?"

"Tomorrow, in the afternoon."

"You bet."

"Just call me before you come, and we'll set it up. Bye."

Slonsky walked to the underground garage, checked out a car, and drove home. He would pay a visit to Channel 6 then chat with the judge.

Chapter 37

Slonsky entered the office of the chief judge. Kelly Francis looked up from her computer.

"Oh, Detective Slonsky. Nice to see you again. What can I do for you?"

"I need to see Judge Carleton. It's very important."

"I'm sorry. Judge Carleton is very busy right now. He can't see you."

"Tell him I strongly suggest that he break into his busy schedule and see me, or he will get a subpoena from the grand jury as a witness to a homicide."

Kelly Francis stared into the eyes of Slonsky.

"All right. I'll tell him."

Francis walked across the room and down the hall, knocking quietly on the door to Carleton's chambers. She entered, closing the door behind her. In a few minutes, she returned.

"The judge says he will see you. Come this way, please."

Slonsky nodded, smiled smugly, and followed her into chambers. Judge Carleton sat behind his desk, stood, shook hands with Slonsky, and waved him to a chair before resuming his own chair.

"I'm glad to see you again, Detective. I still owe you for keeping me from getting killed."

"Thank you, Judge. To protect and serve."

"What can I do for you?"

"Judge, I've got some pictures we took off a videotape of the abortion shooting. Would you take a look at these, please?"

Slonsky handed Carleton several eight-by-ten black-and-white photographs depicting the judge standing at his chambers window. Carleton studied the pictures and looked up.

"I don't understand. These are pictures of me, of course, but what is the point?"

"Judge, those pictures were taken off the videotape running at the time before the woman at the clinic was shot. I watched the tape, and from its sound track, I could tell you were standing at the window at the time the shots were fired. You must have seen the whole thing."

Carleton hesitated. "Just because I was watching the protest doesn't mean I saw anyone shooting that woman. There were hundreds of people there. It was raining and gloomy."

"You said you only saw people running."

"What difference does it make?"

Slonsky took a deep breath.

"The tape shows you standing at the window, looking down at the crowd milling around, but when the woman was shot, you were still at the window, and only then did the people start to run. You must have seen something before the shooting."

Carleton leaned forward.

"I think this conversation is over."

"Tell me, or tell the grand jury."

Carleton sat back.

"All right. You saved my life. I owe you. Look, I'm in the midst of a high-visibility case involving these abortion protestors. For me to say that I saw the shooting means I have to disqualify myself. I would be an eyewitness, not a judge. Some other judge would take my place who would be completely unfamiliar with the facts or the law in the case. While the chief judge was trying to find another judge to replace me and without any judicial supervision of the parties in the meantime, another woman could have been killed. The parties needed to know that I would enforce an order immediately if there were another incident. If I'm off the case, there is no protection."

"But you didn't sign an order right away."

Carleton paused.

"Detective, both lawyers knew I would eventually sign an order. Amstead knew it. Richardson knew it. But they both have constituencies. Giving both sides some breathing room by agreeing not to sign an order immediately and letting the picketers voluntarily stop protesting gave the pro-choicers a small victory. No demonstrations. The pro-lifers could voluntarily stop their demonstration without any order from me. That would show how reasonable they are. Both sides can crow. After a few days, I could sign the order, and everyone would be happy, reasonably happy."

"And so would the president."

"Yes, it was good for me too."

"But did you see the shooter? Whoever shot the victim had to be close and have a clear shot."

Carleton leaned forward on his desk. He nodded his head.

"Yes, I did see the shooting, but I can't identify anybody. All I saw was some guy carrying TV cables, wearing a raincoat and a hat over his head concealing his face. He pulled out a gun and fired. Other than that, he looked like hundreds of others on the street. When the chaos started, I don't know what happened to him. I never saw his face."

"Judge, you know as well as I do, information like that can be helpful even if you can't ID the guy. In the first place, it was a man—not a woman. In the second place, it looks like he acted alone. And third, you could see his hands. What color were they?"

"White."

"So we got a white male. That cuts out a lot of other folks."

"Maybe. But there's whole universe of men out there that fit that description."

"OK. Did you notice anything else?"

Carleton paused.

"Yes, I did notice one thing. He had a limp, but it may have been from carrying heavy cables. And he did wear a ponytail."

"You don't think that substantially reduces the number of suspects?"

"Yes, I suppose so. But even if it narrows the field, where does it take you?"

"Maybe nowhere. But it sure gives us a lead. We have computers, you know, and most of the people who would pull this kind of job are either on parole or probation. So we got an adult white male who walks with a limp. That helps. How tall was he?"

"Hard to say. He was in a crowd, so he didn't stand out."

"Average height?"

"Yes. I'd say so."

"Have you ever seen him again?"

Carleton hesitated again. He folded his hands.

"I'm not sure, but during a hearing in court sometime after the day of the shooting, I noticed this man staring at me as I left the bench for a recess. He turned around and walked out, limping."

Slonsky leaned forward.

"What did he look like?"

"Nothing distinctive. And I'm not sure he was the same guy who killed that woman. I only got a glimpse of his face before he turned around. He had his coat turned up."

"Would you recognize him again if you saw him?"

"I have no idea. Possibly."

Slonsky stood and carefully removed the photographs from the desk.

"I wish you had told me this before, Judge. We just got word there's going to be a protest at the clinic the day after tomorrow."

"But I issued an injunction."

"And the pro-lifers think you have no right to prevent them from speaking out. They're prepared to get arrested."

"Well, let them."

"It isn't that easy. Suppose the shooter shows up again. If you had told us this before, we could have alerted everybody to be on the lookout for a man fitting that description even if unclear.

Now we have to scramble. We may not get this covered in time. Now, if you'll excuse me, I have work to do."

Slonsky buttoned up his coat, turned, and walked out the door.

Chapter 38

Eddie Mathes sat alone in the rear booth of Red's Diner, a steak joint run by his brother. As Latinos and blacks moved into the neighborhood, whites moved out, and the bar matured into a hangout for anyone trying to prevent detection by police. Red had set up a small surveillance team who loitered outside the restaurant, and others staked out further down the street. Supplied with cell phones, beepers, and binoculars, they assured no stranger got within one mile of the restaurant without detection. Red paid his scouts well, most on parole or probation, and he held that condition not too subtly over their heads. Any problems with them, and Red notified the police. In the back of the restaurant, pimps openly used cell phones to place calls and arranged for potential customers to meet with women. Bookies manned the phones daily.

Despite the reputation of Red's Diner, police could never effect an arrest. Cell phones alerted Red to a potential raid of the premises. And Red tolerated no minors, drunks, or rowdy customers to alert Alcohol and Beverage Control. Getting an informant inside was suicide. The Feds had no jurisdiction here, the local cops were stymied, and no one could infiltrate.

But Red held his ace in Eddie Mathes, who kept track of any departmental action involving the restaurant or its clientele. Eddie punched in numbers on his cell phone and spoke, "Honey, I'm at Red's."

Honey Wissman answered, "How did you get my cell number?"

"Hey, Asquith is not too smart, but he does know how to get into the captain's computer. Your cell phone number is in the captain's file. How come you changed your number?"

"I was getting kinky phone calls. Hey, you expect me to talk to you after Maureen McCullough, a.k.a. your wife, was killed and then Sally Thompson?"

"Are you kidding? Look, Gimpy is a computer nerd. When Asquith told me someone broke into his computer, I told Gimpy. Nothing more. I never thought he would follow through, but he did. He broke into city security and found out who had exchanged your computer."

"You expect me to believe that? Liar. Liar."

"You know I don't know squat about computers. I couldn't have done that. He did this on his own."

"You must think I'm really stupid. Slonsky is on this case. He's no dummy. And now he'll be in your face. He's gonna start to put two and two together on the abortion case, and that adds up to me."

"He can't touch you."

"Oh, no? For one thing, he knows more about computers than you think he does. He tried to play dumb with me, but I could tell he was computer savvy. He's on days off now, but when he gets back on this case, you can bet your ass he'll find something."

"You told me he was still using pencil and paper."

"That's what I thought. When I was searching records for Slonsky in the abortion case, I couldn't find the key strokes that would have identified you and Asquith. Very casually, he suggested a different kind of search. For a guy that doesn't know computers, he was right on. He said he just had a hunch. Now I know differently."

"So he knows the department better than you. Probably did a shortcut."

"Well, not only that. He ordered new computers from his friend in the department in exchange for mine. Who else knew that? Nobody but me. And the woman who got them gets killed for it."

"That was in a robbery."

"Oh, right. Very conveniently. A robbery two days later in a two-bit little deli that probably doesn't have more than twenty-five bucks in the till."

"Happens all the time."

"Not like this one. A pro pulled it off. No customers in the store. Kills the owner, who didn't even have a gun. Busts the security camera and takes out the tape. No prints. This was not amateur hour."

"Look, I have a hearing on my case coming up. It's already been continued twice, and the DA says he's ready."

"With what? I thought they had no evidence."

"I don't know. And I can't find anyone on the inside."

Honey paused.

"Where's the shooter?"

"Gimpy? Greasing up his .45, I suppose, to get Slonsky."

"You have to stop him. Slonsky will be at the demonstration tomorrow."

"So what? He doesn't know what Gimpy looks like."

"You think so? By the way, how come they're ready to go to trial on your wife's case?"

"No relation."

"How do you know? Look, I want no part of this tomorrow. I'll deal with pro-lifers my own way."

"It's too late. Gimpy's already jazzed. Looking forward to it."

"Then call him off."

"You don't just call off Gimpy. The guy is a fruitcake. Tell him to call it off, and he'll shoot a few others just for fun. And besides, how come you're worried about Slonsky?"

"I'm outta this."

"Baby, maybe you got something on me, but I got something on you."

Honey Wissman hung up.

Chapter 39

Rain. Black clouds sprawled across the Oregon sky, cloaking the sun and churning the ocean wind that scooped water into the air and hurled it eastward across the shore. The warmth of the earth summoned the clouds, reluctantly releasing their hold, and rain showered the hills and mountains with moisture—not a drenching rain, but a soft, steady, and gentle spray that slowly soaked the land and healed its wounds. Inside the mountain cabin, Honey Wissman listened to the wind rising slightly as the water stirred the air and brushed the pine tree branches against the roof. After three days in Oregon, she recognized the weather pattern. Slonsky had called to say he was delayed. Shutting the unlocked doors left open to the earlier-warm fading sun, she closed the windows to restrain the breeze, turned on the outside porch lights, walked over to the fireplace, gathered up a handful of pine needles and slender wood branches lying next to the fireplace, and carefully laid them on the grate. She lit a match. The flame touched the pile; needles flared and ignited the kindling. Placing a few logs of wood carefully on top of the accelerating flames, she backed away to watch the progress of the fire. Incrementally, smoke drifted from under the logs; tiny flames fluttered at the edges, slowly expanding and bursting into crackling fire. Satisfied, she sat back on the venerable, frayed couch in front of the fireplace and stared hypnotically. The wind subsided, but the rain increased, spattering loudly on the windows and roof. She shivered slightly, reached over to pull a woolen blanket around her shoulders, leaned against the pillows, and closed her eyes.

The warmth of the fire increased, and she dozed in the soft light of flickering shadows.

Behind her back, the door handle turned slowly without a sound, the door opened slightly, and the wind crept through the slender crack and spattered drops of rain inside the room. Honey stirred slightly, shifting her head on the back of the sofa. Minutes passed before the door opened wider to reveal a man wearing a raincoat dripping with rainwater, causing rivulets to spill down on the threshold. A rain hat covered his hair and ears, concealing part of his face, but revealed a pair of piercing eyes underneath the brim.

Silently entering, he could see the blond hair cascading over the back of the sofa, and the face turned slightly to the other side. He slowly raised a revolver, the silencer extending past the burnished barrel, and aimed. He pulled the trigger twice.

The weapon recoiled silently each time and spit smoke, which hurtled upward toward the ceiling, shifting wildly in the wind. Honey Wissman slipped noiselessly down on the sofa, blond hair falling across her face laced in blood. The door closed. Ten minutes later, the phone rang incessantly.

* * *

A telephone call from Slonsky sent local police to the cabin. Paramedics placed her on a stretcher and rushed to the local hospital. Medics carried her into the operating room staffed by three doctors, who looked at the savaged body of the young woman and shook their heads.

The chief surgeon spoke to his colleagues quietly, "We have a long night ahead of us."

Despite the diminutive size of the hospital, several resident doctors had retired from their successful urban practice and moved to this small community to practice medicine, but only in emergencies. All were skilled surgeons and had brought their expertise, and their money, with them. Over the years, they had improved the facilities, employed retired nurses, and developed an experienced staff of local men often unable to find employment elsewhere. Many retired men and women in the community volunteered their time, particularly during the summer tourist season. Although patient volume was low, the skill level of the doctors was high. Trained and eager to serve, nurses and staff appeared immediately upon summons from the doctors and worked diligently at their assignments.

The surgeons donned their surgical clothes and masks, gloved their hands, and studied the body of Honey Wissman closely. Speaking briefly to one another, the doctors initially transfused the unconscious woman, staunched the flow of blood, and administered anesthesia. Rotating their examination on the shattered shoulder, the tattered neck, the unstable arm, they studied X-rays displaying the neck wound. The MRI exposed the wound to display impaired muscles, but the tendon miraculously was untouched. Carefully repairing the neck muscles, they bound together the major strands.

Two hours later, they began reconstruction of the shoulder. Working with shattered bone fragments, they could only pack the wound until the arrival of a neurosurgeon from Portland. Concluding that any delay was not life-threatening, the surgeons removed their masks, gloves, and gowns. Eyes fixed on the screen monitoring heartbeats, they anxiously watched the graph begin to peak slightly higher. All three looked at one another. Their patient would never be the same, but she would live.

When Oregon police called back with their report, Slonsky raced to the airport, flew to Portland, and drove to the hospital, where he stood silently in the waiting room. He had seen hundreds of mutilated bodies in his career, all races, all sexes— gaping wounds, knife cuts, shredded skin—but entering the hospital to see the unconscious Honey Wissman sickened him. The doctors had told him the bullets entered the side of her neck and the rear of her shoulder. She had lost considerable blood. "She will live, but not as a police officer," said one of the surgeons to a relieved Slonsky.

In approaching the intensive care unit, Slonsky swallowed, wiped a tear from his eye, and bit his lip. A doctor walked out of the operating room.

"I'm Dr. Stone. I'm the chief surgeon here. Are you Sergeant Slonsky?"

"Yes."

"Ms. Wissman is alive, but the injury has destroyed too many nerves, and she will undoubtedly lose the mobility of her arm. We can tell more in about twenty-four hours. Are you her superior officer?"

"No. She's my partner. We are involved in a major homicide case in Los Angeles. She came up here for protection because we needed to put her in a safe place. Now it doesn't look like it was safe enough."

"I'm very sorry, Detective. We'll do all we can. Here is the draft of a medical summary if you would like to read it. We have the original, but your department might want it for disability purposes."

Stone handed Slonsky the report.

"Thank you, Doctor."

"You're welcome. You can visit her now, but only for a few minutes."

Slonsky nodded and paused at the door to the intensive care unit. Pushing open the door, he saw an unconscious Honey Wissman, who painted a desolate sight. Her face was as pallid as the sheets she lay on, her entire side, shoulder, and neck covered with bandages. An IV drip slowly entered her traumatized body. The doctors had cut her flowing blond hair during surgery, leaving her partially bald. A nurse hovered nearby to assure that no one touched her. Slonsky hesitated when the nurse held up her hand to signal "No contact."

With tears welling in his veteran eyes, he hurriedly wiped them away with his sleeve and walked near the bed. He looked helplessly at the nurse, who offered him a tissue. He shook his head and wiped his face again. The nurse pointed to her wristwatch. Detective Basil Slonsky quietly turned and walked away, shaking his head in frustration and sorrow.

Returning to the waiting room, Slonsky read the medical report carefully. The doctors, although uncertain in their diagnosis, concluded that the first shot had struck the victim in the left shoulder, which jerked her body downward, as the second shot passed through the side of her neck. Oregon detectives discovered both slugs lying on the cabin floor, each having torn through the flesh, causing shreds of skin clinging to the metal. Slonsky studied photographs of the slugs prepared by local police and recognized them as similar to those found in both the bodies of Maureen McCullough and Sally Thompson. Recalling evidence of the death of both women, he wrote in his report that the assassin in each case was probably the same person who shot Honey. He called Joe Rutledge.

"Joe, it's BS. I guess you know about Honey?"

"Yes, BS. Hey, I'm really sorry. The captain told me you wanted it kept quiet. No press coverage. No one in the department even knows about her yet."

"Thanks. I appreciate it. I need to know whether anyone knew she was going to Oregon."

"Not that I know of. She asked for a few days off. I told her she was assigned to your case and to touch base with you."

"She didn't tell you where she was going?"

"Nope. None of my business either. Wait a minute. I think she did say something, but I really didn't pay attention. I guess she must have told someone."

"I just need to know if there are any department records of her time off at Wilshire Division."

"Nope. Once she transferred to Homicide, she was out of our jurisdiction. You should be able to get that information from downtown."

"I don't want anyone to know what I'm doing. This is an Oregon case, so LAPD is not doing the investigation. She's my partner, so department policy prevents me from investigating the crime anyway."

"Understood."

"OK. Thanks. Let me know if you hear anything."

"No problem. Hey, how's she doing?"

"Not too good. Intensive care. I just got out of there."

"We'll say a prayer."

"Thanks, old buddy. Talk to you later."

Chapter 40

The doctors prohibited any visitors from seeing Honey for one week, and Slonsky flew back to Los Angeles. Entering the Wilshire Division station, he walked over to the office computer sitting on Wissman's desk. He had watched her log on when they were looking for records and noted she used an ordinary password: her last name. He logged on and waited for the computer to boot up. The menu flashed on the screen, and he opened her files. Nothing but a few reports. Guessing that she used the same password for her e-mail, he connected and entered her name. Clicking on a departmental e-mail, he read a short message to the Criminal Courts Building. "Going to Oregon for a few days. I'm taking the train." Slonsky printed out the message but knew it was undoubtedly hopeless to trace this mail through the thousands of daily messages. But she had told someone. He grabbed the phone and asked for the Computer Section. A recorded voice answered, asking for the caller to leave a message.

Slonsky replied, "This is Detective Slonsky. Could you ask Mike to call me? I need that computer genius up here right now."

Mike Winkelmann probably invented the computer. His greatest joy in life was the challenge of determining what the computer had done wrong. He brought sanity to bewildered cops, secretaries, and deputy chiefs who raged against the computer. Repeatedly lured by private companies, he turned down lucrative offers to work in a private lab. Money was not an object in his life. He wanted to use his talents to help law enforcement. When Slonsky called to say he needed help on the Wissman case, Winkelmann dropped everything and drove to Wilshire Division. When Slonsky briefed him and showed him the e-mail message, his face clouded.

"BS, this is not going to be easy, but I think I can find it. Last week alone, the department recorded over five thousand e-mail messages, although not all were interdepartmental. If Honey had erased this message you showed me, we could never find it. But these messages are coded by station. You can't see it on the screen, but we can track where she sent the message." Winkelmann hit several keyboard strokes, stopped, and pointed to the monitor.

"Look, BS. See that letter *W* in the upper left-hand corner? That means the message was sent from this station, Wilshire Division. Now let's see where it went."

Winkelmann typed. He looked up.

"Hey, we got lucky. She e-mailed someone in the courthouse."

"In the courthouse? Who?"

"Let's see. She knows that in our department, you generally can't trace e-mail because the person receiving it frequently deletes it. E-mail is easier than the phone. She probably figured the person receiving the e-mail would delete this kind of message after reading it, but apparently he or she didn't. But she didn't know we coded messages."

Slonsky looked at his printout of Honey's e-mail telling someone she was going to Oregon.

"Somebody at the courthouse knew she was leaving LA and going by train?"

"Looks like it."

"When was this message sent?"

"Ten days ago. 6:30 a.m."

"The train leaves Los Angeles at 10:30 a.m. The first major station is Santa Barbara. So anyone could leave here early and get there before the train arrives at noon. Santa Barbara is a fifteen-minute stop. I know because I drove there."

"You drove to Santa Barbara?"

"Yes. I had a hunch someone might want her dead, so I drove up there in an hour and a half. I couldn't reach her by phone, but I got there before the train arrived, boarded, and told her to be careful."

"Did you see the train leave?"

"Yes. I jumped off after it started."

"Did you come in a police car?"

"Unmarked, but cops can recognize them. God, someone could have already been on the train or got on in Santa Barbara. They had lots of passengers. Mike, I am going to give you a big kiss."

"You do, and I'll file a sexual harassment charge."

Slonsky hugged the shy computer nerd and ran out the door.

"What's the rush?"

"Gotta do some record checking."

Chapter 41

Slonsky sipped black coffee, while Sergeant Rutledge quizzically shook his head.

"You know, BS, after all you told me, how did anyone know exactly where Honey hid out at a remote cabin in Oregon? The state is pretty big."

"I can't prove it, but somebody did."

"Maybe that somebody just wanted her dead for any number of reasons: a parolee, a gangbanger, some john she busted."

"She would have told me that or told somebody."

"BS, she could have had a boyfriend. Maybe she made him jealous."

"Of me? Are you kidding?"

"Yeah? Lots of guys get female partners, and hanky-panky occurs."

"First of all, she never said she had a boyfriend. Second, I'm not the type."

"That's what they all say when they pay alimony."

"Joe, get serious."

"OK. Sorry."

Both men fell silent. Rutledge stirred his coffee.

"BS, did you know that after Honey was shot, the captain cleared out her desk and put her stuff in a locker? Boy, did she have a lot of feminist crap. Kinda dated stuff, but a real pro-choicer, a glass ceiling type, and a bra burner. Or at least she used to be one."

"Honey?"

"Yeah, man, big-time. Even the captain was surprised."

"Funny. She never said a word to me about it."

"Hey, you never know about private lives."

"What else was in there?"

"I don't know. I didn't really pay too much attention. Maybe you should ask the captain."

"Not yet. I don't want to make waves."

"I guess you could look in the locker where the captain stored her stuff."

"Isn't it locked?"

"Sure. But look at this."

Rutledge held up a ring of keys, fingered one, and held it up. Slonsky beamed.

"A master key?"

"Goes with the turf."

"Do you suppose . . ."

"I do suppose."

Slonsky and Rutledge abandoned their coffee and hurried to the locker room. Rutledge reached in his pocket and pulled out a list of locker numbers and found the number for Honey's locker. His master key turned the lock easily, and he opened the door slowly. He and Slonsky removed a stack of random papers and articles from magazines extolling the virtues of femininity and urging women to seek greater freedom. On one side of the drawer lay a clipped article recounting the abortion shooting and the panic that had seized the crowd. Underlined in red were the words *unidentified assailant*.

Rutledge mused out loud, "BS, why would she underline this article? She had nothing to do with the investigation at that time."

"Until I got her assigned to it."

"So? That was later. What's the purpose of underlining those words? She knew you had no suspect."

"Maybe she wanted to start a file."

"With no suspect? I think this lady may know more than we think."

"Maybe so. Joe, keep this under your hat. I want to check something out."

"No problem. I just hope Honey's not involved. She's a nice broad."

"Yeah, I hope so too."

Chapter 42

Slonsky drove up to the courthouse, parked his car in the lot reserved for detectives, and took the elevator to the fifth-floor courtroom of Judge Murphy, who was delivering a dose of liberal pap about rehabilitation, albeit not as sappy as before his daughter was killed. John Marcum was reading a file in the back of the courtroom, and Slonsky tapped him on the arm. Marcum smiled in recognition. Slonsky waved for him to come outside. Marcum got up, and both men exited the courtroom.

"BS. I thought you weren't coming. That trial with Mathes is on the ten thirty calendar."

"Sorry, I got hung up. Can I see the file?"

"Sure."

Marcum thumbed through several files he held under his arm and removed the Mathes file, handing it to Slonsky, who perused it quickly and handed it back to Marcum.

"No change."

"Right. And there's no way I can get a continuance again."

"Then answer 'Ready for trial.'"

"What? With no witnesses?"

"Look, you know the trial won't start for a few days. The courts are backed up. I need a little more time."

"BS, you're putting my ass on the line."

"You can handle it. If you aren't ready in the trial court when the case is called, the judge will dismiss it."

Marcum stared at Slonsky.

"OK, BS. But this is a gold bullet I'm firing for all the help you gave me in the trial with Murphy's daughter."

"Fire away."

"BS, Is there something I should know?"

"Not yet. But you'll be the first to know."

Slonsky tapped the prosecutor on the shoulder and walked out the courtroom behind the shaking head of John Marcum.

Chapter 43

The Oregon surgeons released Honey, and an LAPD helicopter flew her back to Los Angeles. Slonsky had offered to fly to Oregon and hitch a ride back to Los Angeles on the helicopter, but adding a passenger to the pilot, a surgeon and a paramedic foreclosed including another body on the flight. Slonsky drove to the airport to await their arrival. He watched the helicopter arrive, but security personnel allowed no one near Honey while transporting her toward the ambulance. He asked the surgeon if he could accompany her to the hospital, but the doctor declined. After the pilot and the paramedic loaded Honey into the ambulance, Slonsky watched it disappear down the street, its siren blaring. He would visit Honey that night.

* * *

Night at a hospital changes the ambience of a bustling institution. As the pace slackens, darkness yields its own silence, cloaking the wards and rooms in a sunless environment artificially lighted by bulbs and neon fixtures. Doctor visits end, families and friends depart, and a stillness settles in to create an eerie atmosphere for patients, emphasizing their disability or increasing awareness of the physical pain they suffer.

207

Without the hubbub of the day to distract, patients lie alone to concentrate on an illness or injury, compelling their unhappy presence. For those in a serious condition, the thought of mortality runs through their unsettled minds. Only sleep cures the depression as the restless patient awaits the sun and light of a new day.

Into the somber Queen of Angels Hospital, Slonsky entered and flashed his badge, enabling him to visit after hours. Dreading the experience, he walked into the room of barely conscious Honey Wissman. Her short blond hair touched the pillows awkwardly and revealed the sterile bandages covering her neck and shoulder as she lay restlessly on her back. Pain etched her face, and she had pulled her legs up in a fetal position that stretched her gown up across her thighs. An IV drip hung next to the bed, emptying fluid into her system to replace solid food. A small plastic cup of water sat on a table adjacent to the bed, its flexible straw hanging indifferently over the side.

A nurse signaled Slonsky to silence as he approached the bed and sat quietly in a metal chair. From this position, his head was less than a few feet away from the sleeping woman. As he moved his chair slightly, the legs scratched the floor, and Honey tentatively opened her eyes. The worried face of Basil

Slonsky caused her to smile, which brought tears to his eyes. Her voice was weak and tentative.

"So you do have a heart, you big lug. I thought you homicide dicks were all cold steel."

"Honey, I'm . . . I'm so sorry."

"For what? You did everything you could to help. I should have known he'd find me."

"What do you mean? Who would know?"

"BS, when I get better—if I get better—we can talk. But not now. Not now."

"Honey, look, I know this hurts. But we've got to find the guy that did this to you."

"I can't, BS. Please, it hurts just to talk. Hold my hand."

Slonsky reached over and slid his burly hand into the limp and yielding palm of Honey Wissman. Startled that her fingers were stiff and cold, he inadvertently pulled back but quickly gripped her hand again. Honey, pursing her lips as she felt the warm, solid touch of his hand holding her tightly, murmured, "Boy, you have a good grip. But I always knew you did. Do you know this is the first time you ever held my hand except when we were introduced?"

"Yeah, I guess you're right. I just didn't want to get sued for sexual harassment."

A tiny laugh escaped the lips of the injured woman.

"Slonsky, you can harass me anytime you want. And you won't get sued, but you might get something else."

Slonsky put his other hand on top of her cool slim fingers, his voice shaking.

"Honey, I . . ."

Honey Wissman didn't answer; her eyes closed in sleep. The nurse stepped in, gently nudged Slonsky aside, and placed a blanket over the sleeping woman.

Chapter 44

The graveyard shift—dreaded by some police officers, welcomed by others, depending largely on their personal lives. From 2:00 a.m. to 10:00 a.m., many of the young officers preferred to stay at home with their growing families, in contrast to veteran officers who had tired of their spouses and preferred the street to the bedroom. Eddie Mathes had selected the graveyard shift with its reduced staffing and supervision, enabling him free time for other activities. Slonsky had already checked Mathes's schedule after returning from his sick leave and knew Mathes was on duty the night before his trial.

Court subpoenas for mandatory appearance at trial were delivered to the duty sergeant. Privacy for court subpoenas was irrelevant, so the sergeant merely looked at the name on the pile of documents and placed them in the department mailbox unsealed. Officers merely looked in the box to see if they had been subpoenaed for the next day. No subpoena, no problem.

Officers who worked graveyard picked up their subpoenas, if any, the night before their court appearance and walked to the officers' waiting room in the courthouse down the street after duty ended. The city had provided showers and cots in the basement of the courthouse. The overtime pay helped mitigate the inconvenience. Officers often slept all day without testifying and returned to the station at 2:00 a.m., unless on days off.

At 1:00 a.m., midwatch officers reported for duty and were on the street by one thirty. For the half hour before they left, the pace was hectic. By 2:00 a.m. the entire graveyard shift had replaced the night watch. Slonsky arrived through the back entrance at 1:00 a.m. and went unnoticed into the mail room. Locating the subpoena for Mathes in the department mailbox, he removed it, stuffed the document in his coat pocket, and exited through the same door he had entered. Surveying the parking lot and seeing no one, he walked to his car and drove out of the parking lot. He picked up the car phone and called.

"Hello," came the sleepy voice of Joe Rutledge.

"Joe, it's me, BS. Sorry to wake you. You were right. Mathes told the court liaison officer he might get a subpoena. What he didn't tell him was that he was the defendant, not a witness. Nobody reads those things anyway. So liaison just put his subpoena in the general department box."

"Yeah, BS, but didn't the public defender tell Mathes to call in and see if the case was going to trial?"

"Yes. But it' so chaotic you can hardly get through to the courtroom, so I'm banking on that. When Mathes sees no subpoena in the box, I'm hoping he won't bother calling. He'll probably think the DA dismissed his case in the absence of the victim. The court will continue the case and issue a bench warrant."

"Not a bad gamble."

"I hope so. Joe, thanks for the tip about the subpoena process at Wilshire Division."

"No problem. Anytime. But hey, what about the prosecutor, Marcum? Does he know about this?"

"I told you, you'd be the first to know. Bye."

* * *

Judge Murphy was presiding with his usual informality, calling numerous cases to determine whether the prosecutor and defendant were ready. The barely organized chaos continued for several hours until, slowly, the cases settled or were transferred to a trial court. Slonsky slipped in the door at the backroom and saw Marcum calling for witnesses throughout the morning, noting officers who had checked in and those missing. At eleven thirty, Judge Murphy had sent out almost all the cases and was checking his list for the remainder. He looked down at the public defender, Eleanor Dean.

"Are you ready on the Mathes case, Ms. Dean?"

"We are still trying to locate the defendant, Your Honor. He has made all his contacts with us before, and I was certain he would appear today.

"If he's not here in fifteen minutes, I'll issue a bench warrant."

"Your Honor, could you hold the warrant until one thirty? I'll try to find him during the lunch hour."

"All right. Bench warrant issued. Hold until one thirty. If the defendant does not appear, release the warrant."

The judge turned to other matters as Slonsky walked out the door of the courtroom unnoticed, pumping his fist in the air. At one thirty, the judge called the case and, when no one responded, issued a bench warrant for the arrest of Mr. Edward Mathes.

Chapter 45

Slonsky entered the crime lab and sat in a chair next to Winkelmann. In front of them sat an enormous television screen displaying a crowd scene.

"BS, I borrowed this screen from Narcotics. They use it for reviewing their surveillance tactics. With their projector, which I also borrowed, we can get better resolution and maybe see the shooter. This will show the crowd from a camera angle behind the woman who was shot."

Turning on the projector, both men scanned the crowd at the clinic. Slonsky scrutinized men and women in both groups of demonstrators. As the pregnant woman approached the clinic, Winkelmann froze the scene and expanded the size of the frame. The woman walked slowly in the company of another woman toward the clinic. Slonsky edged toward Winkelmann.

"Blow up the crowd following her."

Winkelmann clicked the computer, and the screen expanded to frame a crowd of people waving banners and screaming. Slonsky grabbed Winkelmann's arm.

"Hold it right there. Bring it in a little tighter."

The picture focused tighter. Slonsky leaned forward in his chair.

"I'll be a son of a bitch."

"What? It's just a bunch of screamers."

"Not everyone is screaming. Mike, can you get me a hard copy of that?"

"No problem."

A click of the mouse, and the printer cleaned itself, while Slonsky waited impatiently. After a whirring sound stopped, it spun out a clear picture of Mathes and Wissman standing next to each other in the crowd, although not near the pregnant woman. Slonsky picked up the phone and called Rutledge, who answered on the first ring.

"Joe, BS here. Can you pull up the duty rosters for the day of the abortion shooting?"

"Sure, BS. What's up?"

"I'm not sure. Depends on what you find."

"OK. I can't do computers, but I can read rosters. Hold on."
Slonsky waited.

"BS? Found it. What do you want to know?"

"Did Honey or Mathes ever report being at the scene of the shooting?"

"No, neither one. What's going on?"

"Just trying to put pieces of the puzzle together."

"BS, Honey's not involved in the shooting, is she?"

"Are you kidding, Joe? Your best prostitute?"

"BS, come on. Hey, maybe you're right. But from those papers in her locker, she was obviously interested in the demonstration."

"Joe, thanks for the help, old buddy. Talk to you later."

Slonsky looked up at the clock.

"I'll watch the rest of the tape later, Mike. Gotta do a security check. Thanks much. I'll call you."

He stuffed his papers in a file, waved to Winkelmann, hurriedly walked to his car, and drove toward Queen of Angels Hospital.

Chapter 46

Eddie Mathes, dressed in street clothes on his day off, parked his Porsche several blocks away from Queen of Angels Hospital and walked toward the entrance, frequently stopping at store window displays and appearing to study the merchandise. Stopping quickly and looking around and seeing no police he could identify, he walked inside the hospital and surveyed the night nursing staff at their desks. He selected a black nurse with the badge name Imogene. Interrupting her note writing, he identified himself.

"Nurse, I'm a police officer," said Mathes, flashing his badge and quickly preventing the nurse from any time to study his name. "We are conducting a serious investigation of one of your patients. It's critical that no one, not even another police officer, knows about this. If anyone should come in, including a police officer, please call me immediately. I will be visiting Ms. Wissman. Can you tell me what room she's in?"

The young nurse, clearly impressed by the immaculate suit covering the powerful upper body of this articulate visitor, smiled easily and picked up the roster.

"Room 655. Sixth floor. Visiting hours are over, and you will have to check in with security up there."

"OK. By the way, is there a hospital security officer down here?"

"Yes, but he's on his break."

"I see. Thank you for your courtesy. The department always appreciates cooperation."

He extended his hand, carefully concealing a one-hundred-dollar bill. The surprised nurse eagerly accepted the gift, tucked it in her bra, and pointed toward the elevators.

"I get off in half an hour in case you need anything else."

Mathes grinned.

"I just might. Don't forget. Call the room while I'm here if anyone asks for Ms. Wissman."

The nurse smiled, parted her lips slightly, and flashed an unmistakable sign with her eyes. Mathes waved and headed toward the unoccupied elevators.

Standing alone in front of a bank of elevators, Mathes watched the numbers blink the floors. He pushed the button and waited for the elevator doors to open, pausing briefly, but no one was inside. He entered and touched the panel light for the sixth floor. The elevator stopped on the sixth floor, the doors opened, and he walked out cautiously into a deserted and dimly lit hall. A nurse sat at the nurses' station at the end of the corridor, her back toward Mathes, looking intently at a computer. Near the elevators stood a public telephone booth. Edging his way down the hall, Mathes entered the booth, closed the door quietly, and dialed the hospital operator.

"This is the operator."

"Security on the sixth floor, please."

The phone rang, and a voice answered, "Police. Officer Nolan."

Muffling his voice and feigning anxiety, Mathes answered, "Officer, this is security at the front desk. Could you come down here? We have a rather unruly drunk in the lobby."

"I'm sorry. I'm not supposed to leave this floor."

"I know. We called 911, but they said it would be fifteen minutes. The nurses are frightened."

"Well, OK. If it's just a drunk, I guess it will be all right."

"Thanks. We'll help any way we can."

Mathes hung up and stood toward the back of the booth concealing himself. In a few moments, a police officer appeared around the corner, walked down the hall toward the elevator, and pushed the button. While the officer waited for the elevator to arrive, Mathes slipped out from behind the telephone booth, crept toward him, slammed a karate chop to the back of the officer's neck, and caught him falling unconsciously to the floor. Mathes looked around and saw the nurse down the hall continuing to work at the computer. Dragging the officer behind the telephone booth and dropping him on the floor, Mathes walked down the hall and around the corner to room 655.

In the night-light of the hospital room, Honey Wissman lay quietly in bed. Her body ached; her head reeled in pain, the medication barely controlled. Footsteps alerted her, but the sound stopped briefly at the edge of her room before resuming. Straining to see the person in the gloom, she could barely see the figure of a man standing in the doorway. She struggled to rise.

"BS, is that you?"

"No, Honey, it's me, Eddie."

Honey fell back on the pillow. Fear flooded her face, and her heart raced.

"What are you doing here?"

"I came to visit you, of course."

"Visiting hours are over."

"Not for me. I came to see how you are."

"Go away. I don't want to talk to you."

"Is that any way to talk to your partner in crime?"

"Go away."

"Maybe you want to talk in private. I'll just shut the door."

Mathes closed the door behind him. Honey tried to scream, but her voice choked. Mathes walked toward her and spoke.

"There. Now we can be alone."

"Eddie, why are you doing this?"

"Because, sweetheart, I don't trust you. You're getting a little too close with that detective."

"I'm his partner. What do you expect? You and I talked this over."

"Sure, and your partner drove all the way to Santa Barbara to talk to you on the train while you're on the way to his little cabin in the north woods."

"Part of my plan."

"Oh, baby. That's good. Real good. Part of the plan to stay with him in some hick town where nobody knows you. Real cozy."

"He invited me. I wanted him to think I was a victim, not a suspect."

"Sweetheart, cut it out. I can read lies all over your face. And speaking of cutting it out, I think I'll do just that."

Mathes walked over to the patient's call button and moved it out of reach.

"Now no one will interrupt. Look, my wife cheated on me, and you were so anxious to embarrass the pro-lifers. The demonstration gave you a perfect setup. I get a hit man to kill my wife, and you get your publicity."

"No one was supposed to get killed. Your hit man was just supposed to scare people."

"But all you wanted from me was some way to get your feminist theory going. All that glass ceiling crap. Well, you got your publicity, but you also got me hanging out to dry. Your so-called partner Slonsky has already checked me out. Somehow I got my trial delayed again. You think he isn't on my ass?"

"He has no suspects. You said so yourself."

"No? You been out of commission, baby. He's working me."

"He'll find nothing. You erased everything on the computer. You're in the clear."

"Except for one thing: you. And I don't trust you. It's time for us to break up our partnership. Only this time, one partner won't be around. And just to make sure you get a good night's rest and don't bother the nurses, have a little sleep."

Mathes reached into his pocket, opened a bottle of chloroform, poured the liquid out on a white towel hanging on the edge of the bed, and pressed it over the frightened face. In minutes, Honey was unconscious. Mathes grabbed the IV, pulled out a knife, thumbed the blade for sharpness, and slit a tiny, short vertical line in the tube. A drop of liquid, almost unnoticed,

223

slipped slowly through the plastic wall. Mathes threw the cloth in the trash, checked the IV, and watched the tiny drops sliding inconspicuously down the tube, dropping slowly onto the floor under the bed. Folding the knife and concealing it in his pocket, he opened the door and hurried out of the room and past the unconscious officer.

With no security officer in sight, Mathes took the stairwell to the first floor and opened the door to the darkened lobby. Two nurses were both intently writing reports at the end of the desk. A police officer was on the phone, and a dozing security guard never saw the shadow of Eddie Mathes as he slipped out the door and into the night.

Chapter 47

Despite the late hour, traffic was heavier than usual, delaying, as Slonsky drove to the hospital that same night. Parking in the hospital zone, he threw his badge on the dashboard and slid out of the vehicle. A police officer in the lobby talking casually to one of the nurses turned toward Slonsky, but he had not been assigned to the security detail assigned to Honey.

Slonsky, dressed in street clothes, yelled, "Who are you? What the hell are you doing down here?"

The officer, not recognizing Slonsky and unable to see him clearly, stiffened and grabbed his baton as the outraged detective came toward him. Slonsky shoved him aside and hurried toward the elevator. The officer, struggling to regain his balance, followed and grabbed Slonsky from behind. An adrenaline-pumped Slonsky threw him off to the side and watched the descending elevator lights. The angry officer recovered and approached Slonsky, gripping his baton firmly in his hand. Out of the corner of his eye, Slonsky saw the swinging overhead arm and ducked, the baton crashing on his lower back. He screamed, "I'm a cop! I'm a cop!"

Unconvinced, the officer raised his baton again as Slonsky frantically attempted to locate his missing badge. He retreated with his hands in the air.

"I surrender. I surrender. Look in my jacket pocket and take out my wallet."

Slonsky held his hands high and leaned up against the wall with his head down. Rough hands ran over his legs and arms, grabbing his pants and shirt. The officer carefully reached inside Slonsky's jacket, removed the wallet, opened it, and released his hold. Slonsky straightened up, evidencing pain running down his spine. The officer put away his baton and helped Slonsky to a chair.

"Why didn't you tell me you were a cop when you first came in?"

"I didn't have time to explain. I thought you knew who I was. What are you doing down here in the lobby?"

"I got here a few minutes ago. I was waiting for Officer Nolan on the sixth floor to call me and take his place because he got sick. The captain sent me, but we both didn't know you were coming, and I had never met you. I don't go upstairs until I get the call from Nolan. It's only been about fifteen minutes, so I figured he probably went to the can."

Before Slonsky could respond, the elevator doors opened, and both men jumped inside. Slonsky pushed the button for the sixth floor. The doors closed. His anger barely under control, Slonsky said nothing to the nervous officer. The elevator door opened on the sixth floor, and both ran down the deserted hallway to Honey Wissman's room.

Entering, they saw her apparently asleep, but breathing fitfully. Slonsky studied her face closely, detecting nothing wrong. The officer, visibly relieved, stood on the other side of the bed. He looked at Slonsky.

"Looks like she's OK."

Slonsky just stared at Honey, felt her forehead, and bent over her face. He reacted.

"Chloroform. She's been chloroformed."

"How do you know?"

"Can't you smell it?"

"I never smelled the stuff before."

Slonsky swore under his breath.

"Get the nurse. Right away. I'll pull the call button."

The officer turned and ran down the hall. In minutes, a nurse and the officer returned. She looked at Slonsky.

"What's wrong? Who are you?"

"I'm Detective Slonsky, LAPD. This policewoman was under security. Did you see anyone in the hall tonight?"

"No."

Slonsky turned toward the officer.

"What about you, Officer? Did you see anyone?"

"No. I've been downstairs."

"Where's the guy you were supposed to replace?"

"I don't know. Like I said, I was waiting for his call."

Slonsky looked at the nurse.

"This woman had been chloroformed. Call the doctor."

"What? Let me see."

Leaning over Honey, the nurse immediately looked up.

"You're right. I'll call right way. If that's all there is, she will come out of it in a little while. She's not in danger. But I'll call anyway." The nurse hurried out of the room, while Slonsky and the officer continued to stare at the sleeping woman. Honey stirred restlessly but did not awaken. Slonsky looked at her anxiously. A blue light over the bed activated, and Slonsky could hear the sound of running footsteps. An intern rushed into the room, immediately removed his blood pressure pump, affixed the band to Honey's arm, pumped the pressure, and listened carefully. He yelled into a small microphone hung around his neck, "Get the doctor here! Now!"

Slonsky, startled, touched the intern on the shoulder.

"It's only chloroform. She'll come out of it."

"It's more than that. Her blood pressure is low. She needs a doctor right away."

He shouted into his microphone again. More footsteps, and another nurse and a doctor entered the room. The intern released the blood pressure band.

"Low, Doc, real low."

The doctor immediately checked Honey's eyes, felt her pulse, and inspected her mouth. Honey began to tremble, then shook. The doctor opened his bag and withdrew a hypodermic needle. Expertly injecting the fluid into Honey's vein, he yelled at the intern, "Get the cardiologist! Go!"

As the intern disappeared, the doctor kept his finger on Honey's pulse and watched the trembling woman closely. In minutes, she ceased shaking but rolled from side to side restlessly. Motioning Slonsky to step back, the perplexed doctor palpated her abdomen and chest. Moving away from the bed, Slonsky slipped and almost lost his balance. Looking down at the floor, he saw a pool of clear liquid trickling around the base of the IV stand. He tapped the doctor on the shoulder and pointed to the floor. Impatiently, the doctor looked down. Seeing the pool on the floor, he looked at the IV. Tiny beads of liquid slowly dripped down outside the tube. He grabbed the tube, studied it, and shouted at the nurse, "Get me an IV replacement right now! Right now!"

The nurse flew out of the room. The doctor pointed to the tube. "Look, this tube is leaking. No wonder she doesn't respond."

The doctor taped the tube directly above and below the leak and thrust the two overlapping ends together, one inside the other. The leaking stopped. He turned to Slonsky.

"I understand you're the police. Come here. Hold on to this tube above and below the leak. Keep the ends together. Don't pinch it. Let the fluid flow as much as possible."

Slonsky carefully took the tube and monitored the flow, while the doctor returned to take a pulse.

"Better. Better. It's picking up. Where's that damned nurse?"

Simultaneously, the nurse rushed in with an IV stand in her hand.

"The damned nurse is right here, Doctor."

He laughed.

"Nancy, you are the fastest thing on wheels. I could kiss you."

Nancy blushed. She and the doctor removed the severed IV tube and replaced it. The doctor reinserted the needle in Honey's trembling arm, and the fluid flowed into the veins of the unconscious woman. In minutes, Honey Wissman lay quietly in bed, breathing regularly and registering normal blood pressure. Basil Slonsky never left the room that night.

Chapter 48

"Oh, I remember you, Detective Slonsky," said Agnes Franklin, director of the clinic. You came in and asked for a file on the woman who was killed at the demonstration in front of the clinic."

"That's me. You were kind enough to give me her fingerprints. Could I see your file again?"

"Detective, we have so many women in our clinic who will not give their true names that I can't remember the person you're looking for. Tell me her name."

"Maybe you would remember this one. Maureen McCullough. Here's her picture."

Slonsky opened his file and handed a photograph to Franklin, who studied it briefly.

"Yes. This is the woman who was killed. Of course, now I remember her. She was in here about a month before her death. But she had been killed, so we obviously never submitted a report."

"Do you still have her file?"

"Yes, I think so."

Franklin walked over to a file cabinet and began thumbing through folders. Her brow furrowed. She closed the drawer and opened a second file cabinet, repeating the process. She turned toward Slonsky.

"As you can see, we are not exactly on the cutting edge of technology. I can't seem to find her file. Wait a minute. I remember now. A man came in and identified himself as her brother. He produced a death certificate and said even though his sister was dead, he wanted to take the file to the police. To be honest, one less file in this office is a blessing."

"Did the man identify himself?"

"No. He gave me a business card, but I really can't remember what he said or what I did with the card, for that matter."

"What did he look like?"

"Hmm. In police lingo, a white male, about forty. Nothing special about him. Wait. He limped. I remember he limped. I thought he had been in an accident but didn't think it polite to ask. He volunteered a donation—which I accepted—and I handed him the file. With all the violence that goes on in this city, I never gave it a second thought."

"Anything peculiar about his speech?"

"No. Normal."

"OK. Thanks, Ms. Franklin. If you think of anything that might be helpful, please call."

Franklin nodded. Slonsky handed her his business card, shook hands, and started to leave the room when Franklin interrupted.

"Oh, Detective. There is one other thing I do remember, but I don't know if it's important."

"Yes."

"After the man left with the file, I walked down the hall to get a cup of coffee, and I saw him reading the file with another man."

"Who was he?"

"I don't know. I just remember he was black, and they were talking animatedly. They looked up as I approached, closed the file, and walked away quickly."

"Thank you, Ms. Franklin. Thank you."

Chapter 49

Judge Carleton walked into the courtroom in his usual confident manner, stepped up to the bench, and sat down. Surveying the audience, he smiled ingratiatingly and welcomed counsel.

"I understand, Mr. Amstead, you want a modification of the order I issued."

"Yes, Your Honor. Several weeks have passed since you restrained defendants from demonstrating outside the clinic, and no violence of any kind has occurred. Some of my clients did threaten a demonstration, but their leaders persuaded them to desist. You will note that I have submitted several affidavits from police officers who report no crowd control problems of any nature and that my clients are scrupulously following your orders."

Carleton interrupted, "Even if they disagree with them."

"Yes, Your Honor. Of course. It is a tribute to them that they're obeying the law rather than engaging in the usual left-wing stunts of civil disobedience."

Richardson interrupted, "I object, Your Honor. My clients are not left-wing nuts, Mr. Amstead."

"All right, feminazis."

Carleton grimaced. "Mr. Richardson, please do not interrupt counsel. And, Mr. Amstead, let's stick with the facts in this case without personal charges. Continue, Mr. Amstead."

"We are asking for only a slight modification. You have prevented defendants from coming within twenty-five yards of the clinic. In effect, that compels them to remain across the street. That distance, plus the traffic, renders their message virtually nonexistent. Unions are frequently allowed to picket on the sidewalk. And of course, the courts always give deference to certain people in these cases. I respect your decision, Judge, but frankly, the only people who cannot invoke the right to free speech are abortion protestors. Unions have a more violent history, but only my clients are restricted. All we ask is that the defendants be allowed to cross the street and stand on the corners. They will not disrupt traffic or disobey traffic signals. They will remain silent and only hold up signs."

Carleton leaned forward.

"Counsel, my only objective is to preserve the safety of everyone involved. If your clients cross the street, they will come in very close contact with the clinic, its employees and patients. I don't want to have another homicide on my hands or, for that matter, on the hands of your clients, Mr. Amstead."

"Your Honor, my clients agree to submit to a search of their person by police officers at any time and will sign consent forms to that effect. I can bring them into court, and they will sign in your presence and under penalty of perjury. If they are found in violation, you can hold them in contempt."

"I doubt if the police want to constantly have to search these folks. They can't be sure whether someone else is sneaking through. It's too risky."

"Suppose we identify only a limited number of pickets. They can wear armbands, and only those specific demonstrators can walk across the street."

"Oh, they can hand their armbands off to someone else."

"Not if there are only ten or fifteen. The officers could easily recognize them."

"And what if they get tired and want to substitute another person? This will drive the police crazy."

"Your Honor, we are trying to be reasonable and allow a limited right to free speech. If you deny your motion, then I will have to seek review."

"Of course. But you know the appellate judges in this county. They are not disposed to the pro-life cause. I'm aware of that, you know. All right. Your motion is denied, Mr. Amstead."

Judge Carleton signaled to his law clerk, who came up to the bench to talk to him. Only a handful of the press had sat in the courtroom, unsurprised at the result everyone had anticipated. While they drifted out of the courtroom, a smiling John Marcum stopped Amstead briefly and spoke quietly to him as he was leaving.

"Nice try, Percy, but this judge will never move off his order. He wants the Supreme Court and knows he needs the support of those left-leaning liberals."

"I have to try. When we appeal, maybe the court of appeals will see that free speech is not only for dissidents, atheists, flag burners, and minorities."

Marcum could only shake his head. The bailiff interrupted and signaled for quiet while court was in session. Carleton pulled out another file.

"*People v. Mathes!*" he called out.

At the same time, Slonsky walked in and sat in the back of the courtroom. Marcum and Public Defender Eleanor Dean approached the counsel table. Carleton reviewed the file and entered his notes, while Marcum and Dean waited without speaking. Carleton handed his file over to the clerk and swung his chair around to face counsel.

"Let the record reflect counsel for defendant is present. People are represented. Ms. Dean, where is the defendant?"

"Your Honor, the prosecution generously agreed previously not to require his appearance today. My client told me yesterday when I called him that he never received a subpoena to appear and was willing to come in and testify to that if necessary. Mr. Marcum will not seek enforcement of the warrant."

Carleton looked at Marcum.

"Is that so, Mr. Marcum?"

"Yes, Your Honor. I informed Ms. Dean she had accommodated us before in this case and we would accommodate her client today."

Marcum picked up his file.

"Your Honor, this case has been continued several times. But this is a domestic violence case, and on the assumption the public defender will move for a dismissal, I would ask Your Honor to grant the motion but delay its effect for one week. If we cannot proceed in one week, your order to dismiss stands. The defendant is out on bail, and we would agree he need not return if we are unable to proceed."

Dean stood up.

"Your Honor, this is ridiculous. My client has always been available. We move to dismiss."

Carleton interrupted, "Except when he didn't show up for trial."

"A failure of communication, Judge. He never got the subpoena."

"Judge," said Marcum, "what's the harm of taking the motion to dismiss under submission? If we can't proceed next week, the case stands dismissed, and the defendant is not even required to come to court. In fact, I'll even dispense with counsel's personal appearance if she gives us a telephone number where she can be reached."

Dean grinned.

"Well, that's a very gracious offer, Judge. I guess under those circumstances we agree. But if they are able to proceed, we want the trial immediately."

Carleton looked at Marcum, who nodded his head affirmatively.

"We agree, Your Honor."

"All right, counsel. Are you moving to dismiss, Ms. Dean?"

"Yes, Your Honor."

"Motion granted. Case dismissed. Order delayed until one week from today. The record will reflect no appearance by counsel or defendant is necessary unless requested by the court. And, Mr. Marcum, this is the last time. You must inform me and Ms. Dean the day before trial that you are ready to proceed."

"Thank you, Your Honor."

As Carleton stood for a recess, he noticed a man in a ponytail with his back toward him limping out of the courtroom. Unable to see his face, Carleton shuddered slightly. The judge spoke briefly to his law clerk before returning to chambers. The law clerk waved Slonsky to come forward, opened the door to the hallway, and led him down the hall toward chambers.

Opening the door and entering the chambers of Judge Carleton, Slonsky walked toward the judge and extended his hand. Carleton stood and shook hands.

"We meet again, Detective."

"We do indeed, but under far better circumstances."

"Yes. I agree. Please sit down."

Slonsky eased himself into an overstuffed chair, studying the judge.

"Detective, I realize you are investigating a murder, but I must ask that what I am about to tell you must be in confidence and cannot be revealed. If you are uncomfortable with that, I will understand but cannot go further."

"You have my word."

Carleton studied Slonsky intently.

"I accept that. Please come over here to the window."

Slonsky eased out of the chair and walked over to the window directly behind the desk. "Step back a few feet and to the side of the window. Look down on the street and tell me what you see." Slonsky walked over to the window, leaned forward slightly, and peered down at the intersection abutting the clinic.

"OK, I'm looking down, but I just see a tree and a lot of people."

"On the day that woman was murdered, I was standing just where you are. I told you I was watching the demonstrators and I saw a man in the crowd with a gun standing next to the TV camera. He looked like he was using the camera to shield himself on one side. I told you he pulled out a gun and shot the woman. I never saw his face. His back was facing me."

"Judge, you told me this. Why are you telling me this again?"

"I'm coming to that. Candidly, I was more interested in my career. I'm on the short list for the Supreme Court, and my involvement could derail me."

"As a witness to a murder. Why?"

"Detective, you probably aren't familiar with the world of politics. I issued an order forbidding pro-lifers from coming near the clinic. The administration is run by liberals, and they like that kind of order. I could have been stricter, but they can live with it. They don't like it when we issue orders against some people, of course. But this they like. Don't tell me I'm self-centered. I know that. Even judges are human, you know."

"Judge, with due respect, I appreciate your coming forward, even if it's confidential. But why today?"

"Although I couldn't identify the assassin, do you remember I told you the man limped visibly? Well, I think he was in the courtroom today. When he left the courtroom, I saw the back of his head. He was wearing a ponytail. It could have been him. But there were so many people in the crowd that's all I could see."

Slonsky stared hard.

"What did he look like?"

"White, in his forties. Five ten or so. I only noticed him as I left the bench and got a side view. I'm not even sure I could recognize him if I saw him again."

"Was he alone?"

"I think so. I didn't see him in the courtroom until the Mathes case was over. He left after that, but I didn't see him talking to anyone."

"Do you think he knows you're involved?"

"Only intuitively. The only person I talked to about this case is my longtime political friend."

"What was the man wearing today?"

"Boy, that's tough. A sport coat, I think."

"When is the Mathes case back on calendar?"

"The case I just called? Continued. The defendant didn't show up. Next week, the lawyers will agree on the new date, and the clerk will let me know. But the victim didn't show up again either, so I dismissed the case but delayed the order to dismiss. If the victim doesn't show, Mathes doesn't even have to appear."

"Judge, do you know who the victim is?"

"No. Who?"

"The victim in that case today was probably killed by the same man you saw in the street near the clinic."

Carleton gripped the desk.

"Are you certain? The same woman? How come the press hasn't said anything about this? I thought the woman who was killed was named Maureen McCullough."

"That wasn't her married name. The press think the victim is dead and buried, which she is, of course, but the name of the victim on the amended court file is her married name, Jeri Mathes. The only person who knows the real story is the prosecutor. I can't tell you why she was killed because it might jeopardize your role."

"But the man I saw at the clinic was white. I read the police report in our case, and the defendant in the domestic violence case is described as a black male."

"Yes. We don't think Mathes shot the woman himself. But I can't tell you any more."

"Then it's obvious the victim won't appear. Why does the DA keep asking for continuances?"

"Judge, with due respect, I can't tell you. I do wish you had talked to me about this earlier. It might have saved a young policewoman from assault. I don't know. We may need to talk some more. Where can I reach you?"

"Here. Call me at the court. I'll tell my clerk to put your calls through."

"Thanks. I appreciate it. By the way, you might have to disqualify yourself in this case if, for some reason, it becomes necessary."

"You knew that when you told me about the victim and the defendant."

Slonsky grinned.

"Yes. Actually, it takes the heat off you. Unlike the abortion case, you are not in trial, and any other judge can try this case in the unlikely event that should ever happen."

Carleton laughed.

"You know more about the law than most lawyers."

The two men shook hands.

Chapter 50

Eddie Mathes ended his night shift, quickly changed clothes, and drove to Queen of Angels Hospital. In response to a call he had placed to the hospital, Mathes learned that the nursing shift ended at 1:30 a.m., and by busting a few red lights, he arrived while several nurses were leaving. When Imogene came out, Mathes quickly exited his car and walked toward her.

"Imogene, what a surprise. I didn't realize you nurses worked so late."

Momentarily startled, the nurse studied Mathes carefully.

"Officer . . . I'm sorry, I forgot your name."

"Madigan. Edward Madigan."

"Yes, of course. Why are you here so late?"

"We're still doing an investigation. I just came by to check a few things out."

"Did you know about the accident with Ms. Wissman?"

"No, I went on vacation and just got back today. I haven't checked with my partners. What happened?"

"The IV tube leaked, and she almost died."

"Really? Hell, they don't tell us anything anymore. I think they don't trust black folks."

"Probably not. Anyway, there was a big fuss. Doctors and nurses running all around."

"Man. Our investigation is top secret. Is she OK?"

"Yes. I think the hospital wanted to hush it up. They don't want to get sued for using a defective IV tube, so there was no publicity."

"I see. Say, can I buy you a cup of coffee or something?"

"I don't know. It's late."

"Fifteen minutes. Promise."

"OK. We can go across the street to the coffee shop. It's open all night."

* * *

Rudy's Diner was empty except for the staff. Mathes ordered two cups of coffee and leaned back casually in his chair.

"How long have you worked at the hospital, Imogene?"

"Two years. I can work there forever if I want to. They got an affirmative action program and are afraid to fire blacks."

"Hey, we deserve it. Whitey has held us down long enough."

"You got that right."

The waiter brought over the coffee and set the cups on the table. Without another word, he left.

Mathes grimaced.

"Not too friendly, is he? Imogene, I think we may need your help, but I'm very reluctant to ask."

"What do you mean?"

"Ms. Wissman is a suspect in another matter. We think that's why she was shot in Oregon."

"I didn't know she was in Oregon."

"Hiding out. We're working undercover, and I'm afraid someone will try to kill her."

"Whoa, that's awful."

"Right. I know there's security in place, but I'm worried it may not be enough. I can't be seen because I don't know whom to trust. Somehow, I think I can trust you."

"I know you can."

"Good. Here's what I want you to do. No risk to you at all."

Mathes reached into his pocket, pulled out a tiny round object, and held it in his open hand.

"You may not know it, but this is a tape recorder with a powerful battery."

"You're kiddin' me."

"Nope. Trust me. All you need to do is put this underneath Ms. Wissman's bed where nobody can see it. Don't put it where the cleaning women will find it, but I can see you're sharp enough to figure that out."

"Of course."

"Whenever someone comes into the room, this device picks up the voices and records the conversation. If someone tries to kill Ms. Wissman, we can use this as evidence."

"Boy, that is fancy."

"You bet. Will you do it?"

"I don't know. It's kinda dangerous."

"Nope. Just wipe the top off of the little recorder, and when I come to pick it up, there will be no fingerprints. You can't tell anyone, including other police officers, because we don't know whom we can trust. This is top secret."

Imogene hesitated. Mathes smiled and reached across the table to touch her hand. She felt the strength when he leaned closer to speak confidentially.

"There's just one more condition."

"What's that?"

"That we have dinner together."

Imogene breathed in deeply, eyes sparkling. Mathes had a date.

Chapter 51

Honey Wissman sat up in bed for the first time in three weeks. Holding a mirror to her face, gingerly applying makeup, she grimaced at the reflection of spiky blond hair shooting out from her head. Doctors had removed the bulky neck bandages, replacing them with gauze to cover the stitches. Her left arm hung lifelessly on the bed despite her best efforts to move it. Police officers in the department had flooded her hospital room with flowers and balloons, get-well cards, and notes that lay stacked across a cabinet. Slonsky had visited every day, checking on security personnel and questioning nurses and staff about visitors. No one had seen anything unusual, but Slonsky demanded a list of names of everyone who came into the room.

The sound of his impatient footsteps brought smiles to the injured Wissman.

Slonsky swept into the room, delighted to see a woman with a smiling face wearing lipstick and makeup and her hair brushed. He leaned over and put his hands on the edge of the bed.

"If I didn't know you were a police officer, I'd proposition you."

"Why, Basil Slonsky, how you talk. And here I am, in bed and waiting for you."

Slonsky grinned, touched her hand, and sat down.

"What a change. You look terrific."

"You like my hair? Kinda kinky, wouldn't you say? Does it turn you on?"

"Not like the bandages. Very sexy."

The two police officers laughed, and Slonsky launched into department news. When he finished, they both looked at each other in silence.

"Honey, our computer genius, Mike Winkelmann, gave me some photos of the crowd at the clinic on the day of the shooting."

"I know, I know. I can tell you now."

"I need to warn you."

"I have a right to silence, and anything I say can be used against me."

"Yes. And you have the right to an attorney."

Slonsky's voice clutched. He swallowed hard, his eyes blinking when she looked at him.

"Basil, I understand. You probably know, or guessed."

Slonsky could only nod his head up and down; his voice failed him.

"Basil, I should tell you something first. When I was roaming through the computer one day after we met, I punched up your name, read your record. You testified at the trial of Judge Murphy's daughter that you had retrieved e-mail from the defendant's computer, that you found messages in his Recycle Bin enabling you to retrieve information from his floppy disks. Not bad for a guy that doesn't know much about computers."

"So I took a basic course."

"Mike Winkelmann came by to visit yesterday. He said he showed you some photos that a few narcotic officers had taken of the crowd and that you wanted copies because you hadn't seen them before."

"Yes. I got his message."

"It's OK. I already knew you needed to test me. Originally, you realized I was skipping computer strokes on the computer when I was searching. Then you saw Mathes and me together at the rally in the photos."

Slonsky's head popped up.

"Don't worry, Basil. Winkelmann didn't know what you saw in the picture. But I knew you were working with him. So I just casually asked him how you were doing on the investigation. He told me you had watched a tape of the crowd. I said I was working the case with you and could I see what he had screened for you. 'Sure, no problem,' he said. He e-mailed me the photos of the crowd. And there I was, standing with Mathes. Of course, he didn't notice that among all the people. He just said you wanted copies."

"Why, Honey? Why?"

Honey sank down in the bed.

"Mathes suckered me in with all his talk about racism. I bought into it with feminism. One thing led to another. But here's why I really thought I could trust him. Remember when I told you three guys robbed my father's bank and one of them killed my father?"

"Yes."

"They were all black. When I told Mathes about this, he started to dig around. He knows the streets. He found out who killed my father and was going to do him in. I told him not to, 'Let's tell Homicide.' The following week, the guy was found dead in an alley. I had mixed emotions. I wanted the SOB dead, but not this way. My job was on the line because he would drag me in and I would never get those other two guys."

Slonsky leaned forward, his head in his hands. He looked up to an anguished face. Tears were streaming down her cheeks as Honey wiped her eyes with one hand.

"Anyway, after I got myself assigned to the abortion case—"

"You got yourself assigned?"

"Joe Rutledge and I are good friends. He owed me one and talked to the captain before you did. He didn't know anything about this issue. I told him I needed to get out of the prostitution business, and we both saw this as a way. He did it as a favor, BS. He never knew. Basil, if you don't believe me, there's no sense going on."

"No, no. Go ahead."

Honey laid her head back on the pillow, clearly tiring.

She continued, "I had another life. I wanted to disrupt the pro-lifers. I've changed my mind about abortion since then, but at time, I needed a media event. Eddie said he had a way. One of his cronies would come to the demonstration and fire a shot in the air. Everyone would scatter in chaos, but no one would get hurt. We knew the media was pro-abortion and would report it as an attempted murder by a pro-lifer. Turns out, it was Eddie's wife, whom I had never met, came to the clinic, and Eddie's hit man killed her. Obviously, Eddie knew what time her appointment was at the clinic, and he set it up. At that point, I wanted out."

"Why didn't you?"

"Without my knowledge, Mathes had our conversation about the demonstration plans on tape. If I backed out and reported the conversation to the department, he sends them the tape. I'm terminated and probably arrested. My chance of finding my father's other two killers ends. If Mathes gets arrested and talks, I'm charged as an accomplice, and he can use the tape against me."

"But isn't he on the tape too?"

"Not on the edited version. He retaped it and dubbed in stuff that lets him off the hook. It looks like the whole thing was my idea and he tried to talk me out of it."

"Why didn't you tell me this before?"

"BS, I was in a bind. If I had told you what I just said before we started to work together, what would you have done?"

"Arrested you as an accomplice for murder."

"Exactly. Remember you told me you worked Robbery/ Homicide. I thought I could divert your investigation away from me. If possible, I wanted you to help me find the two guys who robbed my father's bank, but without involving myself with Mathes. At that time, I had no case against the other two robbers. If you could find them, I would have vindicated my father's murder and taken the consequences. Frankly, it was stupid."

"Instead, you nearly got yourself killed."

"I knew the risk and was willing to take it."

"But you suckered me in."

"Yes. But something happened during the investigation."

"What?"

"I fell in love with you."

Speechless, the veteran detective fell back in his chair, staring incomprehensibly at Honey.

"I never—"

"Eddie could tell. He knew something was going on. When you showed up at the train station in Santa Barbara, he figured it out."

"He knew where you were going?"

"Not the address. Just Oregon. He must have read my request for vacation time. He had me followed to the train station by bugging my car, and then someone trailed me to the cabin in Oregon."

"I set you up."

"Don't be silly. If not in Oregon, Mathes would have slammed me somewhere else. He was afraid I would tell you the truth or else go to the department."

Slonsky slumped forward, his hands covering his face. Honey said nothing. Moments later, wiping his eyes on his sleeve, Slonsky walked over to the bed and kissed the woman with spiky hair. With one arm, she curled it around his neck and held him closely. Slonsky looked up.

"Maybe there's a way around the legal problem. You're an accomplice even if the jury believes that you just wanted someone to fire a shot in the air. You planned to disrupt the demonstration with Mathes, but you are responsible legally for the consequences despite not foreseeing the murder. So we need an independent witness to testify to the shooting to convince the jury that you did not actually pull the trigger. We have a tape of you and Mathes in the crowd, but neither of you were near the woman who was killed. If someone else could identify the shooter, you could honestly say you were off duty and watching the demonstration. The only person to contradict that is Mathes."

"But the tapes show Mathes and me in the crowd."

"Yes. But not at the same time of the shooting, Honey."

"So how do you get at him if he's charged with the crime of setting the shooting it up? He'll play the tape when he takes the stand and try to lay the blame on me. And according to you, I can still be charged with murder."

"You won't be charged."

"Why not?"

"Because the DA will give you immunity. Mathes knew you could turn on him when he came to your hospital room. But he also knows the jury will have to believe he chloroformed you and cut the IV instead of just visiting a patient. His lawyer will ask, 'Why would a fellow police officer want to kill you? What motive? He was just visiting, and no one else saw him other than you.'"

"And then he plays the tape."

"Any sound guy can tell a tape is doctored. We can show the jury the interrupted sound waves on television."

"That's still close. And remember, I never reported his attempt to kill me in the hospital. I was unconscious and didn't see him cut the IV. And there's no evidence he chloroformed me except my word for it."

"That is a problem, except we got one more card to play. I kept the IV tube that leaked. My expert says it was sliced."

"So how do you prove who sliced it?"

"A guy who wasn't as smart as he thinks he is. Mathes's prints are on the tube. Fingerprints come off real good on a rubber surface."

"But he'll just say he moved the IV so he could talk to me, or some other excuse."

"Let the jury decide that."

"But you still don't have the shooter."

"I'm hoping Mathes will tell us in exchange for a lighter sentence and an agreement to testify against whoever it is that shot his wife."

"There's another problem, as in 'Who is my witness to the abortion shooting?'"

Slonsky hesitated. Honey Wissman smiled knowingly.

"It's OK, BS. I understand. I have to earn your trust."

"Let's just say I was told in confidence. The bullets that killed the woman at the clinic came from the same gun that shot Sally Thompson. But there is one other problem."

"What's that?"

"As you said, you haven't reported that Mathes tried to kill you at the hospital."

"I told you. There was nothing to report. I didn't know you had fingerprints until just now. Even so, Mathes can come up with some explanation for the prints on the IV. Basil, if I report it, your case will fall apart. I will have to explain why he tried to kill me, which means I will have to explain everything about the abortion case, and you lose a witness when I'm arrested and become a defendant. Look, BS, Eddie knows he didn't kill me at the hospital. So the chances are, he'll try again soon. According to the doctor, I'm scheduled for home release. Eddie will call his shooter to do me. He needs to know where I am. Let him find out. I'll be a decoy."

"You're not going to be a decoy. No way."

"Basil, I don't think you can prove who the shooter is. He won't necessarily tell you even if you get Eddie for attempted murder. Who knows what a jury will do? And maybe Mathes will just risk a trial."

The phone rang. Slonsky picked it up.

"Slonsky here."

"BS? Hi. Fred Southers from the coroner's office. Sergeant Rutledge said to try this number. Can you talk?"

"Sure."

"You remember that autopsy we did on the woman who was shot at the clinic?"

"Yes."

"One of the family members from back East showed up. A real pro-life believer, and she wanted a separate burial for the fetus. She got a court order, believe it or not, exhuming the dead body. I examined the fetus, and guess what? I found a third bullet lodged in its stomach. Almost unbelievable. The shot must have gone through the mother's umbilical cord. With a pregnant woman, her belly button often gets distended. When she was shot, the skin

259

must have folded over the entrance wound, then the skin closed, and the slug lay concealed in the fetus."

"You mean there were three shots?"

"Yes. But here's the tricky part. Not from the same gun."

"Wait a minute. Two separate slugs that killed the victim came from the same gun, and a different one lodged in the fetus?"

"Right. Two from a handgun. The other from a rifle. Either one could have killed her."

"Could you tell the angle of entry?"

"I thought you'd never ask. The two shots in the woman entered laterally, right to the stomach. The other one in the fetus entered at a forty-five-degree angle. Someone shot her from up above."

"Like from a building?"

"Exactly."

"Save the slug."

"That's another interesting issue. This bullet is tiny, really tiny, and according to the ballistic guys, probably goes right through and through the human body when someone is shot. So when you do an autopsy, you probably would never find it. In this case, it went through the stomach and got stuck in the fetus. And we ordinarily don't autopsy the fetus when a pregnant woman is shot and killed."

"Where is the slug?"

"It's in jar with your name on it."

"Fred, thanks. I really appreciate it."

"No problem."

Slonsky hung up the phone and looked at Honey.

"They found another slug inside the fetus of the woman who was shot at the clinic."

"Three shots? I thought there were only two."

"From different guns."

"Two shooters? How?"

"Was Mathes with you all the time during the demonstration?"

"No. Shortly before the shooting, he said he wanted to check a few things out. He said he was tired of all the people pushing and shoving. He was gone about half an hour."

"Was he there when the shooting started?"

"No. The place was chaos even before that. I didn't see him until later."

"I'm gonna take another look at those TV tapes. I might have to bring some in for you to look at."

"No problem."

Slonsky smiled wanly. He reached in his pocket for his notebook, scrawled in a few entries, and replaced it.

"Honey, you have to report what Mathes did to you in the hospital. Fortunately, the doctors saved you. We have an attempted murder."

"Basil, I'm too weak to report anything. And what do you have? I told you, I get arrested, and you have no case, no witnesses, an IV tube that leaked."

"You should still report it. Mathes tried to kill you."

"Please, Basil, don't . . ."

Honey Wissman was asleep.

Nurse Imogene Booker knocked on the door, apologized, smiled broadly at Slonsky, looked at her watch, and signaled him that visiting hours were over. She needed to straighten up the room.

Chapter 52

Mathes popped the tiny tape into his car sound system after profusely thanking Imogene for cooperating with law enforcement. Backing his car out of the hospital parking lot shortly after 3:00 a.m., he drove on surface streets in order to concentrate on the tape. Angrily cursing, he stopped at a liquor store, picked up the public phone in a parking lot, and dialed. An answering machine activated, and he waited through the routine response.

After the beep, he spoke softly, "We have a problem that needs solving. Meet me tomorrow night just before I go on duty. Usual place."

Mathes hung up. He called another number.

A voice answered, "Asquith."

"It's Mathes."

"Where have you been?"

"Never mind. I'm leaving town tomorrow. I'm sick again."

"What about your court date?"

"I don't have to appear. The judge is going to dismiss the case."

"Unless the DA tells the court otherwise."

"What do you mean?"

"Seems like they did another autopsy. The coroner found another bullet in the fetus."

Mathes hesitated.

"Another slug? Now the department will really get hold of this and find out I'm a defendant in my wife's case. There goes my job."

"Exactly."

"I got no choice. I gotta turn in Gimpy."

"Gimpy? The guy you told me that Honey set up for the abortion shooting because you did her a favor? Are you nuts? He'll burn you."

"No, he won't. First of all, he's an ex-con and knows how to keep his mouth shut. Second, he'll never know how the cops found out about him."

"How do you know that? What if the DA offers Gimpy a deal? No death penalty if he talks. He opens up on you and Wissman."

"What proof does he have? My word against his? I'll fix it. Don't worry. I can lead Slonsky to him without me getting involved. Trust me."

"The last guy who said that got impeached."

"Look, Slonsky and Honey are a pair. I've got an inside track to her through one of the nurses. I also have some very valuable evidence against Honey."

"What?"

Mathes removed a tiny round object from his pocket and spoke while he studied it approvingly.

"Technology, babe. She spilled her guts to Slonsky, and I've got it all right here on tape."

"You taped her in the hospital? How did you do that?"

"I'll tell you later. I know where Gimpy lives, and I'll tell Honey just exactly where he keeps his gun every night: under his pillow. She tells Slonsky. He gets a warrant and finds Gimpy and the gun. That's all the DA needs, and they'll match the bullets with the gun. Honey's a smart woman and can play to a jury. She'll never testify against me because she knows I got the goods on her. The DA will give her immunity if necessary, and Slonsky doesn't have to testify against her. Plus the fact he doesn't have a tape of her conversation with him. I do."

"Slonsky gets Gimpy. Honey might go down. And you skate all because you might lose your job?"

"You got it."

"There's only one problem. I thought there were only two shots fired. The coroner found another bullet in the fetus."

"So they screwed up the original autopsy. What do I care? My wife is dead, Gimpy gets hung, Slonsky gets his killer, and I go free. What could be better?"

"You think Slonsky will buy that? He knows you're involved. And Honey Wissman sure doesn't sound like she's the type that would set all this up. Like I said, where did that other bullet come from?"

"How should I know, man? Look, I gotta go. See ya."

Asquith heard the dial tone. He put down the phone slowly, returned to his desk, and looked at a file that one of the employees in the coroner's office had surreptitiously sent him. Fred Souther's autopsy report discussed the discovery of a third tiny slug in the fetus unlike the other two in the victim's chest. The angle of entry was forty-five degrees and dissimilar from the other slugs Southers had found in the body.

Putting the report back in the file, Asquith removed a sheaf of papers from his desk drawer. He noted Mathes's locker number and its departmental issued combination lock. Looking in his calendar book, he read the numbers to the lock that Mathes had given him several years ago in case of his death. Shutting the desk drawer, Asquith got up and strolled casually past the night watch commander, who was just leaving his duty.

Asquith entered the locker room and, after assuring himself it was unoccupied, quickly dialed the combination to Mathes's lock. The door swung open to reveal a pair of binoculars and a department jacket and a hat hanging on a clothes hook.

He removed a raincoat from a hanger and lettered on the back Special Weapons Team. Asquith took down a folded uniform lying on the upper shelf next to a cell phone, a baton, and handcuffs. Concealed under the uniform lay an unusually shaped rifle and a box of tiny ammunition.

Asquith took out his smartphone and photographed all the contents. Closing the door and locking it, he returned to his desk, sat down slowly, and slumped in his chair.

Chapter 53

The department placed Honey Wissman on the disability list, overlooking an injury not caused in the line of duty. But she knew her disability status would expire in three months, and her benefits—and her job—would cease. Without enough time on the department to establish eligibility for a pension, she calculated her savings would last approximately two months. The doctor had arranged for her final tests, removal of stitches, and discharge from the hospital. Tears flowed freely as she lay alone in her hospital bed, contemplating her future. The phone rang. She picked up the phone and answered.

"Hello. It's me, BS."

"Oh, Basil, it's so good to hear your voice."

"I've got good news. I found a place for you to stay after you're released."

"What are you talking about?"

"Small house, kitchen and two baths, living room with fireplace, and two bedrooms."

"What's the catch?"

"It comes with a live-in companion."

"Some nice old lady, I suppose."

"Nope. Middle-aged, active, and intelligent bachelor with strong sexuality."

"I think I can guess."

"I will be your faithful companion."

"At night."

"At your service."

"What kind of service?"

"Whatever your heart desires."

"My heart?"

"Whatever."

The tears came again. Her voice choked.

"After all I've done? Basil, I don't deserve it. And besides, you'll only get yourself in trouble. You can't live with an accomplice to a murder and a fugitive."

"Well, nobody's perfect."

"Get serious, BS. You have a duty to arrest me right now based on what I told you. When they find out I'm living with you, they'll charge you with concealing a known criminal. I haven't even reported an attempted murder on my life. How would that look for you, let alone me? I won't do that to you. I made my bed, and I'll lie in it. When I'm strong enough, I'll turn myself in. I love you for wanting to do this, but the answer is, I love you too much to say yes. Look, wait until I get to my place, and then we'll talk."

"OK. OK. I understand. But you'll need protection. Mathes tried to kill you once, and he'll try again."

Honey paused.

"You know, maybe you're right. I'll stay at your house just for a few days until I can sort this out and then go home and find another place to live. Nobody will know I stayed with you."

"Good. Just stay with me until then."

"Thank you. I love you, Basil Slonsky."

"And I love you, Honey Wissman."

Honey collapsed back on her pillow, laying her arm over her head. The door to the room opened to Imogene.

"Excuse me, Ms. Wissman. I just need to take your pulse."

Honey listlessly extended her hand, and Imogene began counting the beats. As she did, Imogene looked up.

"I understand you're leaving us tomorrow, Ms. Wissman."

Honey nodded.

"I guess you'll be talking to Officer Madigan before you leave."

Honey sat up.

"What do you mean?"

"He said you were an important witness and needed protection."

"Who is Officer Madigan?"

"Why, he's the police officer that was working here on your case the night you got sick and almost died."

Wissman slumped back in her bed.

Imogene leaned over her and whispered, "Yes, ma'am. I'm not supposed to tell no one. He said he was working undercover."

"Of course. I understand."

Imogene started to clean up the room. Noting her patient had fallen asleep, Imogene reached under the bed, removed an object, and placed it in her pocket.

Chapter 54

Slonsky held Honey Wissman tightly by the arm as he guided her up the sidewalk to his tract house in West Los Angeles. The fatigued woman, walking with the aid of a crutch under her armpit, walked slowly, clenching her teeth in pain with every jolting step to her neck and wounded shoulder. Tears flowing down her face, she leaned heavily on the burly detective. She was barely able to lift her legs to ascend the threshold. The pain shot through her neck, and she cried out in agony. Slonsky reached down, picked her up, and carried the exhausted woman into the house. In the bedroom, he gently placed Honey on the bed, laid down her purse, and covered her with a light blanket. Through her tears, she murmured, "I guess you're going to have your way with me."

Slonsky choked and laughed.

"Right. I know a sex object when I see one."

Wissman could only bite her lip.

"Basil, get me some of my pain medication. It's in my purse."

Slonsky reached into her purse, removed the pills, and handed them to her.

"I'll go get some water."

"I'd rather have brandy."

"No problem. I'll be right back."

Slonsky hurried to the kitchen, poured a small amount of brandy into a glass, and returned to the bedroom. Honey gratefully swallowed the pills and the brandy.

"That will hold me for about an hour. Time enough for sex and brandy."

"Good. I'll be back as soon as the medication takes effect." She grinned.

"What a guy."

Honey fell asleep within minutes. In order to protect her paycheck and change her status, Slonsky had received permission for her to get time off under the guise of the Protected Witness program, although no one knew what she had witnessed. Chief Riley, wondering why she couldn't stay on disability, approved the order after ten minutes of ranting and raving.

Slonsky placed the chief's order on the table and opened the refrigerator. Inside sat one half-opened loaf of bread, a quarter pound of butter, a half gallon of milk, and a carton of beer. He stood back and talked to the refrigerator.

"How am I going to feed this woman with bread, butter, and beer?"

The refrigerator did not respond. Slonsky cracked open a bottle of beer and drank some of it briefly. He put down the bottle and checked the small pantry. He twirled around a few random jars aimlessly. He shut the pantry doors and went to the telephone, picked up the telephone book, and scanned the yellow pages. Under *groceries*, he found the section on *home delivery*. He picked up the phone and called.

A voice answered, "Benny's Home Delivery. May I have your order, please?"

"Uh, I'm a little new to this. Can you give me some direction?"

"Of course. Do you have our grocery list?"

"No."

"Oh, well, do you know what you want?"

"Not exactly. I'm taking care of a sick friend, and I don't cook."

"Oh dear. Can you come into our store?"

"Not today. I can't leave her alone."

"Why don't we do this? If your friend is sick, how about milk, some ice cream, potato salad, orange juice, coffee, and some bottled water?"

"All of the above."

"Good. I'll include our grocery list in the bag, and then later, you can consider what else you would like to order. Maybe your friend knows something about cooking."

"I'll ask. Thanks very much."

"What is your address?"

Slonsky hesitated.

"Deliver it to the police station on Wilshire Boulevard. Ask for Sergeant Rutledge."

"The police station?"

"Yes. My brother is a police officer, and he'll bring it over when he comes to visit."

"I will need a check or credit card."

"He'll pay for it."

"OK. Half an hour."

Slonsky hung up and called Wilshire Division.

Rutledge answered, "Wilshire Division. Rutledge speaking."

"Joe, BS here."

"BS? I thought you were off duty."

"I am but need some help. The grocery store is going to deliver some stuff. Would you pay for it and bring it over to my house when your shift is over?"

"Is your credit any good?"

"Of course not."

"No problem. How's Honey?"

"She hurts. By the way, how did you know she was here?"

"I didn't. I just strongly suspected you would not be too far away from her."

"Joe, this is strictly confidential."

"Understood. How soon are the grocery people coming?"

"They didn't say. Probably about half an hour."

"No problem. Your delivery boy will handle."

"Thanks, buddy."

Slonsky hung up. He began locking all the doors and windows, closed the blinds, and returned to the kitchen. The taste of the beer had not improved, and he poured the contents of the bottle down the sink. After checking on a soundly sleeping Honey, Slonsky removed his holstered weapon and tossed his coat onto the couch. He unlaced his shoes, leaned back against a faded leather sofa, and stared at the ceiling, his eyes tracing the thin cracks that meandered from one side of the room to the other. The wind had risen in the last hour, nudging the clouds across the sky and signaling rain. Dark clouds slowly replaced the fluffy marshmallow-white balloons and covered the evening skies.

A car door slammed. Slonsky jumped up, grabbed his gun, and raced to the window. Pushing aside the weather-faded curtains, he peered out and saw his neighbor across the street walking up the sidewalk to his house. Slonsky studied the entire street, searching for anything unusual. Streetlights blinked on, casting more shadows than light; a house light next door glimmered behind curtains and shades. In the distance, a siren wailed, a familiar sound during rush hour. An unexpected rustle on the roof startled him. He ducked instinctively while the slender branches of the birch tree in the backyard swept across the roof. After checking on Honey, he walked into the den and turned on the television.

A commercial break. He settled into an easy chair and dozed. Half an hour later, he awoke just as Channel 5 news reporter Carmen Susa announced breaking news.

"Police Officer Honey Wissman, one of the first female officers on the Los Angeles Police Department, has been shot in Oregon and hospitalized here in Los Angeles. No one has reported the attempted murder of a police officer, and we are asking questions. Sam Henry has the story."

The TV set cut to reporter Sam Henry.

"Yes, Carmen, Officer Wissman was on vacation in Oregon when she was shot and critically wounded. None of the media had been alerted to this shooting until she was released from the hospital today. Police sources report she is on disability, but Police Chief Riley refuses to say what occurred or where she is staying. This story is definitely unusual, and we will follow up. Sam Henry, *Channel 5 News.*"

Susa resumed, "Thank you, Sam. We attempted to interview hospital personnel in Oregon, but all nurses and doctors refused to talk to us. The hospital administrator referred us to LAPD. Local police in Oregon did the same. We'll stay with the story."

Slonsky waved the remote, and the television died. He checked on Honey again, but she was still sleeping, fitfully and restlessly. He started toward the bathroom to get her medication when the doorbell rang. Whirling around, he unholstered his gun and concealed himself behind the door. The bell rang again, and he heard the voice of Joe Rutledge.

"BS, are you there? Open up."

Relieved, Slonsky holstered his weapon and opened the door to a weary Rutledge, his face hidden by two grocery bags.

"You know, I don't pump iron anymore like you did, but I think I'll start again with these groceries."

"Sorry, Joe, I'm a little on edge. Here, let me help you."

Slonsky grabbed both bags from a grateful Rutledge.

"Jeez, man. I didn't know you ate all this crap."

"I don't, but at a time like this, Honey needs comfort food."

"How's she doing?"

"Not too good. Lot of pain. She's asleep now. Come on in and have a pretzel with ice cream."

"OK, just for a minute. Mary Lou is expecting me."

"Speaking of expecting, how's she doing?"

"Good. Doctor says she should pop in about three months."

"Glad to hear it. Give her my best. But I thought you said you were a little short in the sex department."

"Something came up."

"Apparently."

Rutledge fell heavily on the couch, loosened his tie, and sat back.

"You know, I feel guilty about helping to assign Honey to this case. She could have been a great cop. I know my whores, and she was super."

"Don't blame yourself. She wanted to help. She knows the risk of being a cop. Sounds cold, but she told me to say that if anybody asks."

"She's a real trooper."

Rutledge paused.

"BS, Honey left a dress in the gym, so I thought I'd bring it over. It's in the car, so when I leave, I'll give it to you."

"Thanks, Joe. I appreciate it."

"But I should tell you I found some notes in the pocket. She had a list of names and phone numbers. Didn't make any sense to me, but I thought it might to you."

Rutledge fished out a crumpled and worn piece of paper and handed it to Slonsky. Unnumbered, the list had eight names; two were underlined: Jean Carleton and Kelly Francis. He reread the names out loud to be sure.

"You're sure this came from Honey's clothing?"

"Check the label on the dress after I leave it with you. Her name is stitched on the collar."

"Thanks, Joe. I'll ask her about this."

"Hey, gotta go see Mama. Give Honey my best."

Slonsky said nothing. Rutledge repeated his request.

"Hey, BS, you OK?"

"Oh, sure, sure. I'll tell Honey. Thanks, Joe."

"No problem. Call me when you need another delivery."

Rutledge opened the door and started out into the night. He yelled over his shoulder, "See you later! I'll just leave the dress outside the door here."

"OK. Thanks again, Joe."

Slonsky closed the door. He studied the list once more but heard Honey calling him.

"BS, are you still there?"

"Yes, Honey. Coming."

Honey waited until Slonsky walked in, carrying in the groceries.

"I thought I heard voices."

"Joe Rutledge. Came by with some groceries. He says to give you his best."

"How thoughtful. I didn't know he knew we were here."

"He didn't. I called him and asked him to pick up some food."

Slonsky opened the bag. Honey watched.

"Basil, you got chips, dip, ice cream, and junk food?"

"You got it. Food for strength."

"What a guy. I'll bet you're a great cook."

"Yep. Chicken pot pie, canned soup, milk, and cookies."

Honey collapsed in laughter.

"I'm feeling a little better. Can I have some ice cream?"

"Coming up."

Slonsky dished up a bowlful and handed it to Honey. She ate eagerly. Slonsky watched, the list of names in his hand. He started to remove it, paused, and stuffed it in his pocket.

Chapter 55

"Ms. Booker, I'm Detective Slonsky, LAPD. Do you remember me? I visited with Ms. Wissman."

"Oh, yes, nice to see you."

"I spoke to your administrator, and he said I could review the nurse's notes and doctor's report on the night Ms. Wissman almost died."

Slonsky handed her a business card from Steve Corlin, director of hospital administration. On the note were scribbled the words "OK for Detective Slonsky to review Wissman files."

Imogene read the note and handed it back to Slonsky.

"Sure, I remember that night. My shift was over when all the ruckus started, but I sure heard about it."

Imogene opened the file drawers, thumbed through the files, located the Wissman file, and handed it to Slonsky.

"I'm not supposed to let anyone know about Ms. Wissman, but if Mr. Corlin said it's OK, then I guess it's OK. These files are private, but sometimes we have to check them out. Is Ms. Wissman still a suspect?"

Slonsky looked up from reading the file.

"A suspect?"

"Yes. Officer Madigan said she was a suspect in an important case. I suppose that's why you're here."

Slonsky looked down at the files, concealing his face and reading.

"I didn't know you knew about that."

"Yes. When Officer Madigan was here, he said it was very important to let him know if Ms. Wissman had any visitors because people were looking for her."

"That's true. I guess he trusted you to tell him."

"Oh, yes. I'm surprised he didn't tell you."

"Ma'am, we have so many cases that it's hard to keep up-to-date."

"Of course. Did you see that little tape recorder he gave me to put under Ms. Wissman's bed? He came several days ago and picked it up."

Slonsky stopped reading and looked at Imogene.

"A tape recorder? Oh, yes. I'm going to have to speak to him about that."

"I never knew they could make such things so small."

"Technology is wonderful, isn't it?"

"Sure is. Don't tell anybody, but I really like Officer Madigan."

"I'm not surprised. He's a fine man."

"We have been dating, you know."

"No, I didn't know that. I really don't like to get into his private life. You know what I mean."

"I do, I do. But I'm so excited because he's taking me with him on his vacation."

"Really? Are you going someplace romantic?"

"Mr. Slonsky, it's a secret. But I'm sure we are. We leave tonight right after my shift ends at 2:00 a.m."

"Wonderful. By the way, why did he say he wanted you to put the tape recorder under the bed?"

"Well, he asked me to put it there so no one would see it just in case someone tried to hurt Ms. Wissman. You were in to see her several times, so I just thought you knew about it. Come to think about it, I don't think he ever mentioned your name, Mr. Slonsky."

"Well, he's very busy. Ms. Booker, you've been very helpful. I'll tell Mr. Corlin you are a credit to the hospital."

"Oh, thank you."

"And I can see why Officer Madigan is interested in you, if you don't mind me saying that."

Imogene Booker blushed.

"I'll tell Officer Madigan I met you."

"Oh, you don't have to. He knows me. Now if you'll excuse me, Ms. Booker, here is your file. Thank you, but I've got to get to work."

"You're welcome."

Slonsky hurried down the corridor and out of the hospital to his car. He called Records Department on his cell phone.

A voice answered, "Records."

"This is Detective Slonsky. Who is this?"

"Bob Turner."

"Bob, will you pull up the names of officers currently on vacation or on sick leave from Wilshire Division, please?"

"Sure, no problem."

"Whom do you want?"

"Just the names of all the officers not on duty."

"Hold on. Here it is. Seven guys and one female."

"Just the guys."

Turner read the names. Eddie Mathes was on sick leave and leaving tomorrow on vacation.

* * *

Slonsky parked his car down the street from the hospital, away from the streetlights, but with a clear view of the hospital entrance. Checking his gun, he broke it open, looked at the chamber, pressed the bullets in place, laid it on the seat next to him, and slumped down. At 1:45 a.m., no one was on the street; only the security guard was visible. Ten minutes later, Imogene Booker came through the entrance carrying her suitcase in one hand and her purse in the other. Alone under the entrance lights, she looked up and down the street, checked her watch, and set down the suitcase. Removing a cell phone from her purse, she held the phone to her ear for several minutes, closed the lid, and returned it to her purse. A few minutes later, a car approached, and she looked up. Touching up her hair, she picked up her suitcase and waited until the car stopped. She opened the door, tossed in her suitcase, and entered the passenger side. Moments later, the Porsche accelerated and drove away from the hospital.

Slonsky started the engine without activating the headlights and followed the car out of the hospital parking lot. The Porsche turned the corner, and Slonsky switched on the lights, keeping his distance. Without any other cars on the street, he could easily drive hundreds of yards behind the Porsche. He saw the car drive into an all-night gas station, but the driver remained inside the car, talking briefly with the attendant who came out of the station. Slonsky drove past the station and continued up the highway to a side street and turned off. Negotiating a U-turn and again turning off his lights, he waited. No car drove by. He drove to the edge of the highway and looked in the direction of the gas station. No cars. Accelerating, Slonsky drove down the highway looking for the Porsche. After driving several miles, he pulled over. No Porsche in sight. Slonsky picked up his cell phone and called. A sleepy Honey Wissman answered.

"Honey, it's BS. I don't have time to explain. Give me Mathes's home address."

"What's happening?"

"Please, I don't have time to explain."

"805 Washington Street in Culver City."

"Thanks. I'll call you later."

He hung up, swung the car around, and raced down the highway. With no traffic and only slowing for red lights, Slonsky quickly reached Culver City. Blowing another red light, he looked up at the street signs when he heard the sound of a siren and saw red lights in his mirror.

"Son of a bitch."

He pulled over and got out of the car, arms in the air with his badge in one hand and his wallet in the other.

"Police officer. Emergency."

Two young officers were not entirely convinced. Slonsky assumed the position, holding his badge and wallet in the air.

"I'm Detective Slonsky, LAPD. I'm trying to follow a car. This is critical."

The officers walked slowly toward Slonsky. One officer looked at the badge, removed Slonsky's wallet, and read carefully.

Slonsky shouted, "Look at the registration! It's an unmarked car!"

The other officer opened the glove box. He shouted to his partner, "Looks OK. Let him go."

Grabbing his wallet and badge from the officer, Slonsky jumped back in the car. Ten minutes later, he turned onto Washington Street. The house at 805 was dark, and no Porsche parked in front. He ran toward the house and looked inside the front window. In response, a dog barked loudly.

Chapter 56

The following morning, Slonsky stood at the Santa Monica pier, talking to a California Highway Patrol officer. The dead body of a black woman lay covered with tarp laid on the sand surrounded by yellow strips of homicide tape. The coroner's van sat nearby. Numerous officers were searching the area. Slonsky lifted up the tarp to see Imogene Booker in death.

The CHP officer looked at Slonsky.

"I was exiting the freeway, BS, when a guy waved me down. Said there was a dead body on the beach. I found her under the pier about seven o'clock this morning. But this is not your jurisdiction. How come you're here?"

"I met the woman at the hospital where my partner was recuperating. When I read the daily homicide reports, I recognized her name. Cause of death?"

"Two gunshots to the back of the head. Close range."

"Did you find the gun?"

"No. Clean job. No witnesses. Her purse, if she had one, is gone. Probably robbery."

"Yeah, sure. Will you tell Fred Southers to save the slugs for me when he does the autopsy?"

"You starting a collection, BS?"

"I know. People keep dying. I try to find out why."

Slonsky retreated to his car and called Marcum on his cell phone.

"Marcum here."

"John, it's BS. I'm still working that abortion case. I need a search warrant."

"For where and for what?"

"A house. A nurse just got murdered. I need probable cause to search."

"Search for what?"

"I'm not sure."

"BS, you know I can't get a warrant on that. What do you need?"

"Evidence—you know, guns, dope, stolen property. I don't know yet."

"Sorry, BS. That's not enough. Call me later when you get more facts. Hey, gotta go. My kids are waiting for me."

Slonsky heard the dial tone. He dialed again, and a voice answered, "McClosky."

"Only Slonsky could call me on Sunday at my house. BS, you need me."

"Yes, I do. I need to find out where someone lives, and I don't want to do it through the department or her employer. Then I need to search it."

"No problem. But why can't you get a warrant?"

"If I could get a warrant, would I call you?"

"You're right. Give me the name, rank, and serial number."

"Imogene Booker. Nurse. Queen of Angels Hospital in LA."

"Hold on."

Slonsky waited on hold. McClosky came back on the line.

"1020 Monroe Street, Santa Monica. Do you need me to get in?"

"If you don't mind."

"I'll meet you there."

One hour later, a car and a panel truck arrived and parked next to each other at 1020 Monroe Street. McClosky and a man dressed in a telephone-company uniform exited their vehicles. Slonsky, already parked across the street, walked toward them. McClosky smiled.

"I heard there was something wrong with the telephone line at this address, so Jimmy came with me. I'll let you know when you can come in."

McClosky and Jimmy went to the front door and knocked. After a few moments without any answer, they both disappeared around the back. Several minutes later, the front door opened slightly, and McClosky waved Slonsky inside. Looking around, he saw Jimmy putting on work clothes. Wearing a belt stuffed with tools, Jimmy went outside and climbed expertly up the telephone pole and appeared to work on the line.

Slonsky walked through the neat two-bedroom house with McClosky.

"BS, what are we looking for?"

"I'm not sure."

"Fine. I'll look for that."

Both entered the bedroom. Imogene had taken lots of pictures, and they flooded tables and chests. But one photograph of Imogene and Mathes together had been taped on the mirror and a paper heart placed over it. Slonsky removed it. McClosky was dumbfounded.

"That's it. A picture?"

"Yes."

"Who is it?"

"A dead woman."

"Who's the other guy?"

"A cop. I got what I wanted. Let's go."

"I guess I can tell Jimmy we fixed the phone in here. And to think you were my partner," laughed McClosky, "who unlawfully entered a house to find a paper heart."

Chapter 57

That evening, Slonsky showed the picture to Honey while they shared food from the grocery.

"Do you recognize her?"

"Yes. She was the nurse that took care of me in the hospital.

"And in more ways than one," said Slonsky.

"What do you mean?"

Slonsky leaned forward in his chair. Honey swung her legs over the side of the bed, wincing slightly, but resolute in sitting up. Her hair had partially grown out and fell around the edge of both ears. She had combed it into short curls with one hand, but the other hand hung limply at her side. Slonsky had offered to help, but she tactfully declined, although he insisted on holding the mirror. He pointed to the picture of Imogene and Mathes.

"Mathes told her that his name was Officer Madigan and you were under investigation, highly secret and not to tell anyone. That's how he got her to put the bug under your bed. Mathes knew you were cooperating with me and couldn't be trusted. Imogene said he picked up the tape. They've got everything you told me on tape."

"They?"

"Mathes has got someone helping him in the department. I suspect Asquith, but I have no proof."

"Asquith? I never heard Eddie mention Asquith's involvement when we were planning to interrupt the demonstration at the clinic. What do you plan to do next?"

Slonsky hesitated momentarily.

"You're still not sure about me."

"It's not that, Honey. It's . . . Joe Rutledge gave me a paper he found in your dress when the captain put your things in a locker. I read the names and phone numbers of Jean Carleton and Kelly Francis written on it. Jean Carleton is Judge Carleton's wife and getting a divorce. Kelly Francis is the court administrator in the courthouse. From a friend of mine, I suspect that Jean Carleton wants to upset Judge Carleton's appointment to the Supreme Court. The president will go bananas if he learns something shaky about Carleton, and he'll appoint someone else."

Honey began to tremble, but Slonsky continued.

"The note says 'We're all set, Honey. See you at the clinic tomorrow. Hope no one gets hurt.' Signed, Kelly."

Honey sat up and composed herself.

"Yes, I know both those women. We planned the disturbance at the medical clinic, but not to kill anyone. Look, Basil, there's only one way to prove I'm trustworthy. If Eddie arranged to kill that nurse, he won't rest until he finds me. You need to use me as a decoy."

"Forget it."

"Look. Three women—Maureen McCullough, Sally Thompson, and Imogene Booker—were killed in this case. All innocent. And you know I'm next on his list. You said he had a tape of everything I told you. That means he knows I'm the only one who can identify him. If I'm out of the way, he's home clear. Can't you see that, Basil?"

"I won't let you do it."

"If I don't, we'll never get together. You will never know whether I'm telling the truth or not. You want to marry someone under those circumstances?"

Slonsky felt his throat clutch.

"Honey, that's not fair. You don't have to put your life on the line. We can find other ways."

"See? You really are not sure of me. And what other way are you thinking about, Sherlock? You have no witnesses, at least none who are alive, and the only connection you have to Mathes are his prints on the IV. As I told you, I'm sure he can come up with an innocent explanation. He's no dummy. He can just say he moved the IV so he could talk to me. And he can say anyone in the hospital could have chloroformed me. No one ever saw him in the hospital except Imogene, and she's dead, Mr. Sherlock Holmes. You still don't have the shooter even if you get Eddie."

"I might have a witness."

"Who?"

"I told you, I can't tell you."

Honey fell back against the pillow, tears flowing down her face.

"You're lying. You're lying. Go away. No, I have a better idea. Take me home. I don't want to stay here anymore. You can't order me around. Get the car and take me home."

"Give me twenty-four hours."

"For what? So you can check me out?"

"Please."

"All right, get your ass in gear because the clock is ticking now."

Slonsky stood up, gently placed Honey's legs back on the bed, and carefully pulled the covers over them.

"You son of a bitch, BS, I love you."

Slonsky reached up to her hair and pushed back a stray curl. She turned her head toward him and threw one arm around his neck, pulling him down.

"You should see what I could do if I had two arms."

And she turned away to hide the tears.

Chapter 58

Slonsky leaned over McClosky's desk and handed him a photograph.

"OK, McClosky. Take a look at this. That's a photograph of Judge Carleton watching the abortion demonstration, courtesy of a tape from Channel 6. The judge misled me originally, but after I showed the photo to him, he told me he had seen the killer at the clinic and failed to report it. But he can't identify the shooter. The photograph taken from the Channel 6 tape ends the confidentiality I promised the judge."

"Do the Channel 6 employees know about this photo?"

"No. They just gave us the tape. Mike Winkelmann from forensics transferred it to a photograph."

"So Carleton saw the shooting in a crowd but can't identify anyone. Big deal."

"But how does that explain why he didn't inform the police he had seen the shooting? He says that kind of evidence would cast doubt on his integrity and the president could never appoint him."

"BS, that's not the only reason."

"I know, I know. If I disclose the photograph, the murderer would know, or infer, the judge witnessed the shooting and render him vulnerable."

"You told me someone tried to kill him in Mexico, which means someone already knew what he saw."

"But how would anyone know of his potential testimony so soon after the shooting? I'm the only one he told. And even if Mathes was involved, who fired the gun that killed Maureen McCullough? And where did the third bullet come from?"

McClosky handed the photograph back to Slonsky.

"BS, we got a problem. If I told Mrs. Carleton about this, she wouldn't just jump for joy. She would pay me whatever I asked. This would dump Carleton for concealing evidence or some other excuse. But that has nothing to do with the divorce—except she'll make it a big deal. Frankly, I told her I liked Carleton, and God knows who that liberal weenie in the White House would appoint in his place."

"What are you going to do?"

"Quit."

"You're going to quit?"

"Yes. I've finished my investigation anyway, and Carleton isn't playing around."

"I'll be a son of a bitch."

"Yes, you always were."

* * *

In the late afternoon, the sun disappeared behind hazy clouds, and the first tinge of dusk crept in. Slonsky accelerated, realizing he had driven toward home slower than usual, mulling over theories in his head. He turned into his driveway and noted no lights shining in his house. Switching off the car motor, he walked up to the house, unlocked the front door, and entered.

"Honey."

No answer.

"Honey, I'm back."

No answer. Slonsky hurried into the bedroom only to find Honey Wissman gone, the bed made, and his clothes hung up neatly. He looked around frantically. A note pinned to the bedcovers fluttered slightly. He picked it up and read it.

"You still have the original twenty-four hours. I just decided to wait somewhere else. I'll call you when your time's up."

Slonsky crumpled up the note and flung it on the floor. He picked up the phone and called Wilshire Division.

"Sergeant Rutledge, please."

Rutledge came on the line.

"Joe, it's BS."

"Aha, you want another delivery."

"No. This is serious. I need Honey's home address. She told me, but I forgot it."

"BS, she's on the protective-witness list. I can't even tell you."

"Protective witness? Who put her on the list?"

"The chief, of course. She called him and asked to be put on the list because of the shooting in Oregon. So he did."

"Is Asquith the watch commander tonight?"

"Yes. You want to talk to him?"

"Yes. Now."

"Hold on."

The line went on hold, then a voice came on.

"Asquith here."

"Sergeant, this is Slonsky. I need to talk to Honey Wissman. Did you put her on the protective-witness list?"

"No. The chief approved it."

"I need her address."

"Sergeant, I can't do that. You know the regulations."

"Dammit, her life is in danger."

"That's why she's on the list."

"Who's on backup?"

"She didn't want any. I told her I couldn't do that without approval. She said just put her on the list and she would wait for me to assign someone. I said I'd call her."

"Whom did you assign?"

"Nobody yet. The lieutenant went downtown for a meeting and got stuck in traffic. He told me not to do anything until he got back."

Slonsky slammed down the phone, picked it up again, and punched in McClosky's number.

"This is Detective Slonsky. Is Mr. McClosky in?"

"Just a minute."

McClosky came on the line.

"Slonsky, you're in trouble again."

"OK, I'll grovel. I need another address. A cop's."

"That's a tough one. I might have to make a few calls. Who is it?"

"Officer Honey Wissman."

"How come you can't find her?"

"She gave it to me once, but I can't remember. I don't want to call the department. It's a long story. Can you do it?"

"And in return?"

"Nothing. I got nothing. We got a cop's life on the line."

"Good enough. Where can I reach you?"

"At my house."

Half an hour later, McClosky called and gave Slonsky the address.

He replied, "I might need some help. Can you come with me?"

"Sure. Are you still a son of a bitch?"

"Oh, for God's sake."

"Good enough. You're a religious son of a bitch. I'll be right over."

Chapter 59

Slonsky waited impatiently at every red light, accelerating the moment the signal changed. McClosky, sitting in the front passenger seat, said nothing. Both men struggled to see the house addresses on the curb.

"There it is," said McClosky.

Slonsky swerved into the driveway and jammed the gear into park. Both men jumped out of the car and ran toward the front door of a tract home familiar in Southern California.

Slonsky banged on the door frantically.

"Honey, open up. It's me."

No answer from inside the house. Slonsky stepped back, walked toward the side of the house, and looked inside. He shouted at McClosky, "Nothing! We'll have to break down the door!"

"BS, let me see if I can help. Technology keeps improving, and we don't need Jimmy this time."

McClosky reached into his jacket and removed several keys. Carefully placing one in the lock, he turned the key. The lock clicked, and the door opened.

Slonsky barely hesitated, pushed McClosky aside, and rushed in. McClosky followed.

"Hey, BS, this beats climbing up a telephone pole, doesn't it?"

Slonsky ignored the remark, calling out, "Honey, it's me, BS! Where are you?"

No answer. Over his shoulder, he yelled at McClosky, "Check downstairs! I'll go up!"

The two men split up. Slonsky headed up the stairs two at a time. Both bedrooms were empty; the bathroom and family room unoccupied. He called down to McClosky, "Anything?"

"Nope, no one here."

Slonsky walked downstairs, looking around fruitlessly. McClosky sat down.

"BS, do you mind telling me what this is all about since we're both burglars?"

Slonsky leaned against a leather chair.

"OK. Honey Wissman is the target for a fruitcake. And the fruitcake's friend, I think, is a cop who wants her dead. I don't have enough evidence, but she was shot in Oregon. The cop was in LA at the time of the shooting. I checked it out. So it wasn't him. But the cop tried to kill her while she was in the hospital here in LA."

"So why didn't she report the attempted murder?"

"She was chloroformed and unconscious. She didn't see a thing, but the cop cut the IV tube, and she almost died. We just have a hard time proving it was him."

"Shouldn't you have reported it?"

Slonsky sat down.

"Frankly, yes. But it would have compromised the abortion investigation. Honey had other reasons too, but it's not important."

"Basil, I think you're getting your emotions mixed up in this."

"Probably. Paul, look, not now. You have a right to know, but later I'll fill you in."

"Good enough. So why are we in her house?"

"She was staying with me for a while but bailed out. She's trying to prove something by acting as a decoy."

"A decoy? This is getting deep. Who's her backup?"

"She doesn't have any."

"They don't let cops act as decoys without backup."

"I know that. Apparently, the watch commander can't assign anyone until his lieutenant gets back."

"You have no idea where she is?"

"No. She left a note saying she'd call me later."

McClosky surveyed the neatly kept room.

"Is that her computer on the table?"

Slonsky looked over at a solitary laptop computer.

"I suppose so."

"You may as well add to our burglary."

Slonsky got up, walked over to the monitor, and looked at the screen. The computer was still on.

He pressed Enter. The screen lit up to display an e-mail: "Meet me at the courthouse. We'll do lunch. S/Kelly."

Slonsky stared at the screen. Over his shoulder, he said, "Honey told me she knew Kelly Francis. I had met her, though. She's the administrative assistant at the courthouse."

Slonsky turned toward McClosky.

"I need to find out where Mathes is. I'll call Sergeant Asquith again."

"Bill Asquith? Mr. Affirmative Action?"

"Yes."

"Why him?"

"Trust me."

"So do you need me anymore?"

"Not unless you want to help."

"Trust me."

"I don't, but I'll give you a chance anyway."

McClosky bowed ceremoniously. Slonsky smirked.

"Got your wiretapping equipment?"

"Wouldn't leave home without it."

"I'm gonna make a phone call to Asquith from here. Can you bug it?"

"Sure."

"Can you bug any phone calls he makes from the number I call?"

"BS, this is a new world. You guys need to catch up. Of course, I can. Here, put this little gizmo on your phone."

McClosky reached inside his pocket and handed Slonsky a small round object the size of a dime. He pointed to the receiver. Slonsky attached the bug to the receiver and called. Asquith answered on the second ring.

"Asquith."

"Sergeant, this is Slonsky again. Sorry I hung up on you. I guess I'm just a little impatient. I got word from one of my little birds that a nutcase is trying to do Officer Wissman. I know you can't tell me where she is, but I think you should know what's going on. I told the captain, and he said I should call you immediately."

"OK. But the lieutenant came in a few minutes ago and assigned Eddie Mathes as her backup."

"He assigned Mathes? I thought he was on vacation or sick or something."

"He was. Came back today. I was out checking on patrol officers, and when I came back to the station, the lieutenant told me he had made the assignment. Then he went off duty, but now his shift is over. I better call the captain."

Slonsky placed his hand over the phone and whispered to McClosky, "He wants to talk to the captain."

"Tell him to hold on, and you'll get the captain on another line. Who is the captain?"

"Gordon Sanders."

"Sanders? That jerk. Basil, tell Asquith you'll transfer the call. Sanders just got transferred to Wilshire, and Asquith probably doesn't know him yet. Tell him you'll hold on while he calls. What's the captain's private telephone number at the station?"

Slonsky pulled out his address book and looked it up.

"Here it is. 310-464-4200."

Slonsky removed his hand from the telephone.

"Hold on, Sergeant. I gotta turn down my radio."

McClosky wrote swiftly on a notepaper and handed it to Slonsky, who read it: "Tell him you'll transfer the call."

Slonsky looked at McClosky quizzically. McClosky pointed to the phone. Slonsky turned toward the phone.

"Sergeant, I'll transfer the call. You can talk to Captain Sanders."

"Who is Captain Sanders?"

"Your new captain. He just got transferred to Wilshire. I know him well. I used to work for him."

"OK," replied Asquith.

McClosky nodded affirmatively and handed Slonsky another note: "BS, I'll stay on the line. Keep quiet."

Slonsky heard a click on the line, and the phone went dead. McClosky took the phone from Slonsky and punched in some numbers, followed by the sound of a telephone ringing. Answering his own phone, McClosky barked into the mouthpiece, imitating the voice of Captain Sanders, "This is Sanders. What is it?"

Asquith replied, "Captain Sanders, this is Sergeant Asquith. I didn't know you were our new captain. We haven't met. I'm the watch commander. Sergeant Slonsky wants me to call Officer Mathes, the backup for his former partner, Officer Wissman, in a homicide case, but she's on the protected-witness list. I can't give him that information. Slonsky says there's a reported attempt on her life. Is it OK for him to contact Mathes?"

McClosky straightened his bank in pretense.

"Is that OK? Of course, you dumb son of a bitch. Why didn't you call the backup officer yourself? Give Slonsky his telephone number."

"Yes, sir. Yes, sir. Thank you very much."

The line went dead. McClosky, placing his index finger over his mouth, handed the phone back to Slonsky. Another click on the line. McClosky pointed to the phone.

Slonsky spoke into the phone, "Slonsky here. Did you get a hold of Captain Sanders?"

"Yes. He said it's OK. Mathes is using a department phone. Here's his number: 310-454-5577."

"Good. Thank you, Sergeant. I appreciate your cooperation."

"Slonsky, can you wait a minute?"

Slonsky looked at McClosky, who shrugged.

Slonsky replied, "Sure. What is it?"

"I know you want to contact Mathes. After that, can you come by the station for a few minutes? It won't take long."

Slonsky paused.

"Sure. Sure. But I don't have much time."

"Thanks. I'll wait for you."

Slonsky hung up the phone.

"Asquith wants to talk to me. Strange. By the way, McClosky, how'd you know how to imitate Sanders?"

"I worked for him when I was a lieutenant. Total jerk. That's the way he talks to everyone."

Slonsky punched in the telephone number Asquith had given him.

Mathes answered, "Who is this?"

"Sergeant Slonsky."

"What are you calling me for?"

"I'm on special assignment. Captain Sanders says he got word somebody is out to get Officer Wissman and wanted me to call you. She was my partner investigating a homicide. He said you're her backup."

"Who is Sanders?"

"He's the new captain. Just got transferred."

"What the hell does he know about her?"

"I don't know. Someone told him there was a contract out on her."

"OK. What am I supposed to do about it?"

"Be careful. Just letting you know someone is looking for her right now."

"OK. I'll take care of it."

The phone went dead. Slonsky put down the phone. McClosky removed the bug. Slonsky held out his hand toward McClosky. "Thank you."

"What was that conversation for?"

"Mathes knows I'm on his ass. I'm hoping he won't try anything tonight with Honey. If she calms down, I can find her a safe house."

"I hope you're right."

McClosky replaced the bug in his pocket.

"You need me anymore, BS?"

"Yes."

"Well, I can see you need all the help you can get. I'll be your helper."

"I need Mathes's home address."

"Hand me the phone."

For the first time in years, the two men shook hands in friendship.

Chapter 60

Sergeant Asquith waved Slonsky and McClosky to chairs in his office.

"I guess they call you BS. Do you mind if I do?"

"Not at all."

"BS, this will hurt. When you have a really good friend, you almost automatically believe what they say. You want to believe, but sometimes you're not sure."

"I can relate to that."

"Eddie Mathes and I have been good friends, really good friends, ever since we came on the department. You don't know what being black is like on an all-white department, and we formed the Black Officers Union. When Eddie decided to marry Maureen McCullough, or Jeri, as she liked, I was stunned, but no one else knew her real name. And she was white. Eddie had always dated black women. But I stuck with him after they got married. After a while, things between the two weren't working out. Eddie has a temper, and he banged up Jeri pretty good a couple of times. By the way, she kept her real name after they were married, which also pissed him off. But for some reason, she liked the name Jeri, so that's what I called her even though her maiden name was Maureen McCullough.

"She was sleeping around, kept late hours, and threw it in his face. She called the cops a couple of times but then backed down until the last time when they arrested him, and she agreed to prosecute. Eddie knew his career was over if the jury found him guilty. Jeri had taken pictures of her bruised face and sent them to a friend for use at trial. During this time, Eddie met Officer Wissman. Nothing intimate. He pretended he was interested in the feminist bit and said he would help her find the guys that killed her father. Anyway, somehow they both agreed on a way to get some publicity for the demonstration at the medical clinic that would show how evil the pro-lifers were. Eddie would get someone to fire a couple of shots in the air, the crowd would scramble, and the press would go nuts. Great publicity for the pro-choice crowd. To establish their alibi for the shooting, Eddie and Honey would both be in the crowd. He said it was all Honey's idea, but no one would get hurt."

Slonsky interrupted, "Why are you telling me this if that's all they agreed on?"

"I'm coming to that. Eddie and I talked about it, and I said it was a stupid idea, but no one would get hurt. What he didn't tell me was, he had a different plan. When we talked, I was always focusing on his trial and his career. Maybe his wife would back out of the trial. No trial, no problem. But he was focused on his wife. Call me stupid. Call me naive. I thought the whole idea was just helping Officer Wissman out. I didn't see any connection between the abortion antics and his wife.

"When I heard his wife was shot, I never connected that with Eddie because he was in the crowd with Officer Wissman. I wasn't there, so I just figured it was some pro-life fruitcake. Then I discovered Officer Wissman had hacked my computer. Why me? When Sally Thompson was murdered, it was just another robbery. We get jaded in this job. Sally Thompson replaced the computer—at your request—when you were working on the abortion case. It seemed strange that Sally Thompson was killed, and Vice Officer Wissman, who had been transferred to homicide also at your request, was looking into my records. She was also looking up Eddie's records when she found out he and I were communicating. I told Eddie, but he just blew me off. The next thing I know, Officer Wissman was shot.

"Finally, I was at Eddie's house one day to watch football. I went to the bathroom and saw a picture of a nurse posted on the mirror. Someone had written on it 'Love, Imogene.' I asked Eddie about it, and he said it was just a fling he was having with a nurse at Queen of Angels Hospital. I checked it out. Imogene Booker worked at the hospital and was Officer Wissman's nurse. Then she was killed. I added it up. Three women: Jeri Mathes, a.k.a. Maureen McCullough, Sally Thompson, Imogene Booker. Three women dead, all linked together with Officer Wissman."

Slonsky interrupted, "Why didn't you contact me?"

"I couldn't prove Eddie killed anyone, but as you know, every officer can authorize another officer to have access to their locker combination in case they are hurt or killed. Eddie had my name on file, so I opened his locker and found some things in addition to his uniform. The only problem is, you can only open a locker if the officer is hurt or killed, which, of course, Eddie was not."

Asquith swiveled around in his chair and walked over to a cabinet. He removed a rifle, a police jacket marked SWAT, a cap, a pair of binoculars, and a uniform. He showed the items to Slonsky and continued, "Eddie has never worked SWAT. This rifle is not issued by the department. SWAT officers rarely use them unless there is violence, and patrol officers are not issued binoculars."

Slonsky was speechless. He examined the rifle that Asquith had covered with a cloth. He picked up the SWAT jacket, the name tag removed, and studied the binoculars.

Asquith continued, "One more thing. Look at that rifle again."

Slonsky removed the cloth and examined it closely.

"I've never seen a rifle like this."

"Neither have I. The barrel is extremely narrow. And if you look through the scope, tell me what you see."

Slonsky shouldered the rifle and squinted.

"Good lord. Crosshairs and computer numbers in the lens."

"Right. Laser. I checked this out with the manufacturer on the Internet, and this weapon is deadly, extremely accurate. And the bullets are no bigger than your fingernail. Fred Southers in the coroner's office told me the velocity of the bullet is so high that it goes right through an object—like a dummy, for example—and leaves only a tiny hole. Goes through and through the body and out the other side, unless it's deflected."

Slonsky interrupted again, "That explains why the coroner didn't find the bullet originally. It went through Jeri's body but deflected into the fetus."

Asquith nodded. He continued, "The problem is, there are no grooves in the barrel of the rifle. So you can't match the slug removed from the fetus with another shot fired into a target.

That's what the coroner told me when I asked him about this rifle. When I asked Eddie about the third bullet, he just blew me off again and didn't want to talk about it. That did it."

Slonsky rotated the rifle in his hands. He turned toward a crestfallen and dejected Asquith.

"Sergeant, I understand why it hurts to tell us this. I appreciate it."

Asquith handed Slonsky a handful of cartridges sealed in a plastic bag.

"These were in the jacket pocket. Southers said the bullet was fired from an angle. The other bullets were from a handgun and fired laterally into Jeri. My guess is, Eddie wasn't sure the shooter would really pull it off. He wanted to make sure. No wife, no trial, no job loss."

Slonsky leaned forward and put his hands on the desk.

"You know, Sergeant, you are implicating yourself."

"Yes. I have no excuse except for regrettable loyalty. Eddie will just keep on killing or get someone else to do it. First, he'll find Officer Wissman then you. How could I live with that?"

"Sergeant Asquith—"

"Call me Bill."

"Bill, you just solved my case."

"Yes. And I know that you, or someone you knew, impersonated Captain Sander's voice too."

Slonsky responded with a feigned questioning look but said nothing.

"Sanders told me he never talked to me on the phone. And if he finds out who impersonated him, that man's ass is in a sling."

"You got me."

"It's OK. I'll tell no one, ever, on one condition."

"Anything."

"I know you are looking for Eddie or Officer Wissman. Take me with you."

"Why? You've already done enough."

"You said *anything*."

"Deal."

Slonsky handed the rifle back to Asquith, who smiled weakly.

"I'll put this and the bullets away for safekeeping. Let's go."

While Slonsky and McClosky walked out, Asquith reached into the bag, grabbed a few bullets, and folded the rifle into two parts. Concealing it tightly next to his side and under his jacket, he walked toward the car behind Slonsky and McClosky, who were busily talking. Without a word, Asquith eased into the rear seat and laid the rifle on the floor.

Chapter 61

Neither man spoke. Slonsky, driving through city traffic and fuming at cars blocking the streets, followed directions from McClosky. Slonsky wove the car through traffic discreetly, intending to avoid attention, the two men glancing occasionally at each other. Half an hour later, McClosky leaned toward Slonsky.

"This is Mathes's street. Last street at the end of the block, right-hand side."

Slonsky slowed to a crawl, eased toward the side of the street, and parked. Both men instinctively reached for their weapons, checked them, and replaced them in holsters.

Slonsky grunted, staring intently at the house on the corner, its lights unlit and no car in the driveway.

McClosky looked at Slonsky.

"You got a plan?"

Slonsky grunted.

"Of course not."

"Just like the old days."

Slonsky laughed.

"Yeah, you got out your rule book, which you ignored, and I made arrests."

"Well, actually both approaches worked."

Asquith lounged in the backseat, nodding and mimicking sleep. Cars drove by occasionally, lights illuminated houses, several women walked down the sidewalk with children. Mathes's house remained dark. Slonsky and McClosky sat restlessly, each straining to see any activity inside the house. McClosky reached in his pocket, removed a package of gum, and displayed it to Slonsky, who shook his head, simultaneously looking in the backseat at an apparently sleeping Asquith. McClosky broke the silence.

"BS, who is this cop that got shot, and why are you so personally involved?"

Slonsky sat back in his seat and took a deep breath.

"Her name is Honey Wissman, and she's working with me on that abortion shooting. Very savvy on the computer. As Asquith told you, he found out she hacked his computer and his messages to Officer Eddie Mathes. To protect Honey, I got her a new computer from Sally Thompson in the Personnel Department, and that woman got killed for it. I sent Honey to my cabin in Oregon, and someone tried to kill her there, but she was shot from behind and couldn't see anyone. While she was in the hospital, Mathes tried to kill her. We just can't prove it."

"Why Officer Wissman? She didn't kill that woman in the medical-clinic case."

"Not personally, but she was part of the planning process to disrupt the demonstration. Problem is, we didn't have enough evidence to connect Mathes. Now maybe we do."

"You're more than partners with her, aren't you?"

"Sort of."

"Sort of? Your so-called interest in your partner is more than professional, I'd say."

"Hold it. Here comes a car."

A Porsche drove around the corner and parked in the driveway. Slonsky and McClosky reached for their guns and waited. Asquith sat up. All three watched Mathes step out of the car, shut the door, and walk to the passenger side. He opened the door, and Honey Wissman, her lifeless arm in a sling, slowly stumbled out of the car. Slonsky and McClosky quietly opened their car doors, concealing themselves, and stepped onto the street. Slonsky reached inside the car, clicked on the high beams, and yelled, "Police! Put your hands in the air!"

A stunned Mathes whirled around in the glare of the headlights. Slonsky continued to aim his firearm directly at Mathes.

"Turn around, put your hands on top of the car."

Mathes complied. McClosky holstered his weapon and yelled at Slonsky, "Keep him covered! I'll do the search."

McClosky walked cautiously toward Mathes, keeping out of Slonsky's line of sight. He kicked Mathes's legs further apart, searched him thoroughly, and found nothing.

"He's clean."

Slonsky, moving from behind the open car door, holstered his gun and approached Mathes, who stood next to Honey. McClosky backed off. Without warning, Mathes grabbed Honey by the neck, stepped behind her, and twisted her injured arm. She screamed in pain. Mathes shouted, "One step closer, and her arm goes out!"

Slonsky and McClosky stood paralyzed.

Mathes waved McClosky and Slonsky back.

"Both of you, back up, take off your jackets, and drop your guns. In that order. Slowly."

Both men removed their jackets and dropped their weapons on the ground.

"Walk backward so I can pick up your firepower. Keep walking."

Slonsky and McClosky retreated several yards. Mathes came forward to pick up the weapons lying in the street. Slowly he bent down, releasing Honey, who fell against the car and crumpled to the street. Keeping his eyes on Slonsky and McClosky, he picked up both guns and stood with one in each hand.

"Well, well. Now we are three, but soon there will be none."

A rifle shot split the night air. Eddie Mathes staggered backward, grasped his shoulder, and collapsed on the street, while the two handguns clattered on the pavement. Slonsky and McClosky turned around. Sergeant Asquith slowly stepped out from behind the open car door, the rifle in his hands.

Chapter 62

"Have a seat, BS. We've got a little problem with your abortion case," said Marcum as the prosecutor leaned forward on his desk. Slonsky glowered. "What problem? Honey confessed to me. You'll give her immunity. She'll testify at trial. We got Mathes's prints on the IV tube. And we got the binoculars, bullets, the rifle, and the SWAT uniform that Asquith found in Mathes's locker."

"We still have a problem. In the first place, Honey confessed to you while she was in the hospital."

"So what? She was not in custody."

"Even so, that's just part of it. Medical records show the doctors prescribed morphine in the hospital."

"Surprise. She had just been shot."

"I know that. But the defense will argue she confessed while in pain and you exerted pressure on her."

"She volunteered all that stuff about her and Mathes. I never said a word."

"Will the jury believe that? A female cop in the hospital under the influence of drugs freely talking to an experienced investigator? And you have no tape recording of the conversation."

"You talk like a defense lawyer."

"That's part of my job. I gotta fill holes here. But that's not all. Honey didn't pull the trigger. Whoever killed that pregnant woman is still a mystery. If we charge Mathes with murder, Honey's an accomplice, and we can't convict Mathes on her testimony alone without corroboration from another witness even if we gave her immunity, which we haven't. You know that. Where's our corroboration?"

"The prints on the IV tube."

"Two problems with that—one, Mathes will probably find some excuse for holding the IV tube so he could talk to Honey as a visitor more easily."

"Ridiculous."

"Maybe. But it's an issue. Problem number 2: he doesn't have to explain the prints unless we find them."

"What? What are you talking about?"

"The lab lost the prints."

Slonsky stared incredulously.

Marcum continued, "And the slug that Southers found in the fetus? Forensics tells me they can't match the slug in the fetus with the rifle. The weapon is really cutting-edge technology, and the bullets leave no mark in the barrel they can detect. They don't have the technology."

"Is there something going on that I should know about? This was a slam dunk case that is falling apart."

"Nothing, BS, nothing. Shit happens, which brings us to the last problem."

Slonsky looked up. He waited.

Marcum continued, "You made personal arrangements to be alone with Honey in Oregon. You visited her in the hospital repeatedly. You let her stay in your house after she had been shot. The defense is suggesting you concealed her and are involved in the murder. And neither of you reported the attempt by Mathes to kill her in the hospital."

Slonsky sat up in his chair.

Marcum continued, "BS, do you have an alibi for the time Honey was shot in Oregon? How come your prints are also on the IV tube? And after she told you about her involvement in the abortion shooting, why didn't you arrest her? You knew she was legally responsible for the death of that woman at the medical clinic even if you did believe her story."

Slonsky glared at Marcum, stood up, and walked toward the door. Marcum shouted, "Basil, I'm just telling you this case is not a slam dunk! Where are you going?"

A slammed door was his answer.

Chapter 63

Slonsky slumped in the chair and looked aimlessly out of Paul McClosky's eighteenth-floor office window. While rubbing his palms together angrily, a pigeon fluttered down and perched on the sill.

"Perfect. A pigeon visits me as though we were family. Describes me perfectly."

McClosky handed Slonsky a cup of coffee.

"Excuse me for laughing, but it is a good metaphor. Look, BS, I appreciate your situation, but did you just come to visit, or do you want me to help?"

"Paul, you know we were never friends. Frankly, I didn't like your methods more than disliking you. But I have to admit it. You were good, the best. Right now, I need help."

"Enough. What are enemies for if they can't help their friends?"

"You do have a way with words. Honey is the victim of a kidnapping, right?"

"Yeah, BS, that's obvious to us. But if the DA thinks she was involved in the murder, he will charge her. She never reported any attempt on her life in the hospital. She was in the crowd at the time of the shooting. She and Mathes were together at the time Asquith shot Mathes. And she has been arrested as an accomplice along with Mathes in the abortion murder."

Slonsky interrupted, "All bullshit."

"Whoa. Let's sort this out, BS. In the first place, we know that Honey didn't shoot that woman at the medical clinic. The tape shows she is just watching the demonstration and too far away from the victim. Even in her confession to you, she said she didn't want anyone hurt. Just a feminist scheme that went awry. The jury might buy that. What the DA really wants is the shooter. But without that, he needs something to satisfy the media and dampen the publicity."

Slonsky put down his cup.

"Maybe. Maybe. We might have a witness who saw the man who pulled the trigger."

"What?"

"Paul, you're a lawyer, so this is protected by the attorney-client privilege, isn't it?"

"I'm a lawyer, but you're not my client."

"I just hired you."

"What about my fee?"

"Later."

"Agreed."

"The witness is a judge."

McClosky blanched.

"Don't tell me his name."

"What?"

"Don't tell me his name."

"You're my lawyer. You can't reveal it."

"That's not the problem."

Slonsky sat up.

"Oh no. I can't believe this."

McClosky said nothing. He picked up the phone and called a number. Jean Carleton came on the line.

"Hi, Mrs. Carleton. Paul McClosky here. I just completed my investigation and could find nothing to verify your concerns. Some rumors, that's all. It looks like your husband is clean."

He paused and listened to her reply.

"Nope. Not a thing. I hope that's good news . . . Of course. I'll send you my bill. Thanks. Good-bye."

McClosky hung up the phone and smirked.

"Now. Who is your witness? I'll bet I know."

"Ah, the good old days."

"Yes. I thought you might guess whom I was investigating, so I did what had to be done. You were at every hearing on the abortion case in front of Judge Carleton. You went to see him several times in his chambers. And you saved his life in Mexico. And you knew he was probably going to get a divorce."

"How did you know all this?"

"BS, I still have friends in the department who owe me. Big-time. When I need something, I get it. As I said, what are enemies for if they can't help their friends?"

Slonsky laughed.

McClosky continued, "So when you said you had a witness, I figured it out."

"OK. My witness is Judge Carleton."

"I thought so. Carleton is a witness?"

"Sort of. He saw the shooting but can't identify the shooter. 'A white guy with a ponytail who limps' is all he can say."

"Not much of a witness."

"No, but it narrows the field."

"You told me about Asquith. What about him?"

"He's agreed to testify but can't add anything. He's got the rifle and the bullets, but Forensics can't compare them, so the lab guys can't make a match with the slug in the fetus. Asquith said Mathes never told him he was going to shoot his wife. Asquith was trying to save Mathes's job from the wife-beating case."

The telephone interrupted. McClosky picked it up and listened.

"It's for you, BS."

Puzzled, Slonsky picked up the phone and answered, "Slonsky."

He listened carefully.

"When?"

He listened again.

"I'll be right there."

Slonsky cradled the phone.

"Honey's lawyer. She wants to see me."

Chapter 64

Dressed in an orange jumpsuit lettered LA Co. Sheriff, a wan and distraught Honey Wissman walked slowly down the hall, leaning heavily on the arm of Percy Amstead. A deputy sheriff escorted both into an interrogation room and pulled out a chair for Honey. Outside the room, Slonsky handed his gun to another deputy. Taking a deep breath, he walked into the room. Honey smiled weakly, tears forming in her eyes. Amstead walked over to Slonsky.

"Basil, I really appreciate your recommending me to represent Honey. But I have to defend her to the best of my ability. You understand. She's my client, Basil, and you and I may not see eye to eye."

"I do understand, Percy. That's why you were retained. I wanted the best."

"Thank you, BS. I appreciate that. But to the point, this meeting is not my idea. I told my client not to talk to you, and she said she would make that decision, so I'm doing it under orders."

Slonsky nodded affirmatively and sat down across from Honey.

"Honey, are you OK?"

"I've been better, Basil. Seeing you again helps."

"Are they treating you all right here?"

"No problem. One of the deputies said you told him to keep an eye on me. Thank you."

"You're welcome. Look, your lawyer is right. You shouldn't be talking to me."

"I'll make that decision, if you don't mind."

Slonsky smiled, shrugged, and sat down.

"You haven't lost your spunk."

"I'm sorry. It's just a defense mechanism."

"What do you want to say?"

"I told you once I had to earn your trust. You think I lied."

Slonsky said nothing. Honey bit her lip.

"After I left your house, I called Joe Rutledge and said I needed to help you because eventually Mathes would find out I was living with you. Word gets around. You were in danger. Somebody already tried to kill you before in that gas station. Joe gave me the address of a safe house."

Grimacing in pain, she sat up straight.

"After I left your house, I went to the hospital to see the doctor about my shoulder, and one of the nurses stopped me. She said Imogene had told her to keep it a secret but a police officer named Madigan had put a listening device under the bed in my room and did I know anything about it. I tried not to sound surprised and said the detectives must have forgotten about it. Then Sergeant Asquith called me."

"Asquith called you? He didn't tell me."

"Never mind. He had talked to the prosecutor, John Marcum, who told him my statements to you in the hospital might be thrown out by the judge and that would affect any search you undertook. After that, I told Asquith about the device under my hospital bed, and he told Marcum. Marcum talked to the nurse and got a search warrant to search Mathes's house. Police found several tapes. They kept the recorded ones of our conversation in the hospital and gave copies to Percy, as the law requires. Percy, give one to Basil."

Amstead handed Slonsky a sealed plastic bag. Slonsky placed the tapes in his pocket.

"Percy, have you listened to the tapes?"

"Yes, BS, and I will have to ask the court to exclude them. You know, the Miranda thing."

Slonsky grimaced.

Honey resumed, "Mathes knows you will hound him and work him somehow. You're too dangerous. He needs to take you out."

"That son of a bitch."

"Anyway, I left to go to the safe house because Mathes knows I'm alive and his first priority is to do me. I'm vulnerable. He got your address somehow from Personnel and staked out your house. When I left, he followed me to the safe house. As soon as I got out of the car, he grabs me, shoves a gun in my side, drives me to his house, and says this time, no one will rescue me.

"We go inside and make a deal. I told him I would take the fall for the abortion murder. I'll tell the judge I suckered Slonsky in because you were getting too close to me and I thought I could romance you. Mathes goes free. Without me, your case goes nowhere with him. You're no longer a threat."

Slonsky interrupted, "To begin with, this is asinine, incomprehensible, and I would never agree to it. In the first place, how did he know you'd keep your word?"

"Two reasons. First, he knows I love you. Second, he'll either kill me or have me killed if I don't follow through. Instead, you stay alive, and I just do the time."

Slonsky hesitated.

"OK. Let's assume the judge throws out your statements to me. What about the prints on the IV tube?"

"Mathes found out Forensics lost the prints. The prosecutor gets an easy plea from me, and Mathes skates because you have no case against him. But you still can track the shooter."

"What about the bullets, the rifle, the binoculars, and the SWAT jacket that Asquith found in Mathes's locker?"

Amstead interrupted, "BS, I talked to Marcum. He's a decent prosecutor. He told me Forensics got no match. Forensics says they can't match the grooves in the rifle with the slug in the fetus. So the rifle and the bullets are irrelevant. It's not illegal to own this weapon. And anyone can buy those SWAT jackets at the police department sports store. Marcum said he told you that."

Honey continued, "Percy, let me finish. After Mathes put me in his car, he phoned someone he called Gimpy. Mathes said he would help him change his name from Frank Bellings to Frank Anthony. That's probably the name of the shooter you're looking for."

Slonsky leaned forward and looked directly into Honey's swollen eyes.

"This is going to be difficult. You're forgetting Mathes tried to kill you in the hospital. And he probably set you up in Oregon when you got shot."

"BS, I've told you this before. You have no case against whoever shot me or, for that matter, against the other women who were killed either. No witnesses. Assuming Mathes gave the orders to kill, how are you going to ever prove it? He'll never confess.

He'll deny cutting the tube and want to know where the prints are. The DA has no prints, so all you have is a big nothing."

Amstead placed both hands gently on Honey's shoulders.

"BS, I talked to the DA's office. They'll take a plea to second-degree murder, twenty-five years."

Slonsky scowled.

"Twenty-five years? Honey never killed anyone, Percy."

"She's an accomplice, Basil. She and Mathes cooked up a deal to start a riot at the medical clinic. Well, you know the law. If you plan some scheme and somebody gets injured or killed as a result, you're responsible even if you never intended harm."

"I have no evidence that she planned to start a riot. No witness will testify to her plan except me."

"And Mathes. Call it a diversion then if not a riot. Makes no legal difference. But you don't have to testify. I don't agree with Honey, but if you want to, just confirm to the DA before trial what Honey told you in the hospital. When he hears that, he'll assume you'll testify to it at the trial—assuming the judge allows it. At one point, you did advise Honey of her Miranda rights, and the judge might allow that part in evidence even if she was taking morphine for the pain. Now the prosecutor thinks he has a strong case against her. Honey agrees to the plea—over my objection—and there's no trial."

"So Mathes and the shooter go free. No way."

Honey sat up and braced herself against the chair.

"Percy's right about the law, BS. That pregnant woman got killed because of me."

Slonsky interrupted.

"What about Imogene, the nurse at the hospital? And what about Sally Thompson, who got killed because she did me a favor and ordered computers? And what about yourself?"

"BS, you can't prove any of that against Mathes or anyone else."

"I am not going to let you go to prison for a murder you never committed. I am going to get whoever killed innocent women and tried to kill you."

"Basil, you can't stop me."

Slonsky suddenly smiled, leaned back in his chair, put his hands behind his head, and roared. Honey and Amstead looked dumbfounded.

"You know what, folks? If I ever doubted Honey Wissman, that doubt is gone. I'm gonna marry that woman as soon as she's released from jail."

Honey and Amstead were speechless.

Slonsky took a deep breath.

"I have a witness."

Amstead leaned forward.

"You have a witness?"

"Yes. The witness saw the shooter but can't identify him. His face was concealed, but Honey was in the crowd when the shots were fired by someone else. That's on videotape. Percy, don't plead your client. Let her tell her story to the jury. Let Mathes tell his story. See whom the jury believes."

"Honey, I think BS might be right. We can prove you didn't pull the trigger. Slonsky has your statement explaining what you did. The judge might throw it out, and we should at least try to exclude it. Even if the judge excludes the evidence, you can still testify to your plans."

Honey shook her head.

"It makes no difference, Percy. No one can identify the shooter except Mathes. I don't know who it was. Besides, I told you Mathes has me on those tapes that make it look like I set the shooting up. The police didn't find that tape.

Slonsky interrupted, "Honey, you said Mathes mentioned some guy's name while you were in the car with Mathes. If we find him, maybe he'll cough up Mathes."

"And who on the jury is going to believe the word of this guy, who's obviously a pro and probably an ex-con, against the word of a police officer?"

"But you can testify."

"I'm a cop who planned a diversion that got someone killed, hacked police files, fled to Oregon, and failed to report an attempted murder on my life in the hospital. I hide out with another cop and am stopped while in Mathes's car. Even Percy can't win that one. I'll represent myself and enter a plea." Slonsky put his head down.

A voice on the intercom from the supervising deputy interrupted, "BS, sorry to interrupt. There's someone here to see you."

Honey and Amstead looked surprised. Slonsky turned toward the window in the interrogation room. Sergeant Asquith, folding his arms and smiling broadly, stood in the adjoining room next to a man dressed in a suit and tie. Asquith extended both hands toward Slonsky and signaled a thumbs-up.

Slonsky left the room and walked out to talk to Asquith. The man in the suit held a jar containing two tiny round objects.

Asquith smiled. "Basil, meet Alan Wright, the president of Guns Inc., the manufacturer of the weapon I found in Mathes's locker. Forensics couldn't match the bullets, so they let me borrow the rifle. The manufacturer's name and serial number had been filed off. I went back to Mathes's locker and found the sales receipt in the inside pocket of his uniform. We never removed that because it was just a standard uniform. I called

Mr. Wright, and his tech guys can match the slug in the fetus of Maureen McCullough with the rifle in Mathes's locker. It's laser technology our Forensics Department doesn't have. Mr. Wright can explain."

Wright removed his company manual.

"Mr. Slonsky, what happens is this. The rifle was invented originally for hunters. Unfortunately, sometimes the wrong people use it. In that case, usually the bullet goes through and through the body and hits another object: a chair, a table, a wall, a door, whatever, and it scratches the slug or defaces it in some way. That makes it impossible to compare with the weapon. But in this case, the bullet was deflected into the fetus, and obviously, no marks are on the slug. Then we can test it. The slug in the fetus came from the rifle that Sergeant Asquith gave us."

Slonsky found his voice and clasped the hand of Alan Wright.

"Mr. Wright, thank you, sir. Thank you."

Wright nodded his appreciation.

A jubilant Slonsky returned to the room and explained to Honey what Wright told him.

Officer Honey Wissman collapsed in tears.

* * *

Honey and Slonsky sat in the back of the courtroom, waiting for John Marcum to complete the paperwork for her release from custody, although the charge of murder had not been dismissed. Pro-life organizations and the police union had raised enough money for her to make bail. She had surrendered her passport. Slonsky touched her hand.

"Honey, look, remember you originally told me you just wanted to create a scene at the abortion demonstration because it would interfere with those demonstrators for pro-life and you would get publicity?"

"Yes. What does that have to do with anything? I'm still an accomplice."

"You didn't do that on your own initiative. Were you part of an organization?"

"Yes. Feminists for Choice."

"Who's the president?"

"Kelly Francis. She works for the chief judge of the court. She wanted the pro-lifers shut down."

"Did she know Mathes?"

"Yes. He took me to a couple of our meetings, and I introduced him."

"She knew you were a cop. Did she know Mathes was a cop too?"

"Sure. In fact, they seemed to get along very well."

"OK. I'll check it out."

The door to the judge's chambers opened, and Marcum came out, walked over to Honey, and handed her a release from custody form.

"Here you are, Ms. Wissman. Just sign here."

Marcum handed her a pen. Slonsky held her shoulders gently while she signed her name on the form. Both men shook hands. Slonsky turned toward Honey. "Let's go home."

Chapter 65

Carleton ushered Slonsky into his chambers, sat in his chair, and simultaneously signaled the detective to sit down.

"Detective, I'm still the judge on the abortion case, so I have to be careful of my answer to your question."

"I understand, Judge. Just let me know when you can't."

Carleton leaned forward, placed his arms on the desk, and folded his hands.

"Fire away."

"Judge, you remember you told me that a guy with a limp was in your courtroom twice when there was a hearing on the abortion case?"

Judge Carleton paused, then nodded agreement.

Slonsky resumed, "The courtroom was packed, and mostly by the media. How would someone who didn't have a press card get in the courtroom?"

"My bailiff lets in a few lawyers he knows, then he passes out numbers and conducts a lottery among the media and the crowd. Pretty crude but fair."

"About how many lottery winners get in?"

"Not many. Maybe fifteen."

"Any other way to get in?"

"No. Not unless you know somebody in the courthouse. Favors happen."

"So the average Joe Blow would just have to get lucky? How do you suppose the guy you saw with the limp got in?"

"Just luck of the draw, I guess."

"Two times he got lucky?"

Carleton sat back, frowning.

"You're right. Really lucky. Probably, someone who works in the courthouse got him in."

"Judge, I need to ask you for a favor."

"If I can, sure."

"Could you step away from your desk for a moment?"

"That's the favor?"

"Please."

Carleton stood up and walked to the side of his desk. Slonsky looked at the phone displaying a rotary dial.

"Judge, where did you get that phone? It looks like it came from the Middle Ages."

"Yes, I know. You put your finger in one of the holes in the dial and twirl it around. My grandfather gave it to me when I was a little boy. I just kept it as a memento."

"OK. I hope technology works on this."

Slonsky reached over the desk, picked up the phone from the cradle, and unscrewed the mouthpiece. Reaching inside, he removed a tiny round object and held it in the air.

"Judge, do you see this? I talked to my tech guy. Someone is tapping your phone."

Carleton stared incredulously.

"I'm being tapped? Is this your idea of getting information from me?"

"Hold on, Judge. We don't tap phones without a warrant, and you know we need one. You can check it out with the chief judge if you want to."

"Who would do this? I will start an investigation immediately."

"Please, now I need that favor. Let me work on this. Give me a little time."

Carleton hesitated.

"OK, OK. But you keep me posted."

"I will. Believe me, I will. I need to replace the bug. In the meantime, just continue using the phone like nothing's wrong. If you have to really make a personal call, go somewhere else."

Carleton nodded.

"Just one more thing, Judge. Maybe we can help."

Slonsky reached in his coat, pulled out his cell phone, and called Mike Winkelmann, who answered.

"Mike, it's BS. I need your brain. Can we trace a phone tap?"

"Sure. Piece of cake. When do you want to do it?"

"Now."

"BS, I'm in bed with my wife."

"Tell her to hold that thought."

"She's already holding something."

"This won't take long."

"That's what she always says."

"Mike, this is urgent."

"OK, she says she can wait. Give me the phone number you want to trace."

Slonsky looked at the elderly desk phone and repeated the number to Winkelmann.

"All right, BS, I'm going to phone you on that number. Don't say anything. Just pick up the phone, listen for a few seconds, but keep the phone to your ear until you hear a click. Then hang up. Then I'll call you again, and you can answer."

"Got it."

Slonsky put down the phone, waited until the phone rang, and did as instructed.

Moments later, Winkelmann called Slonsky back.

"BS, did you hear a click after a few seconds?"

"Yes."

"That's one sign there's a tap. But I called the number you gave me, and both times, an operator answered, 'Superior court.' I thought you would answer the call directly."

"I'm in the courthouse."

"I've got a gizmo here that is tracing the call. Wait a minute. It shows my call to you is going to a different number than you gave me. The tap is putting the call first to someone at the same location you are."

"What do you mean?"

"The main line to your building is automatically transferring my call to the phone number you gave me. But that phone is just an extension line even if it has its own number. Same thing when you call out. Your call goes through the main number. In other words, somebody originally answers an incoming phone call on the main switchboard first before it is transferred to the extension phone I called. Undoubtedly, the phone is in the same building. Let me call you again, and this time, don't hang up."

Slonsky waited until the phone rang, and he answered.

"Mike, OK, the desk phone rang."

"Here's what's happening. There is about a thirty- to forty-five-second delay between the time someone initiates a call and the time it takes to transfer the call from the main number to the extension. The system switches the call automatically to the extension number if the person calls the number, but there is a short delay. The person at the main number sees the telephone number flashing on the board and answers, but of course, that person could just listen on the main line then transfer. Or if you call out, same sequence. The board lights up, and the person at the main line can listen. That person can just leave the line open for as long as they want to listen while the parties talk. Where are you?"

"Sorry, I can't tell you exactly, Mike. How does someone leave the line open when the call goes to the extension line?"

"They have put a little device in that phone if they want to listen, and it automatically leaves the main line open while the parties talk."

"Mike, you really helped me out. Now get back to your work."

"Work?"

"Whatever you're working on. Thanks, old buddy."

Slonsky replaced the phone on the desk.

"Judge, we have a problem. I'll have my tech guy come over to check out the phones. Let me explain what's going on."

"OK. Why don't we order in lunch?"

Slonsky laughed. The two men shook hands.

Chapter 66

Chief Riley's face gradually changed from pink to florid. His body quivered, and the knuckles of his hands whitened.

He spoke slowly, "Slonsky, we have had a similar conversation before. You came on the department when you were twenty-five. You put in your twenty years. I'm going to recommend a disability retirement. You went on a toot down in Mexico and found nothing. You discharged yourself from a hospital without their permission and against their orders. You stole a car—"

"Borrowed."

Riley bellowed, "Stole, as in *thief*! Then you hired McClosky as your new partner and entered two houses without a warrant. And now you want to wiretap the courthouse. If you don't retire, how about an assignment to pedestrian intersection control?"

"Willard, I don't—"

"Don't you 'Willard' me. If anyone deserved a name like BS, it's you. The only reason I don't get your badge and gun right now is 'cause you saved Wissman's life at the hospital. Good god, man, are you moving with the stars?"

A knock on the door interrupted the tirade. A young sergeant peeked in deferentially.

"Chief, sorry to interrupt. The DA said it's important."

"All right, all right. What is it?"

"He said Detective Slonsky's warrant to tap the phone at the courthouse is ready."

Chief Clark put his head between his hands. "I'm going to put in for retirement, Slonsky. Disability. Working with lunatics."

* * *

Slonsky and Winkelmann sat next to a tape recorder in an unused room in the courthouse after having wiretapped the main courthouse telephone of the chief judge in the middle of the night. Both wore headphones while either dozing, reading the newspaper, or watching TV. They waited for anyone to call the main number or call out, listening to innumerable lawyers calling the court about the status of their cases. Winkelmann worked on his computer. He looked up at Slonsky, who was reading the sports page.

"BS, are you sure this is a good idea? How do we know anyone will call about Honey today?"

"Because she was released yesterday from custody. Now she's alone and vulnerable."

"But why the courthouse?"

"Because I think someone here is involved in the abortion shooting."

"In the courthouse?"

"Yes."

"Wow. But we've been here a couple of hours."

"I know. If we don't hear anything by noon, we'll shut down."

"OK. But my wife is expecting me."

"Seems like she's always expecting you."

Winkelmann blushed.

The computer board lit up when the chief judge's line activated and registered an outgoing call. Both men immediately grabbed their headphones, and Winkelmann turned on the tape recorder. The phone rang several times without any answer. A voice mail came on.

"Hello. You've reached Eddie. Please leave a message."

The voice mail activated.

"Eddie, this is Kelly. I haven't talked to you in several days, but I understand your Black Officers Union put up big bucks for your bail on the kidnapping charge. Obviously, I can't be seen with you. I told you that Slonsky talked with Carleton, who described the man he saw shoot that woman at the medical clinic. Carleton still can't identify him but said the guy walked with a limp and wore a ponytail. Somehow Slonsky got the shooter's name. Maybe from Wissman. Slonsky told Carleton he did a computer search on all LA parolees recently released and who had some kind of disability. Came up with your shooter. Partly bald, walked with a limp, wore a ponytail. The parole officer went with Slonsky to question the guy, but they missed him. Call me if you can."

Slonsky and Winkelmann removed their headphones.

Winkelmann looked at Slonsky. "Wow. What was that all about?"

"I can't tell you, Mike, but it did sound interesting, didn't it?"

Winkelmann sat back and laughed. "How about a game of chess?"

"I didn't bring my board."

The computer activated again, and both men grabbed their headphones. The voice of Eddie Mathes came on. Slonsky signaled Winkelmann to turn on the tape.

"Kelly, it's Eddie. Don't call me on my cell phone. I'm calling from a public phone. They may have my phone tapped. Anyway, I don't think there's a problem. Even if they arrest my shooter, he'll never talk. A stupid nurse and an old lady in a market cost me plenty, not to mention killing that pregnant bitch."

The voice of Kelly Francis came on. "Eddie, you don't think there's a problem? Slonsky told Carleton he had called the prosecutor, who said the DA will offer your shooter life without parole instead of the death penalty in exchange for him testifying—that's, of course, if they find him."

"No. He's an ex-con with a record as long as your arm. No jury will believe him. They'll think he's just trying to save his ass. What about Carleton? Is he going to be a witness?"

"Yes. He told Slonsky the president called. The president said he did a great job on the abortion case and will probably submit his name for the vacancy on the Supreme Court. And Jean Carleton hired a private investigator. The investigator said he found nothing on Carleton, but I said just wait until I put out some more rumors. In fact, I might even have to put out myself. If he gets divorced, you can call me in Washington, DC, as wife of a Supreme Court justice."

Eddie replied, "What a sweet thing you are. I can't talk any longer. I'll call you later."

The line went dead.

Winkelmann turned to Slonsky. "Is what you said about Judge Carleton true?"

"Not exactly. Sort of. Not really."

"But you still don't have the shooter guy. Doesn't this conversation put the judge's life in danger?"

"Yes."

Chapter 67

Late afternoon the next day, Judge Carleton and Slonsky sat in chambers, talking earnestly.

"Judge, you're sure you want to go through with this? You can still back out."

"No. Three women have been killed, and you and your partner are in danger. I might have prevented all of this."

"OK. I'm glad we had that long conversation yesterday. Now you know the whole story after listening to the tape we made."

"Yes. I'm ready."

"OK. Make the call."

Judge Carleton switched on the intercom.

"Kelly, I'm going to leave in about half an hour. Taking my daughter out to dinner to talk about college. See you tomorrow."

"Thanks, Judge. Have a nice evening."

Carleton signaled to Slonsky, who picked up Carleton's phone programmed by Mike Winkelmann to listen to outgoing calls from the chief judge's phone. The light on the phone activated, and he put the phone against his ear. The voice of Kelly Francis came on.

"He's leaving in thirty minutes. Get your ass over here."

The line went dead. Slonsky placed the phone down carefully. "Showtime, Judge."

Slonsky walked out the door, waving to Carleton. Half an hour later, Judge Carleton ambled out of his chambers and down the hall to the elevator. He pushed the button for the garage.

The garage lights barely illuminated the cold and darkened cement structure. Few cars remained, all scattered throughout the floor and empty of occupants. Echoes carried the sound of footsteps through the frigid evening air. An occasional motor started up, tires squealed on the cement in the turning of its wheels, and the engine noise increased as the car moved forward. Then, silence as it faded into the night. Carleton walked toward his car.

The outside wall of the garage opened to a skyline view of Los Angeles, and the cars parked along the edge of the rows were reserved for judges. Carleton had parked in the same spot for years, always carrying his venerable briefcase. Opening the trunk, he carefully placed the briefcase inside, eyes glued to the side-view mirror on the driver's side of the car. In closing his trunk, the sound echoed throughout the garage. When Carleton opened the car door, the side mirror reflected a figure clad in an overcoat and wearing a brimmed hat approaching. Limping slowly and silently, the man held a weapon in his hand. The barrel, pointed toward the ground next to his leg, glinted under the overhead garage light. The man stopped, looked around, and resumed walking. Carleton swung around to see the man slowly raise his weapon.

A voice shouted, "Drop it!"

Stunned, the gunman swiveled his head.

Slonsky, concealed under the car, lying on his stomach, with only his head visible, pointed his gun at the man.

The man fired at Slonsky, and the bullet thudded into the car door. A second shot careened off the oil-stained cement floor. Slonsky fired back.

A scream pierced the night air. Several gunshots from the assailant's gun ripped aimlessly into the cement floor as his body lurched, staggered, and collapsed on the floor. A hat and strands of his ponytail lay beside his head soaked in blood. Basil Slonsky crawled out from under the car covered in grease and sweat.

Chapter 67

Chief Riley stood proudly in front of the press, preening and mauling the language, trying to answer questions.

"Basil Slonsky is a credit to the department. He put his life on the line in this case, and I intend to nominate him for the Medal of Valor. I have promoted him to lieutenant, which he richly deserves. He kept me informed of his progress in the case at all times and never let me down. Too bad they didn't have the three-strikes rule when the killer originally went to prison. He never would have been paroled."

* * *

John Marcum waved Slonsky into his office.

"The DA appointed me to try your case against Mathes, BS. But I'm afraid he won't be tried alone."

"What are you talking about? Honey is gonna get immunity."

"The DA says no, and I can't talk him out of it."

"For God's sake, what is wrong?"

"Basil, this is a big case. Really big. The DA does not need any adverse publicity right now. He's running for attorney general, and if he immunizes Honey, they will crap all over him. We can convict Mathes with the gun and ammunition in his locker, the matching bullet inside the fetus, the prints on the IV tube, and the SWAT jacket. The DA says we don't need Honey's testimony."

"What if the judge throws out her statements to me? And the guy who did shoot her is dead? It's Honey versus Mathes. The jury won't believe him."

"Maybe. Look at it this way, BS. Remember what I said? Honey cooks up this disturbance. A woman gets killed at the disturbance. Kelly Francis and Mathes will tell the same story about Honey. She is at the demonstration and takes off to Oregon right away without telling anyone her story. Yeah, she gets shot up there, but she doesn't know who did it. Said she was on vacation. Then, according to her, Mathes tries to kill her in the hospital, and she doesn't report that either. Finally, she and Mathes are in a car together when you and McClosky confronted them, but there is no evidence she was kidnapped except for her say-so. Maybe everything you know is different, but you are not the jury. The best thing for the DA to do is try both of them together. They will hang each other.

"But there's more. Mathes's lawyers filed a motion to exclude the evidence Asquith found on grounds he conducted an unlawful search of Mathes's locker without a search warrant.

If the judge grants the motion, and he has indicated he would, none of the evidence in the locker is admissible. And then, of course, they are objecting to Honey's statements to you in the hospital. I told you this before. With none of the evidence from the locker admissible against Mathes, all we have is Honey's testimony implicating him."

"Who is the judge?"

"Judge Murphy. He finished his tour in the calendar court and is now in a trial court."

"The old liberal shines through."

"Yep. Without the gun and the jacket that Asquith found, we got zip. You gotta admit it, BS, it's a tough case. All we got are the tapes the police found in Mathes's room. But Honey admitted on the tapes she set up the abortion demonstration with him."

"What about the tapes we got of the conversation between Mathes and Kelly?"

"The search warrant authorized you to listen to conversation among parties in the courthouse. That gave you the right to listen to everyone in the building. Way too broad and not individualized enough. Fourth Amendment. The judge threw it out."

"I think I'll go back to lifting weights."

"I'm sorry, but my hands are tied."

"Anything I can do?"

"Say a prayer. Go to see Father Braun. You will probably need to. Two burglaries and a car theft."

"Very not funny."

Chapter 68

"Please remain seated and come to order. This court is in session. Judge Murphy presiding," announced the court bailiff. Judge Murphy waddled up to his ancient chair on the bench, surveyed the packed courtroom, peered down at the counsel table, and announced, "The record will reflect the defendants, and their counsel are present. The people are represented by Mr. Marcum. Mr. Amstead, are you representing the defendant Wissman?"

"Yes, Your Honor."

"Mr. Batone, are you representing the defendant Mathes?"

"Yes, Your Honor."

"Very well. Mr. Marcum, I have read the motion by the defendants to exclude evidence found in the defendant Mathes's police locker by Sergeant Asquith. It is undisputed that Sergeant Asquith did not have a warrant to search the locker, that he had no valid consent from Mr. Mathes to search the locker in the absence of injury or death required by department policy. There was no emergency. I may not like the law, but that is what it is. Motion granted, the evidence seized from defendant Mathis's locker is excluded."

Marcum responded, "Your Honor, would you at least withhold your ruling to give us an opportunity to investigate further?"

"I don't know what else you would find, but that's a reasonable request. You can argue later, but after we select the jury. All right, let's start jury selection."

The tedious process of selecting a jury took two days to complete. At the end of the second day, weary lawyers, spectators, and jurors welcomed final selection of the jurors. Judge Murphy adjourned court until Monday but remained on the bench. When the courtroom cleared, Judge Murphy spoke, "Mr. Batone asked to be heard."

"Your Honor, the defendant Mathes originally posted bail and was released. The judge later revoked the bail because Mr. Mathes could not find his passport. He has now done so. The codefendant, Ms. Wissman, has been released from custody, so we ask the same for him."

Marcum and Slonsky looked at each other.

Marcum replied, "Your Honor, this is now a murder prosecution."

Murphy shook his head.

"I recognize that, Mr. Marcum, but if a defendant posts bail, there is nothing I can do. Ms. Wissman posted bail, and she is charged with the same crime. I suggest you talk to Mr. Batone and Mr. Amstead. The defendant Mathes is released upon confirmation of the clerk that the passport has been surrendered."

Murphy stepped down. Mathes smirked as he rose from his chair, while Batone walked over to the clerk and handed him a document. The clerk read it over and nodded to the bailiff. Mathes and Batone exited the courtroom.

Chapter 69

The trial resumed. After the prosecution had presented evidence of the shooting at the clinic, including pictures of the dead victim, the pictures of Honey and Mathes at the demonstration, Marcum called Slonsky to testify to Honey's confession in the hospital. Murphy allowed part of the evidence over strenuous objections by Amstead, although conceding the evidence was a close case. He advised Amstead to ask for a rehearing.

The prosecution then called Mike Winkelmann to testify to the tapes recorded by himself and Slonsky. Although Batone objected on various grounds, Murphy overruled the objection, noting he had issued a warrant for the tap.

He added, "However, I ruled the warrant overly broad to the outset, but since no other conversations were overheard, no one's privacy was violated. But the warrant was defective from the outset and, therefore, makes no difference. Motion granted. The evidence is inadmissible."

Judge Murphy explained to the jury that Wissman was being tried separately and they should not consider her absence a factor in reaching a verdict in this case.

At the end of the day on Friday, the prosecution closed its case.

When the jury had left the courtroom, Batone turned toward the judge. "Your Honor, we will produce our own tapes when we resume."

With that, Judge Murphy strode off the bench and back into his chambers.

Marcum turned toward Slonsky. "BS, I talked to the DA, and the tapes are enough to convict Mathes, but Wissman's story is pretty weak. And Batone said he had tapes they are going to play of Honey's conversations with Mathes."

* * *

Monday morning, Judge Murphy took the bench to another packed courtroom.

"Mr. Marcum, do you have any further witnesses?"

"No, Your Honor."

Murphy leaned back and signaled to his bailiff. "OK, Frank, bring in the jury."

"Mr. Amstead, do you have any witnesses?"

"Yes, Your Honor. The defense calls Officer Wissman."

The jurors took their seats. The courtroom buzzed as Honey Wissman took the stand and repeated the oath. In her testimony, she explained the information she had given to Slonsky about initiating the abortion demonstration, her trip to Oregon upon fearing retribution from Mathes, the shooting in the cabin by an unknown assailant, Mathes's visit to her in the hospital, and the IV episode. She concluded by adding her kidnapping by Mathes. She repeatedly wiped her eyes, confirming her admission to Detective Slonsky. She agreed to having watched the demonstration but had no explanation for the fatal shooting. Marcum sat down, turning to attorney Batone. "Your witness, Mr. Batone."

Batone eased out of his chair as though he was stalking.

"Ms. Wissman, when did you first meet Mr. Mathes?"

"About a year ago."

"And you discussed creating what you call a disturbance at the medical clinic, didn't you?"

"Yes."

"And you were in the crowd with Mr. Mathes when a woman was shot, weren't you?"

"Yes."

"And within a few days, you left town and went to a remote cabin in Oregon, didn't you?"

"Yes."

"Did you inform your superiors that you had participated in setting up the disturbance?"

"No. I witnessed nothing. I arranged no shooting of the victim. I never saw or did anything at the demonstration except to attend. Mr. Mathes told me he arranged for someone to fire a shot in the air. That's all."

"Did you tell your superiors that Mr. Mathes had participated in the disturbance?"

"No. But he was not in the crowd with me when the woman got shot."

"You did know a woman had been killed, didn't you?"

"Later that day, yes, of course."

"What was your assignment before the homicide occurred?"

"Vice."

"And you transferred to Robbery/Homicide after the murder at the medical clinic, didn't you?"

"Yes."

"Was it your intention to prevent identification of the assassin?"

"Certainly not."

"Why did you ask for the transfer?"

"A woman had been killed. I wanted to find the killer."

"Really? You set up the disturbance that resulted in a death, and you wanted to find yourself not guilty?"

Marcum interrupted, "Objection, Your Honor."

"Sustained. No more questions about personal opinion, Mr. Batone."

"Yes, Your Honor. Now, Ms. Wissman, I apologize for asking questions about your injury, so I hope you understand."

"Yes."

"After you were shot in Oregon, you returned to Los Angles and were hospitalized. Is that correct?"

"Yes."

"And you testified that Mr. Mathes came to your room in the hospital and the police later discovered a severed IV tube."

"Yes."

"Did you see Mr. Mathes sever the IV?"

"No. I had been chloroformed and unconscious. He was the only one in the room."

"No one else saw Mr. Mathes, did they?"

"Not to my knowledge."

"Did you report that incident to your superiors?"

"No. I reported it to Detective Slonsky."

"Did he report it to his superiors?"

"No."

"So Detective Slonsky covered up the confession you gave him later?"

Marcum interrupted, "Objection. Conclusion of the witness."

Murphy leaned forward. "Sustained. I asked you not to ask personal or conclusionary questions, Mr. Batone."

"Yes, Your Honor. I withdraw the question."

Looking at the jury, Murphy commented, "The jury should not consider the question just asked. It is not evidence."

Batone resumed, "You stayed in Detective Slonsky's house after your discharge from the hospital, did you not?"

"Yes."

"How long did you stay there?"

"Several days."

"And as of today, you have not reported the plan to your department for the abortion disturbance or the alleged cutting of the IV tube."

"I reported it to Detective Slonsky."

"The man whose house you stayed in?"

"Yes."

"And finally, Ms. Wissman, you testified that Mr. Mathes kidnapped you after you left Detective Slonsky's house. Correct?"

"Yes."

"When you got out of the car, did he hold you or use any force on you?"

"No."

"You got out of your own accord, did you not?"

"Yes."

"Any witnesses to this alleged kidnapping before police shot Mr. Mathes?"

"No."

"No more questions. Thank you, Your Honor."

Murphy stood up. "All right, ladies and gentlemen, let's take a recess until one thirty."

The jury left the room, but Murphy signaled to the bailiff not to adjourn. Taking off his glasses, Murphy turned toward Batone.

"Mr. Batone, I thought you were going to play some tapes."

"Yes, Your Honor, but unfortunately, we played them to an FBI forensics expert, and we will not be using them. There seems to be some problems."

Marcum and Slonsky both smiled knowingly. Murphy shrugged and stepped down.

"Understood. Court is in recess."

Honey left the witness stand as Marcum turned toward Slonsky sitting down at the counsel table.

"BS, not only did Batone undermine Honey. He pulled you in too. Do you realize he thinks you are covering up? That makes you an accomplice. I told you that might happen."

Before Slonsky could answer, the bailiff handed Slonsky a note.

"BS, Joe Rutledge's wife asked me to give you this note from her."

Slonsky read the note: "Basil, Joe is dying from cancer. Doctor just found out. Joe wants to see you. Urgent."

Slonsky read the note to Marcum, who handed it back to him.

"Go, BS. We only have some additional testimony from the coroner, and we're done for the day."

Slonsky raced out of the courtroom, jumped in his car, and drove away with red lights flashing.

Chapter 70

Slonsky stood at the bedside of Joe Rutledge but hardly recognized the pain-etched face, watery eyes, and swollen mouth. His wife, Ruth, stood on the other side of the bed, gently wiping his moist brow and stroking his hand. She smiled when Slonsky rushed into the room and held up her hand gently to stop him from talking to Rutledge.

"Basil, the chief of police was here yesterday talking to Joe about the abortion case. The chief told Joe that the judge had excluded important evidence from Mathes's locker because Sergeant Asquith had no warrant, no consent from Mathes, and without an emergency. Joe could barely talk but asked me to open the desk drawer in his office at the station and bring him a specific file. Here it is."

She handed the file to Slonsky, who scanned it briefly. Suddenly, he felt a cold hand on his arm.

Rutledge struggled to speak. "BS, I talked to Mathes a couple of weeks ago before his arrest to tell him he had to renew his locker consent form. As you know, under department regulations, every cop has to have a consent form on file with another officer to have locker access. He said he didn't trust

Asquith anymore and wanted me to fill out the form. I was a little surprised because all the cops knew I had been diagnosed with terminal cancer and was going on leave. I wouldn't be coming back."

Rutledge paused, exhausted.

Moments later, he resumed, "I figured Mathes had something important in the locker but didn't want Asquith to know about it. Mathes signed the form, a new one the department issued this year. I put it in my desk and, the next day, went to the hospital. Here I am ever since."

Slonsky interrupted, "But, Joe, the court has already ruled Asquith had no consent to search Mathes's locker unless for death or injury."

"The department changed the form at the first of this year. You probably didn't bother to read it. No one does. It's already on file, so you just sign. But now any watch commander has authority to search an officer's locker without consent whether there's an injury or not. The chief said Asquith probably didn't read about the change. Whether or not he did, Mathes signed the form himself. It's mandatory."

"So Asquith did have the right to go into Mathes's locker without consent in his capacity as a watch commander?"

"Correct. I forgot all about it. Just cosigned it. Figured I'd never need it in my condition."

Rutledge could go on no longer. His head rolled to the side, and he gasped for breath.

Slonsky leaned over and held the cold hand of his friend.

"Joe, you just saved Honey's life."

"You got a winner, BS."

Rutledge smiled and closed his eyes. These were the last words he ever spoke.

Chapter 71

The jurors waited in the jury assembly room, waiting for court to resume.

Marcum addressed Judge Murphy in a closed session of the court, "Your Honor, you may recall you agreed to reconsider the motion to suppress the evidence seized from defendant Mathes's locker."

Murphy nodded agreement.

Marcum resumed, "I have in my hand a police department document signed by defendant Mathes authorizing any watch commander to enter the locker of an officer and without restrictions. I have showed this file to Mr. Batone, and he objects on the ground of hearsay unsupported by any witness. My response is that this document is an official business record of the police department and may be entered into evidence."

Marcum handed the file to the bailiff, who gave it to the judge. Murphy read it carefully. He looked up. "No question this is a business record. Where is the witness who kept this document?"

"He has terminal cancer, Your Honor. He is expected to die in a few days. If you wish, I can bring in the department supervisor to verify the original is on file."

"Well, Sergeant Rutledge may have been authorized to open the locker, but it was Sergeant Asquith who actually did."

"Yes, Your Honor. But look at the back of the form issued on the first of this year."

Judge Murphy turned the form over and read the printed sentence: "Any administrative watch commander officer retains the unlimited authority to open and inspect any locker assigned to any officer within his jurisdiction, regardless of the underlying cause, and remove any items therein. I agree to these terms. S/ Eddie Mathes."

Judge Murphy read the form again.

"Mr. Marcum, is Sergeant Asquith a watch commander?"

"Yes, Your Honor. Mr. Batone has agreed to that fact."

"Any objection, Mr. Batone?"

"No, Your Honor. Mr. Marcum has offered me an opportunity to talk to the supervisor, and he faxed me a copy of the original. Although I am satisfied of Sergeant Rutledge's condition, I object on the grounds of hearsay."

Murphy shook his head negatively. "Objection overruled. My previous order is vacated, and a new order entered. Motion to suppress the evidence found and removed from the locker of Mr. Mathes is denied. The evidence is admissible. Anything else, Mr. Marcum?"

"Your Honor, now that the items removed from the defendant's locker will be introduced in evidence, I do have other witnesses."

"All right, proceed."

Coroner and autopsy expert Fred Southers testified to the location of two bullets found in the body of the victim, the third bullet in the body of the fetus, and the angle of the entry wound. Sergeant Asquith testified to finding the binoculars, ammunition, rifle, SWAT uniform, and cap in Mathes's locker. The manufacturer's representative testified the bullet found in the fetus came from the rifle in Mathes's locker. A distributor for the IV tube testified the product had been cut with a sharp instrument. The product was not defective.

"We have one more witness, Your Honor. We call Judge Royal Carleton."

Heads swiveled as Carleton came through the courtroom doors, walked to the witness stand, took the oath, sat down, and identified himself to the jury. After a few preliminary questions on his job, the time and day he had observed the shooting at the medical clinic, the inability to identify the shooter, he conceded his failure to report his observations.

Marcum asked, "Judge Carleton, just before the shooting started, did you see anyone on the roof next to the courthouse?"

"Yes."

"Whom did you see?"

"A man kneeling down on the roof, a rifle in one hand and binoculars in the other hand."

"Could you see what he was wearing?"

"Yes. He was wearing a jacket and a cap with the letters SWAT."

Marcum picked up a jacket and cap lying on the counsel table. Each contained the letters SWAT.

"Judge Carleton, do you recognize this jacket and cap?"

"Yes, those are identical to the ones I saw the man wearing."

Marcum paused, then resumed, "Judge Carleton, were you able to identify the man who shot Maureen McCullough?"

"No. His face was concealed by a rain hat. All I know he was a white male wearing a ponytail and limped when he walked. Sergeant Slonsky told me about the tapes he and Mr. Winkelmann had recorded between Kelly Francis and Mr. Mathes. I felt I had a duty to help after my failure to initially report my observations at the medical clinic on the day of the murder. I volunteered to help, and Mr. Slonsky, he asked me to tell Ms. Francis I was leaving the courthouse. He said he would lie under my car before I got there and arrest anyone who tried to kill me. I went down to the garage to my car. As a man approached me, I could see him limping. Later on, after he had been shot, I saw he was wearing a ponytail."

* * *

Slonsky, Marcum, Wissman, and Amstead remained in the courtroom after Judge Murphy adjourned for the day. Slonsky looked around and saw no one.

"John, the case against Mathes is now overwhelming. He knows that, but he's out on bail, and that means he can try to kill Honey again. He's got too many friends in the department who know how to find her. We need a safe house for her to stay."

"BS, you're gonna have to find something. We don't have the resources for that. And I don't think the police want to guard a defendant on trial."

"I've got an idea. Let's put her in the hospital. I'll get cops from another division to guard her. They don't know her or Mathes. We can alert them to Mathes and show them his picture."

"The hospital?"

"Perfect place. Easily guarded, and we probably only need one or two nights before the jury finds Mathes guilty. Honey needs the protection. Mathes is the only witness yet to testify, and I doubt if Batone wants to put him on the stand. We've got the wife-beating cases to impeach him in case he wants to testify."

"Well, if you can arrange it."

Slonsky asked Honey, "Is that OK with you?"

"Not my idea of a lot of fun, but OK."

"All right. I'll take you home, get your things, and I'll set it up and drive you to the hospital."

Chapter 72

Mathes punched in numbers, and a voice on the line answered, "Bobby."

"Bobby, it's me, Mathes. What did you find out at the department?"

"A lot of action. They're transferring six cops from Northeast Division to St. Mary's Hospital."

"St. Mary's? Not Queen of Angels? That's not in our division."

"I know. Which means something is going on at Queen of Angels, and they don't want any personnel from Wilshire Division at that hospital."

"Understood. Thanks, old buddy."

Mathes, dressed in full uniform, checked his weapon, put on his hat, and went out to his car. He looked at the clock—1:00 a.m. Arriving at St. Mary's, he parked three blocks away, exited his car, and walked slowly onto the shady grounds of the hospital. Concealing himself behind giant trees, he awaited the hospital shift change. Several minutes later, a van drove up, and seven police officers jumped out the back door. One officer, sergeant stripes on his sleeve, held up his hand, and the others waited. He walked into the hospital and returned a few minutes later accompanied by six different uniformed officers, who all entered the van. The driver shut the doors and drove away.

Led by the sergeant, the newly arrived officers walked into the hospital. Mathes snuck up to the side of the main door, looked inside, and saw the sergeant talking to the other officers, pointing in different directions inside. He was interrupted when Slonsky walked over from the registration desk, joined the group, and passed out something to all the officers. With his hands, Slonsky directed two officers toward the elevators and two others to the door with a sign overhead reading Stairs. The officers took up their posts.

Slonsky beckoned the other officers to follow him toward the elevators. They all approached, waited briefly until the doors opened, and entered. The doors closed behind them. The officers standing by the elevators and stairs pulled up chairs and immediately started talking, but in minutes, the conversation faded, and they began reading or dozing in the dim light of the entrance. Mathes waited for half an hour. Pulling his police hat down over his head as far as possible, he ran into the darkened hospital entrance and shouted, "Somebody is trying to break into the emergency entrance! I need help!"

The officers dozing by the stairs jumped up and followed Mathes out the main doors.

He shouted to them as he pointed toward the rear of the hospital, "By the emergency door. I'll call for help."

The view of the officers near the elevator, blocked by the main doors, stood and waited. Mathes ran over to the nurse's desk and, in a hurried voice, said to the nurse, "I'm supposed to guard Ms. Wissman. What room is she in?"

"231."

Mathes raced back to the unguarded stairway and ran upstairs two at a time. He stopped on the second floor, followed the sign on the wall to room 231, and looked through the window on the door. Honey was nowhere in sight. Removing his revolver, Mathes attached the silencer to his weapon, slowly opened the door, and stood in the doorway of room 231.

The officer sitting in the room looked up. "Who are you?"

Mathes raised his weapon and fired. The officer fell off the chair and slumped to the floor. The crash of the metal chair reverberated down the hall, its echo exaggerated by the silence of the night. Slonsky, standing around the corner of the corridor, came running down the hall toward room 231, trying to draw his gun at the same time. Mathes stepped behind the door, partially concealing himself, aimed, and fired. Slonsky staggered, fell against the wall, and collapsed on the floor. Mathes walked into room 231 and saw Honey Wissman sitting awake in the bed and starting to pull off the covers and reach for the alarm. Mathes raised his hand. "Just stay where you are. Well, Ms. Snitch, you are not going to get any help from your partner. He's lying on the floor outside your room. Are you ready to end the trial?'"

Mathes raised his weapon, the barrel pointed directly at Honey. A shot rang out. Mathes stiffened, crumpled, and fell against the bed onto the floor. Honey Wissman looked up. Basil Slonsky, lying facedown just outside the door, dropped his revolver and lost consciousness in a trail of blood streaming down the corridor.

Chapter 73

A disgusted Detective Slonsky sat in a hospital bed, arms akimbo and uttering a stream of profanity. The white gown he had worn similar to one in the other hospital allowed air to flow up his ass as he kept attempting to close the gap. A knock on the door caused him to look up angrily. Honey Wissman walked in, a bouquet of flowers in her hand and a newspaper held under her arm.

"Feeling better, BS? I see you're enjoying yourself. How's the leg?"

"Very funny."

"Here's the newspaper. Read the headlines."

She handed him the paper.

"President appoints Judge Royal Carleton to Supreme Court.

"City names new police station in honor of Sgt. Joe Rutledge.

"Kelly Francis was convicted of conspiracy. Eddie Mathes was sentenced to life imprisonment without parole for the murder of his wife and attempted murders of Officers Wissman and Slonsky. Prosecutor dismisses all charges against Officer Wissman. Officer Morgan, who was guarding Officer Wissman, has been released from the hospital and is expected to make a full recovery."

One month later, police officer Honey Wissman walked down the aisle of St. Catherine's Church, with one arm in a sling and the other held by Chief Willard Riley. Detective Basil Slonsky sat in a wheelchair at the altar but stood on crutches next to his best man, Paul McClosky, when she reached out her hand. Honey's sister, Marilyn Hathaway, stood as the bridesmaid. Sergeant Asquith sat in the front row next to Supreme Court Justice Royal Carleton and Ruth Rutledge, who gently caressed her baby Joe Jr. When Fr. Braun pronounced Honey and Slonsky husband and wife, the church packed with police officers roared.

McClosky whispered in Slonsky's ear, "Do you think you will need any help on your honeymoon?"

Slonsky hit McClosky's leg with his crutch.